ANGEL OF DEATH

HIDDEN NORFOLK
BOOK 12

J M DALGLIESH

HP

First published by Hamilton Press in 2022

ISBN (Trade Paperback) 978-1-80080-651-1
ISBN (Hardback) 978-1-80080-592-7
ISBN (Large Print) 978-1-80080-921-5

EXCLUSIVE OFFER

Look out for the link at the end of this book or visit my website at **www.jmdalgliesh.com** to sign up to my no-spam VIP Club and receive a FREE Hidden Norfolk novella plus news and previews of forthcoming works.

Never miss a new release.

No spam, ever, guaranteed. You can unsubscribe at any time.

ANGEL OF DEATH

PROLOGUE

THE SONG PLAYING on the radio was distracting. It was a tune he remembered his mother enjoyed. She used to hum it while she was preparing tea. Well, she used to hum a few bars of it and then voice the first line of the chorus over and over again. His mum wasn't someone who could be described as having a sound memory. For faces, yes, but as for lyrics…

The portable stereo was donkey's years old, a leftover from when the site was far busier, but these days staffing levels were a fraction of what they once were. He was amazed the thing still worked and he enjoyed the almost ceremonial twiddling of the dials each time he passed through this part of the site. He turned the dial to off and the crackly tune ceased just as the melody was fading out and the DJ spoke. Late-night radio. The oldest songs were the cheapest to play as royalty payments must be next to nothing for songs that old. Momentarily regretting being so quick to turn it off, he knew that tune was going to bug him until he remembered the title if not the singer. *Was it Dusty Springfield?* He couldn't even picture her in his mind's eye, but he could remember his mum tunelessly repeating that one line over and over. It brought a smile to his face as he made his way out of the old plant room towards the office block.

The night was overcast and muggy. The threat of rain was ever present as thunderstorms were forecast. With a bit of luck, it would hold off until he'd finished his rounds. Once back in the relative sanctity of the office, the heavens could open. It wouldn't matter by then. Most people would believe the rain would drive the opportunists away, keep them at home. After all, no one particularly likes to be out at night in a storm. Decent people don't at any rate. Thieves see it differently. Two sites had been broken into in the past three days alone, stripping the copper from the on-site transformers and making off with it for scrap value.

He was half expecting to find someone charred to a crisp one of these days. It was more luck than judgement that it hadn't happened already. The increased rounds were a by-product. Not that he minded. The overtime rate was decent, and the money would definitely come in handy.

A sound carried in the night air, and he stopped, turning towards it. Peering into the gloom, he struggled to make out a shape. Was it his mind playing tricks on him? Unhooking the torch from his belt, he angled the beam into the shadows. More movement. This time he was certain.

"Hello? Who's there?"

No answer.

He tried to sound commanding, "Whatever you're doing back there…"

A figure stepped out into the beam. She was blinded by the light, raising a hand to shield her eyes from the glare.

"Ben. It's me."

He redirected the beam away and focussed on her. "Angie?" he squinted as he eyed her. "What are you doing here?"

She tentatively took a step towards him. The pitter patter of raindrops struck the gravel at his feet, quickly growing in intensity. Angela was dressed only in a loose cami-vest top, cut away denim shorts and trainers. She pulled her arms close to her as the rain increased. Ben hurried to her, taking her by the hand and leading her to the nearest building. They took shelter in the doorway while he fumbled with his keys. It wasn't much but it was better than being caught out in the open.

The storm was breaking upon them and eventually Ben found the right key, unlocked the door and the two of them bundled inside out of the rain. It'd only been a matter of seconds but the two of them were virtually wet through. Ben looked upon her. Angela's shoulder-length blonde hair was soaking wet and stuck to the side of her face. She deftly moved it aside, away from her eyes, tucking it behind her ear. Her mascara had run but she didn't seem too bothered, smiling up at him as he wiped the warm rain from his own face. Her top clung to her chest revealing the contours of her body. They were close. He could smell a sweet, flowery fragrance on her.

Was it the conditioner in her hair or was it her perfume?

The room was lit by the night lights, every fourth strip light above them was on; enough to see by, but the darkness ventured deeply in between casting odd shadows all around them. Angela smiled at him.

"What are you doing here?" Ben asked again. "You'll get in trouble!"

"I'm here to see you, you idiot!"

"Me?"

"Yes, you!"

She reached out and grasped his shirt at the waist, drawing him towards her. Confused, he mumbled something, but it faded out as their bodies touched. He swallowed hard, staring into her blue eyes. They gleamed in the scant light as she gazed upon him and he felt self-conscious, scared of saying the wrong thing or making a mistake.

"I wanted to say thank you," she said.

"T–There's no need."

She reached up and placed the point of her forefinger against his lips, silencing him. His mouth ran dry, and his nerves were set ablaze. On her tiptoes, she leaned in and kissed him, allowing the touch to linger for a few seconds. Unsure of how to respond, he didn't. He felt lightheaded and dizzy, but in a good way. He would never be able to explain it any better than that, no matter how hard he would try. She drew away from him, smiled again, and he found himself returning it. She tasted of strawberries.

"Thank you," she said quietly.

"T–That's okay," he said, instantly regretting the tone. In his head, he sounded feeble, pathetic.

She touched his cheek, slowly tracing her fingers down the side of his face and placing her palm flat against his chest.

"I can feel your heart beating," she whispered.

He nodded, dumbstruck.

What should he do now?

"Thank you, Ben," she repeated, releasing him and stepping back. The realisation that this was his moment, and it may have passed, struck him. She moved to the side and reached for the door handle behind him. They were still touching.

He should make a move… but how? Do something. Anything.

Suddenly he felt inadequate. The hinges on the door shrieked as she opened it, the sound of the rain striking the ground beyond, carried inside. Angela passed out into the storm. Ben hesitated and then followed, calling after her.

"Angie… wait!"

It was a decision that would play over and over again in his mind – and in the mind of the jurors – in the months to come. It was a genuine sliding-doors moment. A decision that Ben Crake would forever regret.

CHAPTER ONE

Despite the shelter provided by the brick wall encompassing the garden, Tom was still buffeted by the wind as he surveyed the damage. Forced to brace himself against each gust it was no wonder the overnight storm wrought carnage at the back of the house.

The greenhouse had collapsed at one corner, the frame twisted and broken, bent in a seemingly impossible angle that there was no coming back from. The opposing corner was lifted into the air like the hull of a gigantic ship preparing to sink beneath the waves. Fortunately, the panels were Perspex rather than glass or the devastation would have been worse. As it was, plastic pots, bedding trays and polystyrene cups littered the garden around his feet. Many of these were torn or battered into unrecognisable shapes.

"You'll not be getting that down today, I take it?"

Tom looked up and to his right. Raymond, their neighbour was peering over the dividing wall. He had to be standing on something and Tom hoped it was sturdy, just as the next gust threatened to wreak yet more havoc around him. He followed Raymond's eye up to the roof of the garages by which the two houses were linked, and shook his head.

"No, I'll have to wait until the wind dies before I go anywhere near it."

"If I was your age, I'd be up there in a flash, Tom."

Tom smiled. Raymond was in his eighties, six foot tall and as slim as a taper, and had been ever since Tom had known him. He'd also done a few laps of the track working abroad, running his own business and had clearly experienced life. He knew a lot and enjoyed conveying said knowledge, whether you wanted to hear it or not.

"Well," Tom said, his eyes lingering on Saffy's trampoline lodged precariously on the pitched roof, "I'm a bit wider than you and I'd act like a sail. I'd probably come down somewhere in Cambridgeshire if I was lucky."

"Yes, true enough," Raymond said. "Good job I don't have my car in the drive."

Tom smiled. In all the time he'd been with Alice, he'd never known Raymond to park his car in the driveway of his home. He always left it in the road in front of the house. Alice once said it was because the drive was too narrow for his wife to get in and out of it comfortably. Sadly, she'd passed away a couple of years previously and yet the car was still left on the road overnight. Maybe it was habitual, maybe it was a man trying to hold onto his past, unwilling to accept the change in his life.

"I'll get it down as soon as this wind drops," Tom said. "I promise."

"You should have tied it down."

Tom knelt and picked up one length of strap. It had been one of three used to tie the trampoline down to the hooks driven deep into the soil. The connector had sheared off. Once one strap was loose, the pressure on the others was too much and they must have gone one after another. He held the end up for Raymond to see.

"Ah… cheap plastic. I'll bet it was made in China."

In Raymond's world view, everything that broke was made in China.

"Plastic degrades when exposed to the elements, heating and cooling," Tom said. "I must admit, I didn't check the clips, but the straps and anchors were sound."

"They don't make them like they used to, that's for sure."

Growing up, Tom only ever experienced trampolines in the beer gardens of pubs. Great, sprawling blue things with no safety nets, covers for the springs or adult supervision in most cases. The number of times he'd lost the skin off his shins by slipping between the giant springs. These days, every back garden seemed to have one. It was the best purchase he and Alice had ever made though. Saffy was never off it as long as it wasn't raining and often times, even if it was.

"As I say, I'll get it down as soon as it's safe. In the meantime, I'd recommend keeping clear of the drive and the garden. Sorry for the hassle."

"Don't worry, I'm not planning on going anywhere today."

"Not even to the club?"

Raymond went out every night, almost exactly at half past ten, seven days a week unless he was unwell. He'd return half an hour later, on the dot. This was a puzzle that Tom's keen detective mind sought to solve through deduction. Was he giving someone a lift home from work, a family member perhaps? But that'd been ruled out because no one worked seven days a week. Not unless someone else had been murdered, and, anyway, Raymond was a retired decorator not a policeman. Was he meeting someone for a clandestine meet-up? It was possible. Every town had an illicit trade catering to the needs of lonely men, and even women, should they feel the need. However, this too was dismissed. If he had a favourite, then she couldn't be working seven nights a week either. It was a puzzle that Tom couldn't solve.

In the end, Alice grew tired of his constant speculation and asked, much to Tom's embarrassment. The answer was nowhere near as enthralling as he'd imagined. Raymond would call in at the local social club for a swift beer before closing. Every night, like clockwork. The barman had it lined up for him before the front door had even closed upon his entry. For once, real life was honest and simple. Tom liked honest and simple, although too much of that would put him out of work.

"Well, I'll always go to the club. No doubt. Let me know when you are going up and I'll give you a hand."

With that, Raymond dropped out of sight. He had an opinion on everything, but Tom, Alice and especially Saffy, had a great deal of time and affection for the elderly man. He was quick-witted and each cutting remark was said with a smile.

The gate rattled, the bolt shrieking as it was put under tension by the wind. Alice cracked open the French doors, reluctant to allow the wind a chance to catch it but had to as Russell forced his way out at her feet. The Jack Russell terrier set about inspecting the garden and all the new bits and pieces he could play with, or pee on, whichever took his fancy.

"I've made tea!" she called.

"I'll be right in."

There was little he could do to secure the greenhouse. Multiple panels were missing, blown off when the door was torn away from the frame. Much of the roof was now missing, presumably in neighbouring gardens or halfway across Norfolk by now. At least the wind could tear through what was left but not gain any extra lift now. The contents of the greenhouse couldn't leave the garden, hemmed in on all sides by brick walls but it would take some clearing up.

Tom crossed to the door and opened it, allowing the dog to enter first as was customary. Closing the door behind him, he realised just how loud it was outside with the wind howling around the house. He was pleased to be back inside. Alice was leaning over the dining table assembling cuttings she'd made from magazines and brochures judging by the butchered magazines on the chairs beside her. She glanced up at him as he found his mug of tea on the breakfast bar, cupping it to warm his hands.

"Is she salvageable?"

"Which? The trampoline or the greenhouse?" Tom asked.

"The greenhouse. I figured once the trampoline was attached to the roof, it would be terminal."

"Both are terminal, I reckon," Tom said, blowing the steam from the top of his tea and sipping it.

"Does that mean I need a new trampoline?" Saffy called from the adjacent living room where she was watching Sunday morning cartoons in her dressing gown.

"Afraid so, yes," he said.

Saffy came padding through in her oversized Tiger-feet slippers, pouting.

"Can we get one today?"

"Certainly not, young lady," Alice said without looking up. "Otherwise, it will end up on the roof alongside the old one."

Saffy's pout grew and she looked at Tom, rolling her eyes in a snapshot of the exasperated teenager she was destined to become in a few years' time. "I'm not saying assemble it today… but we could *buy it* today and have it ready to go when the storm passes. *It's not difficult.*"

The last comment had to be repetition of something she'd heard from a classmate or, more likely, from a YouTube channel she favoured watching. It was a go-to line that she'd adopted a week previously that was being used more and more.

Alice met her daughter's eye. "Comments like

that will ensure the only trampoline you get to use is in Abigail's back garden, young lady."

"Ugh… I can't stand Abigail," Saffy complained.

Tom frowned. "What's wrong with Abigail? I thought you two were… what do you say, BFFs?"

Saffy took a deep breath. "That was before last week when she told Martha that I'd taken her yellow pen… and then told Jack that I'd said it was him."

"Sounds reasonable," Tom said, sipping his drink. "Had you?"

"Had I what?"

"Taken the yellow pen?"

"No!" Saffy said with such force that he was quite taken aback. "I took the blue one."

"Right… and Jack, did you tell Martha that he'd taken it?"

Saffy looked at him, confused. "Yes. And he had."

"Okay. All of that seems… reasonable," Tom said. Saffy dipped her head in agreement and returned to the living room. Tom smiled. "I'm glad I didn't have to interview the witnesses working that case."

Alice grinned. "They'll be friends again tomorrow morning, I'm sure. They'll have to be as Sylvie and I are meeting for coffee and the kids will have to get on. I think Saffy's just bored and wants half-term to be over. It doesn't do her any good to be cooped up in here all week."

"What's all this then?" Tom asked, coming to stand alongside her and casting an eye over the assembled pictures. There were more than he'd thought. There were cuttings of men, women in an assortment of dresses, prestigious-looking mansions, classic cars and floral table decorations.

"It's my mood board."

"Say again?"

Alice glanced at him and frowned. "I told you the other day. It's research."

"For the wedding?"

"Exactly." She cast an open hand out over the collage in front of them. "And this is my mood board."

Tom paid closer attention, tapping one image that was front and centre. "This looks like a Tuscan villa."

"That's because *it is* a Tuscan villa."

"Well, I don't know if you're aware of a detective inspector's salary constraints but getting married in a villa in Tuscany might be pushing it a bit."

"Who says that's where the ceremony would be?" she said, smiling playfully.

"Ah… so you're not planning a wedding in Tuscany?"

"No," she said, smiling and rearranging some of the images in front of her. "I thought maybe Bali."

"Bali?" Tom asked, open mouthed, just as his mobile vibrated on the breakfast bar, indicating an incoming call.

"Hadn't you better get that?" she asked. "Someone might have died."

He shook his head, crossing the dining area to pick up his phone, silently mouthing the word *Bali* at Alice as he answered. She grinned. He wasn't sure if she was winding him up or not.

"Hi, Cassie," Tom said. "What's up?"

He could barely hear her over the sound of the wind coming through the mouthpiece of her mobile.

"Hi, Tom. Sorry to bother you this early. I know you're on the late shift, but I figured you'd want to know. The storm has unearthed a body… or some of it, anyway, out near Ringstead."

Tom checked Saffy was out of earshot, lowering his voice anyway. "Some of it?"

"Aye. Looks like a tree's come down and the body was pulled out of the ground along with the roots. I think you're going to want to take a look."

"Okay, text me the location and I'll be right there."

He hung up, glancing over at Alice who was watching on.

"You have to go in early?"

"Yes, sorry." He looked in on Saffy whose attention was caught by Caitlyn, a neighbour from two doors down, strolling up the drive waving a hand clutching a number of letters with an artificial smile.

Alice sighed. "That new postie doing weekends must have delivered our mail to Caitlyn's house again. That's two Saturdays running he's done that. I guessed when nothing came through the letter box yesterday. I swear he's the dopiest postman we've ever had!"

Tom smiled. "He does look like he's stoned much of the time."

Saffy hopped off the sofa and ran to collect the post from their neighbour.

Tom took the opportunity where he knew he'd not be overheard by the little girl. "Cassie has found a body."

"She has all the luck," Alice said, dryly. "Suspicious?"

"Aren't they always? Until the examination says otherwise."

Saffy hurried into the kitchen with the letters in her small hands. She tossed all but one onto the breakfast bar and held a promotional leaflet aloft in both hands.

"The circus is coming to town!" she said excitedly, handing the leaflet to Tom. He inspected it.

"Is that something you'd like to go to?" he asked.

Saffy's expression changed, becoming thoughtful.

"If there are animals in cages, then no," she said after a moment of deliberation. "That wouldn't be cool."

Tom examined the details. "It doesn't look like that kind of circus. Acrobats, knife throwers and clowns, by the looks of it."

"Oooh… knife throwers… very cool," Saffy said.

Alice shot Tom a dark look. "As if she needs more inspiration!"

Tom grinned, turning the leaflet towards Alice. "And acrobats."

"And clowns!" Saffy said. "Knife-throwing clowns."

"Might be pushing it, munchkin," Tom said. "I could book tickets?"

Alice agreed with a reticent nod. "If she starts throwing knives at the dog, I'll hold you accountable, DI Janssen."

"Understood," Tom said, high-fiving Saffy, who took off in a hurry. "Where are you going?"

"To Snapchat Abi," she called over her shoulder.

Tom exchanged a look with Alice. "Is she allowed to have a Snapchat account?"

"It's mine, and I monitor the exchanges," Alice

said. "It's the only way I could stop the nagging. All her friends are on it."

"Oh, well that's okay then… I guess," Tom said, looking for his keys. He picked up his wallet and then checked the address Cassie had texted him, before kissing Alice goodbye. "Right, I'm off."

"Keep me posted, would you?" Alice asked as he walked away.

"Will do." Tom turned as he reached the doorway. "And Tuscany looks great."

"It's lovely there," Alice said. "But I was thinking… more of a honeymoon type of place."

Tom inclined his head and smiled. "I love Tuscany."

CHAPTER TWO

TOM PICKED his way along the narrow lanes leading towards Ringstead, a small village a little inland from Hunstanton, separated from the larger conurbation by farmland and the Ringstead Downs, one of the largest remaining chalk grasslands in the county. He knew the area well as it was a safe area of open ground and managed woodland for children to play, and for ramblers to wander in nature. Families would often have impromptu barbecues in a large clearing, surrounded by trees with a low chalk ridge at the back of them. Whether they were permitted to do so, Tom had never found out, but as long as it was done safely and all of the mess cleared away then he figured it was okay.

Passing the turning into the narrow car park for the Downs, he continued on and, as per Cassie's instructions, he turned off before reaching the centre of the village and headed past several farms, moving onto made-up tracks frequented by agricultural vehicles only and feeling the result, as the car's suspension groaned on the unadopted lanes. Where the track came to an end, at the entrance to a field on the left and a thick copse straight ahead, Tom found a solitary liveried police car alongside Cassie's, and a small hatchback which he knew belonged to Dr Fiona Williams.

A uniformed constable climbed out of the car to greet him.

"Morning, sir," PC Marshall said, smiling.

"Morning Sheriff," Tom said, referencing the nickname the constable was known by. He looked around. Gulls soared overhead, shrieking as the storm had driven them inland. This close to the coast, the wind was still roaring but the trees offered them a little sanctuary. It wasn't raining yet, not like the torrential downpours they'd experienced in the early hours but, glancing up at the ominous clouds rolling in off the North Sea, it was only a matter of time.

"DS Knight is waiting for you about a hundred yards that way, sir," Marshall said, pointing towards the trees. "There's a clear route through the trees. Not exactly well trodden but passable. Scenes of Crime are on their way but it's just us and the FME at the moment."

Tom thanked him, looking around as he set off in the direction of the crime scene. The nearest inhabited building would be Hall Farm, which was roughly a quarter of a mile away. Beyond that was another farm and the nearest residents of the village were nowhere in sight. This was an isolated place. In the summer, beautiful, but in November, it was cold, dark and lonely.

"Everything all right, sir?"

Tom looked back, not realising he'd been standing still, momentarily lost in thought. He smiled. "I'm all good, Constable."

He picked up the pace and entered between the trees. Branches were down and the damage was evidently recent, judging by the colour of the exposed wood. The storm had hit the coast pretty hard and it was easy to see where he needed to be. Several trees had been uprooted in a line, the first to fall lay flat with the next two coming down on top of them, almost as if Mother Nature had driven a sharp blade through the woods and hacked three down cleanly. As it was, the surrounding trees were swaying in an alarming manner suggesting they might be next.

Tom found Cassie standing beside the first of the fallen trees, peering into a crater where the roots had once been. It was almost a metre and a half deep, the soil wrenched from the earth in one great clump along with the tree and cast aside on the ground alongside where it must have stood for several hundreds of years.

"She was a beauty, wasn't she?" Cassie said, smiling briefly in greeting. He narrowed his eyes. "The tree, she was a giant."

"Right, yes."

Standing by her shoulder, Tom looked down to where Fiona Williams was crouching in her forensic coveralls, clipboard in hand, examining what looked like a black tarpaulin that had been torn to reveal its contents. She noted Tom's arrival and stood up.

"Morning, Tom." She indicated the precarious-looking trees around them. "Lovely day for it!"

"What do we have?" he asked no one in particular. It was the on-call forensic medical examiner who answered.

"Well, you have a body," she said dryly.

"Do we need a medical degree to figure that out?" Tom replied with a hint of a smile.

"Well, in this case, you just might, Detective Inspector," Fiona said, drawing an inquiring look from Tom. "Perhaps I should rephrase. What you have here, is a *partial* body. Some of it is missing."

Tom cocked his head and then glanced at Cassie. "How much is missing?"

"It'd be quicker to tell you what's here, to be honest, Tom," Fiona said. "You have a torso that remains pretty much intact. Female, white, and likely to be in her late teens or early twenties judging by the condition of her skin; taking into account she's been wrapped in plastic and in the ground for some time."

"Define *some time* for me, if you can?"

Dr Williams thought about it, glancing down at the remains briefly. "From the rate of decomposition, I'd guess you're looking at a month to six weeks, give or take. With so little to examine, it is an estimate. The pathologist should be able to tell you more."

"You said there are parts missing. What else do we have here for us to work with?'

"Besides the torso?"

Tom nodded.

"An arm and two legs..."

"That's it?" Tom asked, failing to mask his surprise.

"Correction, half an arm and most of one leg," Fiona said. "The upper arm is present but the lower portion, including the hand is missing." She raised herself up to her full height and looked around the woods. "I suppose there's every chance the killer deposited other parts of her around here somewhere, but why they'd bother digging multiple graves, I'll never know."

Tom frowned. "And you think she was murdered? Can you be sure?"

Fiona shook her head. "No, without the rest of

the body I certainly can't be definitive, but dismemberment and illegal burial strikes me as a bit iffy, wouldn't you say? Not that I'm telling you how to arrange your investigation."

"Point taken," Tom said. He looked past her at the remains, seeing the plastic wasn't a tarpaulin at all, but heavy-grade refuse sacks, bin liners. There didn't appear to be enough room in the crater for a full body, even one that was missing a head and an arm. Cassie noticed his confusion.

"Yes, that's right. Multiple bags."

He looked at her quizzically.

"It's not just the head and a partial arm that have been cut off. Whoever dumped her here, dismembered the body first. The legs are cut into chunks and have been placed in one bag, the torso in another… the bag of legs has the partial arm in it as well."

"Jeez…" Tom said, grimacing.

"Yeah, nice huh?" Cassie said glumly.

Tom cast an eye over the bags. This was no way for anyone to be laid to rest, cast into the ground like refuse into landfill.

"Any indication as to the cause of death?"

Fiona shook her head. "I've not gone into it too far as we have to wait for the crime scene techs to arrive, but from my initial inspection of the torso, I can't see any wounds or injuries commensurate with a killing blow. Perhaps that's why the head is missing… but I'm only speculating. The cuts to the body where the arms and legs have been severed… are not precise, indicative of an amateur or hasty approach. If someone was proficient with a blade, a skilled butcher for example, then I would expect to see cleaner passes through the tissue."

"What if they were in a hurry then? Could they still know what they're doing?"

"Perhaps, or maybe the edge to the blade was not honed enough. My instinct still tells me this is an amateur, though. Some of the cuts are more ragged than others, suggesting he lost heart in what he was doing and started hacking at it rather than being clinical."

"Nice," Tom whispered.

"Weather warning is still in place for today and through the night," Cassie said, nervously looking at the trees. "It's your call, Boss."

Tom took a deep breath. "We can't leave her out here for the animals. Let's get everyone on the scene and get it processed as quickly as possible."

"I'll make the call," Cassie said, reaching for her mobile.

Tom dropped to his haunches, resting his elbows on his knees and examining the crater. There was something odd about it all but he couldn't put his finger on what it was.

"Penny for them?" Fiona asked him.

He looked around the scene, rubbing his chin with the flat of his palm.

"Why here? And why not all of her?"

Fiona turned the corner of her mouth down and shrugged. "Beats me. But, then again, I've never understood what drives these people to do such vicious things. I mean, I can understand how someone – anyone – could be driven to kill under the right set of circumstances or if they absolutely had to, but doing this," she said, indicating the bags of dismembered body parts beside her, and shaking her head, "it makes my skin crawl. As it would any normal, sane person."

Tom agreed, but only in part. "You'd be amazed at what people can do when they feel they have no other choice," he said, shaking his head, "or if their own life after the event is threatened. Many will do anything to preserve it. Is there anything there that could help us identify her?"

Fiona looked down. "I haven't come across any identification. In fact, there are no personal effects at all. I suppose we shouldn't be surprised by that. There will be no place for jewellery. Sorry to appear crude, but no fingers and no ears, or indeed a head, will explain why. There are no clothes here. No fabric remnants or shoes. Her toenails are not painted though."

"And that's significant?"

Fiona shrugged. "Her nails are well taken care

of. Personally, I never used to bother and therefore when it came to dressing up for a night out, my feet were not looking their best, whereas this young lady took care of hers. I should imagine, she'd have worn nail varnish or something to show them off. Just an observation, one that only a woman would notice. No offence."

"None taken," Tom said, appreciating the insight. "Anything else?"

"We are in something of a natural bowl here," she said, waving a hand around in the air in a circular motion. "The water likely drains from the surrounding chalk ridge down into this valley, so I think the water table is quite high where we are now."

"Meaning?"

"It's helped preserve the body. The ground is cold and wet. We've had quite a bit of rain in the past couple of months as well." She shrugged. "It might help."

"And in terms of identification, we'll be relying on her DNA sample being in the database?"

"I should say so," Fiona agreed. "Once the forensics team are through with the scene and we can get her out of the ground and take a proper look at her, then we'll know if she has any distinguishing marks that might help. Any young women gone missing recently?"

Tom arched his eyebrows. "People go missing all the time, but nothing recent as far as I'm aware."

"Shame," Fiona said. "If she's from out of town, it'll be doubly hard. Hey, do you remember that poor soul who was dumped in the fens… must be twenty-odd years ago now? The one where the killer cut the head off the poor girl."

"Yes, I remember reading about it," Tom said. "Sex worker, wasn't she? From Eastern Europe."

"That's right," Fiona said. "It was a devil of a task to identify her, but they managed it. But she was reported missing."

"That's always where the problem lies," Tom said. "If no one misses them, then no one comes looking and asking questions. That's why some people just vanish into thin air."

Cassie reappeared alongside him. "I spoke to Tamara. She's going to get a few more people down here and get this done as quickly as possible. I've asked Eric to start looking at all the missing persons cases going back six months to see if anything leaps out at us. I hope that's okay?"

Tom nodded. "Fingers crossed we get a DNA hit or the rest of her turns up around here somewhere."

"Cadaver dogs are coming as well," Cassie said. "If we're lucky, the rest of her won't be too far away."

"Oh, thinking about it, there is one thing that

strikes me as odd, Tom," Fiona said. Both Tom and Cassie looked down as Fiona lowered herself closer to the bag containing one of the legs and a partial arm. "This rather odd abrasion on the skin of her thigh. Do you see it?" Tom could just about make out what she was referring to, but he couldn't see detail from this distance. It was a patch of skin, perhaps half a handspan in width, slightly longer on one edge than the other and roughly the length of an index finger. It had a discolouration to it in comparison with the surrounding tissue.

"What is it?" he asked.

"That's just it. I have no idea." She shrugged. "The skin appears to be somewhat leathery… but you'll understand that is not, strictly speaking, a professional medical term. Rather odd though. Just thought I'd mention it."

Vehicles could be heard approaching along the nearby track. The rain also began to fall. Cassie drew her coat about her, shooting a despairing glance at the heavens.

CHAPTER THREE

Tom Janssen pulled into the car park in front of the police station. The side entrance was currently blocked by two vans offloading a group of rowdy individuals, so the rear parking wasn't accessible. He hesitated to walk through the front door, focussing on the commotion at the side of the building but the officers seemed to have it in hand. Whoever this bunch were, they were voicing their displeasure at being detained, but no more than that.

One woman, in her late sixties, Tom guessed, sat down on the ground next to the front wheel of the second van and began singing an old protest song from the days of the picket lines. Tom saw PC Kerry Palmer bend over to discuss the woman's refusal to move, only for several people around them to mimic the move and subsequently join in the singing, much to Kerry's frustration. She put her hands on her hips and looked skyward for inspiration.

Rain drops began striking the ground around them, another shower coming in on the stiff breeze. Showers were forecast before the tail end of the storm would make land later in the day. Tom doubted anyone would be choosing to sit outside when it did.

Leaving the scene, and pleased to no longer be dealing with such events, he avoided it entirely by entering through the main lobby. Raised voices greeted him.

"Stop lying to me!"

Tom was taken aback. A lady was at the front desk haranguing the constable, who protested his innocence with his hands up in supplication. Neither of them paid him any attention, although the younger man standing beside the woman looked nervously over at him. The woman was dark haired, in her early fifties, slim and quite tall even considering she was in heels. The younger man beside her was twenty-something, a similar height and build and sported the same angular jaw and cheekbones. Her son, perhaps?

"As I've already told you, Mrs Dale," the constable stated evenly, deliberately keeping his tone measured, "the detective inspector is no longer stationed here…"

"Why wasn't I told?" She slammed her balled fist onto the counter. The constable pursed his lips, taking a half step away. Tom felt the officer had lost the heart and mind in this particular battle.

He approached.

"Excuse me."

All eyes turned to him. Mrs Dale, a name Tom thought familiar but couldn't place, glared at him. Despite the obvious anger in her expression, he could also see she'd been crying, her eyes were red-rimmed and puffy. The young man looked even more the image of her, standing alongside, reinforcing his assumption they were mother and son.

"I'm Detective Inspector Janssen. I succeeded DI Reynolds when he moved on to another role. Can I help you with something?"

That small sliver of information appeared to cut through and he watched her anger dissipate, if only slightly.

"I'm Marie Dale," she said firmly. "And Benjamin Crake murdered my daughter, Angela."

Now it clicked. The Crake case made headline news across the country. Tom silently berated himself for remembering the murderer's name rather than the victim's, such was the way of these things. Although, he'd always made an effort with his own caseload to do the opposite. But Angela's murder was before his time in Norfolk CID.

PC Nichols, standing behind the counter, looked grateful at Tom's intervention. "Tom, Mrs Dale has come in to see why Ben has been released from prison and also to find out—"

"Why weren't we told, DI Janssen? Do you not think we have the right to know?"

Tom raised a hand politely. "Let's find somewhere where we can have a proper talk, okay?"

Reluctantly, Marie Dale agreed, although she was in full flight and didn't appear keen to ease off. Tom led them into a visitor room just off the lobby, holding the door open for the two of them and offering them a seat as they entered. Marie Dale remained standing, arms folded defiantly across her chest. Her son pulled out a chair for her and, after a brief hesitation, sat down.

Tom had barely sat down himself, when she asked the question once more, only this time without the overt anger she'd already demonstrated.

"How can Ben be out of prison, Inspector? I don't understand it."

Tom was at loss to explain. He was unaware of the case since its conclusion which must have been four or five years previously.

"Forgive me for asking such a daft question, but how do you know that he is out?"

"Because, Inspector Janssen, I've just bumped into him on the bloody high street! That's why. Clear as day, strolling along like he hasn't a care in the world. How is that possible?"

Tom took a breath, wracking his brain to recall the details of the case.

He recalled a contentious trial, and the killer, a local, was convicted by a majority verdict of the jury after more than a week of deliberation. He was one of only a handful of people ever to have been convicted of murder in the absence of a dead body. Angela Dale's remains had never been found. Even after conviction and sentencing, Ben Crake refused to reveal where she was buried, flatly denying his guilt at every opportunity. The sentencing judge took that stout refusal into consideration when giving him thirty-five years with a minimum period of thirty before he would be eligible for parole. Tom remembered the judge summing up and making it very clear that he'd considered a whole-life term, but the guidelines didn't allow it.

To think that Ben Crake would be out five years later struck him as very odd, but Marie Dale was adamant.

"I'm not aware of his release, Mrs Dale," he said. "Is this your son?"

"Yes, this is Jack."

"Hello, Jack." Tom glanced at him and the

young man nodded, smiling politely. "Were you with your mother?"

"I was alone, Inspector… but I didn't imagine it," Marie Dale said, cutting in.

"Please, call me Tom," he said, keeping his tone calm, "and I'm not doubting you."

"How can this be?" she asked, her voice quivering as she spoke. This was the first time he'd seen a crack in her armour since they'd entered the room.

"If you can bear with me, I'll go and make a couple of calls," he said.

"You mean you don't know?" Jack asked, incredulous.

"The probation service or HMP service are under no obligation to inform the police, so, no, I really don't know," Tom said honestly. "But I will try and get to the bottom of this for you as soon as I can."

Excusing himself, Tom left the room, ensuring the door was closed behind him. He crossed the small lobby to the front desk. PC Nichols rose from behind his desk and came over to meet him.

"How is she doing?" he asked.

"Upset would be an understatement," Tom said. "What do you know about this?"

Nichols shook his head. "Last I heard, Crake's defence team were going to appeal, but we all expected that. I hadn't heard anything more, and certainly not recently. But..."

"But?" Tom asked, fearful of the answer.

Nichols took a breath and glanced over his shoulder to ensure they were alone. "I called my brother-in-law. He works in the probation service, for his sins, and he told me it's true, Crake's out."

"How come?"

Nichols shook his head. "Beats us both, but he is and that's that. Released yesterday, by all accounts."

"Bloody hell. And no one saw fit to tell us?"

"Right hand doesn't talk to the left hand, you know that Tom!"

"Isn't that the truth," Tom said, sighing. "I'd better get some more detail before I go back in there," he said, looking over his shoulder.

PC Nichols buzzed Tom through the security door and he hurriedly made his way upstairs. The forensics officers were processing the scene and although Tom was keen to speak to Eric and see if he'd come up with any prospective names for the victim they'd discovered, he was well aware of Marie Dale and her son waiting on him to provide answers. He knocked on Tamara's door and entered without waiting to be bidden; they didn't work within formal constraints and seldom waited.

Tamara looked up, surprised and seated behind her desk.

"Tom, I was expecting—"

"Hi, sorry to speak over you but I've got Marie Dale downstairs and she's got herself all worked up over—"

"Ben Crake's release?" a voice said from behind. Tom turned to see Chief Superintendent Watts sitting on Tamara's sofa. It was positioned behind the door and Tom hadn't realised Tamara was not alone.

"Yes, sir. Sorry," Tom said. "I didn't see you there, sir."

"That's okay, Tom," he said, standing up. "Damn mess, this Crake situation." He gestured to Tamara. "We were just discussing the impact of it all."

"On whom, sir?"

Watts appeared taken aback by the comment. "Well… the constabulary, obviously. Questions are being asked Tom. It won't do. Not at all."

"Quite hard on the Dales, too, sir."

Watts frowned. "Yes, I'm sure it is. Marie is downstairs, you say?"

Tom nodded. "Along with her son Jack."

"Hmm… Jack. Decent lad as I recall. It was hard on him when he lost his sister. They were close, I understand."

"You know them, sir?" Tom asked.

"We spoke during the investigation, yes. I was a lowly DCI back then," he said, glancing at

Tamara. "Far from as distinguished as you, Tamara."

She politely tilted her head with a slight smile, acknowledging the clumsy, backhanded compliment.

"Would you like to have a word with Marie, sir?" Tom asked. "I'm sure she'd appreciate a word from a familiar face."

Watts glanced at his watch. "Hmm… if only I could. I have to brief the assistant chief constable, and she's an impatient woman at the best of times. I'll leave it in your capable hands, if you don't mind, Tom? You're very good with people. It's one of your strong points."

"Thank you, sir," Tom said.

Watts made his way to the door before turning back and looking past Tom at Tamara who rose as he left.

"Do bear in mind what I said, Tamara. I think it's in all of our interests, don't you agree?"

"I do, sir. Leave it with me."

Something about her tone made Tom believe she felt the exact opposite, but he remained stone-faced.

"Good, good." Watts turned to Tom. "I understand you have a body out at Ringstead?"

"That's correct, sir. A young woman… most of her anyway."

The senior officer's forehead creased in concern.

"This is not good. Not good at all. We could do without this, especially this week. Do try to get it roped off quickly, won't you Tom?"

"I always do, sir. It's one of my strengths."

"Good man."

Watts clapped Tom gently on the shoulder and departed.

"Keep me informed, won't you Tamara?" he said over his shoulder.

"Will do, sir," Tamara replied but Watts had already left. She sank down into her chair, running a hand through her hair. "Close the door, would you, Tom? Feel free to lock it."

He did as he was bid. There was no lock on the door and he shot her a quizzical look. "What did Teflon want?"

Tamara smiled at the in-joke, the name most people informally used to refer to the chief superintendent because nothing ever seemed to stick to him. How he'd risen to his current rank was a mystery to most but, then again, most people didn't know how to play the political game and the upper echelons of the police service were just as political as any other institution. Watts was exceptional at playing pass the parcel, particularly if the parcel in question contained an explosive device. He was never the one left holding it when it went off.

"He got wind of Ben Crake's release this morning," Tamara said. "He's worried about how it will go down locally if he chooses to come home."

"Worried about how any strife will look for him, more like."

Tamara sat forward in her seat, resting her elbows on her desk, interlocking her hands and pointing both forefingers directly at Tom. "I think there's something in that, Tom. I gather that case generated a passionate reaction amongst the locals when Crake was arrested."

"So I understand," Tom said.

"I think he's worried someone will take matters into their own hands."

"How come he's out?"

Tamara sighed. "From what we can gather, the court of appeal has ruled the conviction was unsafe. Crake's defence team has uncovered inconsistencies in the evidence presented at trial along with information that wasn't disclosed to the defence, so Teflon – Watts – just told me, and it has cast yet more doubt on the conviction. I'm not abreast of the detail, but couple that with how tight the decision was anyway, they've allowed him out on licence, a bail of sorts, until all of this can be ironed out."

"That's unusual," Tom said. "In a murder case the suspect still remains incarcerated until cleared in court—"

Tamara spread her hands wide. "I'm only telling you what he's just told me."

Tom shook his head. "That's asking for trouble."

"There might be if he comes back here."

"Well, brace yourself then," Tom said. Tamara looked at him sternly. "Marie Dale just bumped into him in the town!"

"Oh, bloody hell!" Tamara said. "How is she?"

"I'd say ninety percent angry and ten percent distraught," he frowned, "or swinging back the other way. If her reaction is anything to go by, then this could get messy. I think she was caught off guard this morning."

Tamara took a deep breath. "Watts wants us to have a word with Crake if he shows up. I sort of hoped he'd stay away judging by the depth of feeling."

"What does he expect us to do, run him out of town before the burning pitchforks come after him?"

"Something like that, yes."

Tom crossed his arms. "He does know we're policing in the twenty-first century these days, doesn't he? Innocent until proven—"

"Guilty. Yes, I know. The thing is, in most people's minds, he was found guilty and got off lightly."

"That's not for us to judge!"

"No, it isn't. But I doubt the good burghers of Norfolk will agree with you once word gets out."

"That's another thing," Tom said. "This case was headline news not so long ago. How have the journalists missed this?"

Tamara shrugged. "Beats me! Now… what do we have going on at Ringstead?"

"I'll fill you in once I've spoken to the Dales, if that's okay?"

"Yes, yes, of course," Tamara said, dismissively waving him away. "Sorry. I forgot. What are you going to tell them?"

Tom shook his head. "Justice must run its course… or something lame like that. What can I say to a woman who thinks their daughter's killer has got away with it?"

Tamara rubbed her eyes with the tips of her fingers. "You'd better make it clear for her to steer clear of Ben Crake, for her own wellbeing."

"And maybe for his," Tom said quietly.

Tamara nodded.

CHAPTER FOUR

TAMARA GREAVE STOOD at the front of the room casually scanning the information boards as they were slowly populated with information as it came in. What they had already was scant to say the least. Her mobile rang. Glancing at the screen, she saw David's number flash up. It was the second time he'd called today, not that she'd taken the first one. This time, she answered.

"David, everything okay?"

"Yes, of course. I was wondering what your plans are for the weekend?"

"Sounds like you're making some," she said playfully.

"I was hoping to come up to the coast. I know the weather is dreadful, but I figured we could get the wood burner going... a bottle of wine. I could cook us a lovely meal."

"You had me right up until the *you cook* part," Tamara said.

"Ah, yes... fair enough, but it was a good start, right?"

Tamara was distracted by Cassie walking into ops, removing her jacket and shaking the water off before hanging it up. Her hair was wet through and clung to her face. Cassie ran a hand through it, shaking the excess water off moments later.

"And I thought it rained a lot in the northeast," Cassie muttered as Eric smiled at her.

"T... are you there?" David asked.

"Yes... yes, I'm here. Sounds good. Let's do it."

"Great!" David said enthusiastically. "Shall I book our usual place?"

"Er... no need. Mum and Dad are away to Bristol for the weekend to catch up with friends, so I have my place to myself for once."

"If you don't mind me intruding?"

Tamara laughed. "Of course not."

"Great. I'll see you Friday evening or would you prefer Saturday?"

"Whatever works for you, honestly. Just let me know."

"Will do," David said. "I..."

"I'll see you then, bye!" Tamara said, quickly

hanging up as Cassie came to stand on her shoulder.

"Still avoiding the *I love yous*, are you?" Cassie said quietly, with a wry smile.

Tamara frowned as she slipped the mobile into her pocket. "Am I that obvious?"

"Yes."

"Terrific." She turned to Cassie. "What's wrong with me? He's a nice guy. I like him, his company… he can't cook but," she shrugged, "he's a divorced middle-aged man, so that's not a surprise."

"There's nothing wrong with you. You're perfect just the way you are. Don't force it, even if he's trying to."

Tamara perched herself on the edge of the nearest desk. "How did you get on in Ringstead?"

"The body has been removed and transported to await the keen hands of Dr Death," Cassie said, sniffing loudly. "You know, if I get pneumonia, I don't want any questioning of my sick pay."

"I'm through with the database search,' Eric said, coming to join them. "I had to widen the parameters because there hasn't been a matching disappearance locally in the last three years. A few missing teens but no one over the age of fifteen, and Dr Williams set her as older, right?" he looked at Cassie for confirmation. She affirmed it with a nod. "Well, I've gone through all reported missing persons, anyone who has absconded from care, tied in known sex workers; all of which needed to match a white woman aged seventeen to twenty-seven—"

"What about tattoos?" Cassie asked.

Eric looked disappointed and then fearful. "I don't remember you mentioning tattoos."

"That's because I didn't know, Eric," Cassie said, taking out her mobile. "It was only when we were able to recover the body, the torso part, did we find a tattoo on the lower back." She tapped on the screen and brought up her saved pictures before turning the image so Tamara and Eric could see. "Here, at the base of her spine where it meets her bottom. I think it's some sort of Celtic pattern or tribal symbol."

The tattoo started centrally at the base of the spine and spread out in a mirror image to the left and right, stretching beyond the middle of the hips. It was a solitary colour, black or perhaps dark blue. It was difficult to tell in the light provided within the woods on Cassie's mobile.

"Distinctive," Tamara said. Looking at Eric, she nodded towards his computer. "Can you add that to the search and see if it brings up any more possibilities?"

"Yes, of course," Eric said. He glanced at Cassie and Tamara thought he looked irritated. She looked at Cassie once Eric was back at his desk.

"Everything all right between the two of you?"

Cassie shrugged. "Fine by me, but I can't say for Eric." She lowered her voice. "He's been a bit out of sorts recently."

"How long?"

Cassie raised her eyebrows. "Weeks. Haven't you noticed?"

"No, I can't say I have. Anything to worry about?"

Cassie smiled. "Where Eric's concerned, there's always something to be worried about. I'm sure he's fine. I asked him how George was yesterday and he bit my head off."

"They've not found it easy going, have they, Eric and Becca?"

"Aye. Can't see them trying for another anytime soon."

"Got it!" Eric announced triumphantly, looking over at them and gesturing for them to come to him. Both women came alongside and he angled his screen towards them. "Here she is," he said smiling.

The image of a smiling teenager stared out of the screen at them. She was pretty with finely chiselled features and large round grey, blue eyes, unusual for a brunette. The picture would have been taken at a party of some description. She was smiling into the camera, it looked natural rather than artificial as these shots often could be. Eric looked at them in turn.

"The tattoo is an exact match. I give you, Angela Dale."

Tamara felt her heart skip a beat.

"You have got to be kidding me?"

The smile faded from Eric's face and he looked at Cassie who shrugged that she had no idea either. Tamara straightened up.

"Call Tom and tell him to drop whatever it is he's doing and get back here, would you?"

With that, Tamara walked away. Eric and Cassie exchanged glances. It was Cassie who spoke first.

"Who's Angela Dale?"

Eric sat back in his chair. "She went missing a few years back. A local weirdo was convicted of killing her but we never found a body."

"You were on the investigation team?" Cassie asked.

Eric shook his head. "No, I'd just joined. I was in basic training. Nowhere near the case, but everyone felt it. Angela was only a year or two younger than me when she went missing. Not that I knew her, mind you. But it sent shock waves through the community. We hadn't had a murder for years that I can recall."

"Right," Cassie murmured, watching the door Tamara had walked through. "So, what's spooked the DCI?"

Eric shrugged. "Not a clue." He turned back to

his screen. "I'd better get all this written up before Tom gets back."

"Where is he anyway?"

"Not a clue."

"Eric, you're repeating yourself."

He looked at her and shrugged. Cassie examined his face. The darkness under his eyes, the lines on his face. Up until recently, Eric had always looked more youthful than his years. In a short space of time that had been tipped on its head.

"Are you okay, Eric?' Cassie asked.

"Like you care."

The edge to his tone was cutting, and she felt it. Pursing her lips, she placed a hand on his shoulder and gently squeezed it. He didn't respond but neither did he shrug the touch away.

"I guess I should dig out the old case file, seeing as we've just solved a murder that has already been solved," she said. "Quickest murder case I've ever worked."

"Hey, Cass?" Eric said as she moved away. She turned back. "I'm sorry. It's just… George hasn't been sleeping well… and neither has Becca. It's all a bit much sometimes, you know?"

Cassie smiled. "I know, Eric. Let me know what I can do to help and I'll be there. Okay?"

He smiled appreciatively and turned back to his screen.

"WHAT DO we know about the Angela Dale murder?" Tamara asked. "And I want to know actual case facts and not what we can find on the internet from the time."

Cassie read from the notes in front of her. "Angela went missing on a Saturday night, following an evening out with friends. She left her group around seven o'clock saying she had someone to see."

"Who was it she was meeting?" Tom asked.

Cassie shook her head. "No one seemed to know at the time or, if they did know, they weren't telling us. After she didn't return home that night, her parents reported her missing to police the following afternoon."

"How old was she?" Tamara asked.

Eric answered. "Seventeen."

"Seems an overreaction for a seventeen-year-old spending the night away," Tamara said, thoughtfully. "I was forever disappearing at that age."

"And your folks didn't mind?" Tom asked playfully.

Tamara cocked her head. "No, they frequently hit the roof… not that it stopped me, mind you."

"There you go," Tom said.

"They never called the police on me, though. Didn't you ever stay out?"

Tom smiled. "I was always home early for church on Sunday."

Tamara rolled her eyes. "Somehow, I doubt that." She turned to Cassie. "Sorry Cass, go on."

"As you pointed out, police at the time fobbed the parents off… sorry, explained the need to allow her time to return home, assuming she was staying with a boyfriend. The following day, the mother, Marie Dale, returned to the station and pushed hard. Apparently, the family had been round to the boyfriend's place and he claimed not to have seen her since the previous afternoon. Seemingly they'd had a falling out, but the parents were unaware."

Tamara chewed on her lip, looking at the picture of Angela pinned to the information board. She pointed at her casually. "So, the investigation wound up from there?"

"Yes," Cassie said, revisiting her notes. "When it became clear that Angela was actually missing, her mobile was no longer active and there were no hits on her cash card or bank account, and none of her friends had seen or heard from her, the team was set in motion and quickly scaled up. Her clutch bag, that she'd been carrying the last time she was seen, turned up a couple of days later, followed by her mobile phone. There were no calls or texts to or from any number, in her contacts or unrecorded names, after that Saturday night where she'd last been seen."

"Where were the phone and bag found?" Tom asked.

Cassie shrugged. "Handed in at the local nick. Passers-by found both of them in the street. There was a lot of news coverage locally at the time, apparently."

"What led them to Crake?"

"Ah... yes, Ben Crake," Cassie said, nodding knowingly as she switched to another file. "One of Angie's friends, that's what they called her, told an investigating officer that Ben had been at school with Angela and had something of a thing for her. They used to joke that he was her shadow... a stalker type of thing."

"Any evidence for that?" Tamara asked.

Cassie shrugged. "Just hearsay from what I can tell. Anyway, Ben had left school the previous year and not gone on to college like many of his peers." She checked her notes. "He took a job working shifts as a security guard for a local business."

"Didn't he say he had an alibi?" Eric asked, his brow furrowing in concentration. Cassie nodded. "And it was confirmed at trial, I think."

"Aye, it was," Cassie said. "He was at work the time of her disappearance. However, the prosecution presented CCTV footage from Crake's workplace showing him chasing a woman matching Angela Dale's appearance across one of the sites that he was monitoring."

"He'd abducted her while he was at work?" Tom asked. "That's one way to get an alibi."

"Interesting thing was, he never denied being with her the night she disappeared," Cassie said. "Only, he said she came to see him at work. The team didn't believe him and obtained a warrant to search both his workplace and his home. He lived with his mum at the time and maybe she hadn't washed his jammies and stuff because they found Angela's DNA on his uniform, the clothes he'd been wearing that Saturday night."

Tamara drew breath, eyeing the mugshot taken of Ben Crake the day of his arrest, also now pinned to the board. "What was his explanation for that? Did he have one?"

"Oh aye, he did. He claimed she came on to him and that's how their bodies came into contact and her DNA got onto his uniform. He swore blind."

"Ah, the old *we were an item* defence," Tamara said. "The only way to explain away incriminating trace evidence. Presumably, the jury saw it differently?"

Cassie shrugged. "Enough of them to convict, yes."

"Was there no CCTV footage to corroborate his account?" Tom asked.

"Much of the security footage was damaged or lost," Cassie said. "The prosecution argued this was rather convenient for the defendant but, of course, the defence barrister argued the opposite. The CPS barrister presented Crake as a skilled manipulator who covered his tracks well, leaving only one bit of footage intact; the video that saw him chasing Angela across the site that night."

"They reckon he destroyed the other recordings?" Tamara asked.

Cassie nodded. "Stands to reason. It was his job. No one knew the system better than he did but that particular camera was linked to a different hard drive. Had he known, then he could have destroyed it and there might not have been enough evidence to convict."

Eric cleared his throat. "What about the DNA though?"

Cassie smiled. "That warrant was obtained after the footage was viewed, thereby giving the magistrate a reason to grant the search of his home. Without the footage, there was nothing to link him bar school friends pointing a finger."

Tom looked troubled. Tamara noticed and got his attention. "What are you thinking, Tom?"

"Only that I can see why Ben Crake has been released."

"Really?" Tamara asked. "You think he's innocent?"

Tom shook his head. "Now, I didn't say that. It's just, if I was heading up a murder inquiry, I'd prefer to go to the jury with more than..." he waved his hand at the information, "more than five seconds of grainy CCTV footage and a bit of forensic analysis as the basis of my case. Seems flimsy at best."

"Risky," Tamara had to agree. "You're relying on the jury to believe your version of events over his."

Cassie nodded along. "By all accounts the emotions on this one were running high. Angela Dale was a popular local girl. Lots of friends, intelligent and not to mention beautiful. Whereas Ben Crake was quite the oddball. He kept himself to himself, didn't mix well, few friends. He didn't have anyone in his corner."

Eric looked glum. "I remember people at the time really wanted someone caught. There was something of a frenzy about public safety going through the community. They pulled all of us trainees out of school for a while and buddied us up with active officers to swell the street presence; cuts in numbers were beginning to bite and the bosses wanted to make a visual impression. Let residents know they were safe."

Tom looked at Cassie. "Marie Dale was in here earlier asking for DI Reynolds. Was he heading up the inquiry?"

Cassie returned to her files, flicking through the pages, tracing the lines with her forefinger. She stopped, looking up in surprise. "No. The senior investigating officer was DCI Watts."

"Teflon himself?" Eric asked, quickly averting his eyes from Tamara's stern gaze.

"None other," Cassie confirmed. "Well, as the kids say these days; *that's a bit awks*."

Tamara felt her chest tighten. Taking a deep breath, she thought on the next steps. This investigation could very easily become a mad hatter's tea party if she wasn't careful. Once the media got wind of this case, it could blow up in her face.

"Right. First things first," she said firmly, looking around and making eye contact with her small team in turn. "Word of this does not leave this room or the four of us until I say otherwise. Is that clear?" No one objected. Eric nodded profusely, Cassie curtly and Tom remained his impassive self, arms folded across his chest. "I don't know how long we'll be able to contain this but I want us to get as far along in this case as we can before word gets out. To begin with we'll need to go back over the original investigation, speak to every witness, review every statement, every piece of evidence."

"In that case, it'll not be long until the penny drops what we're doing," Tom said, shaking his head. "Once we've a confirmation of Angela's remains through DNA or otherwise, people will want to know who she is and as soon as we start interviewing the same people it'll be obvious." He took a deep breath. "And based on Marie Dale's reaction this afternoon, I don't think she'll keep it quiet once we tell her we've eventually found her daughter."

"Well, we'll have to do the best we can up until that point, Tom."

She was frustrated and her tone was harsher than she'd intended. However, Tom was right, as usual. Although, that precious time could mean making some headway prior to all the pressures that would inevitably come their way.

"Okay," she said quietly, "let's gather as much evidence as we can from the initial investigation into Angela's disappearance but, as Tom rightly says, we will have to be sly about it or they'll be all over us in minutes—"

"The press?" Cassie asked.

"Press, family, Joe public… and not to mention our colleagues," Tamara said. "Every minute I spend batting them away is less time that I'll have to find Angela's killer."

"When did Angela disappear, Eric?" Tom asked.

Eric thought hard. "Crake was sentenced five years ago… take off eighteen months for the investigation and the time he spent on remand… six and a half to seven years ago."

Tom's frown deepened. "So, where's Angela been for the last six years?"

All eyes turned to him.

He indicated the information board. "Fiona Williams has her death occurring within the last month to six weeks." He shrugged, looking up at Angela Dale's photograph. "Where's she been all this time?"

"That's what we're going to find out, Tom," Tamara said, drawing in a deep breath and exhaling heavily. "Okay, let's get organised. I want a briefing in three hours with everything there is to know about the investigation into Angela Dale's disappearance: suspects, motives, friends, work history, social media if she was into it… everything." She glanced at Tom. "I'll leave you to carve out the assignments."

Tom nodded. "Right, get yourselves prepared, call your loved ones and let them know they're likely to forget what you look like because we're not going anywhere anytime soon… assignment briefing in five minutes."

Eric and Cassie went back to their desks. Cassie picked up the telephone, presumably to call Lauren whereas Eric hesitated, lifted the receiver but Tamara noted he put it straight back down and set about organising his desk instead.

"What are you going to do?" Tom asked.

"Well, Watts has been the chief superintendent here for how long?"

"Four years, give or take. Why?"

Tamara lowered her voice to be inaudible to Eric

or Cassie. "How does a man with such limited skills rise through the ranks?"

"Connections or by catching a big case and getting a result," he said, realising what she might be getting at, he smiled ruefully. "You think this was his big case?"

"Would stand to reason why he doesn't want anyone digging over it," she said.

"You're a cynical woman, Tamara. Cynical," Tom said, grinning.

"Doesn't mean I'm wrong though. I'm just going to have a little root about, see what turns up, just so I know what we're getting into."

CHAPTER FIVE

A LITTLE OVER three hours later, Tamara re-entered the ops room to find the team were waiting for her.

"Sorry to keep you," she said, but that was as much of an apology as she was going to offer. She glanced at Tom and raised her eyebrows in a gesture that only he would likely notice and would certainly be the only one to interpret it.

"So, who had Angela Dale?" she asked.

"That's me," Cassie said. "Like I said before, Angela was a popular girl. She had a lot of friends, notably Lucy Minors, who was her closest confidant. She also knocked around with her brother, Jack. They weren't twins but they were barely a year apart in age, so they may as well have been."

"Was she ever in trouble?" Tamara asked.

Cassie shook her head. "Not with us, no. Lucy, her

friend, did offer up in her statement that Angela was something of a party girl; she drank fairly heavily but not to excess. Largely what one might expect from a seventeen-year-old." Cassie flicked through her notes. "She also partook of recreational drugs; a little weed, some more trippier substances when she went clubbing or partying. Keen on dancing, apparently. Nothing that raised any alarm bells at the time."

"Okay," Tamara said. "You mentioned she had a boyfriend. What do we know about him?"

'That comes under suspects, Boss," Eric said. "And I had those."

Cassie offered Eric an open hand to pass the floor to him and he stood up, notes in hand and crossed to the board where Angela's picture was mounted in the centre. Taking a marker, Eric first stuck another picture of a young man up on the board and began annotating around it as he spoke.

"Charlie Babcock was Angela's on-off boyfriend. He was a few years older than Angela, twenty-three at the time of her disappearance. Her parents knew of their relationship but, by all accounts, they didn't approve of it—"

"Why not?" she asked.

Eric shrugged. "That was never clear, but it was said by Charlie himself and backed up by Lucy Minors. Anyway, Charlie was also known locally as a bit of a womaniser, liked a drink and was quite a full-on character. Their relationship was a passionate one but also volatile, although there's no evidence of any violence."

"Who's offering all of this up?" Tom asked.

"Multiple people, her brother Jack, his girlfriend at the time, Susan Brock. Not to mention Charlie himself."

"Okay, Eric," Tamara said. "What can you tell us about Charlie Babcock?"

"He's still in the area. I ran a check on him just now and he's got a drink-driving conviction, a couple of other entanglements with the law, often outside of a pub, if you know what I mean?"

"A drinker with a passionate and volatile temperament?" Tamara said.

"Yes, that about sums him up," Eric said. "Curiously, the year after Angela's disappearance, and just before Crake's trial began, Babcock entered the Royal Military Academy at Sandhurst."

Tom was surprised. "He applied for a commission?"

Eric nodded. "And he was accepted."

Tamara did a rough calculation in her head. "Even if he went in on a short-service commission, he shouldn't be out already. What's he doing back here?"

"I couldn't get that information from his file," Eric said, glumly. "However, he was back in town within eighteen months, so either he was forced out medically or—"

"Kicked out for some unspecified reason," Tamara finished for him. "Look into that, would you, Eric?"

"Will do," Eric said, making a note.

"Was Charlie ever considered a suspect?" she asked.

"In the early days, I believe he was, yes," Eric said. "Although there was some ambiguity about whether they'd split up in the run-up to her disappearance, he didn't confirm that, saying quite the opposite. Although, to be fair, their relationship was so off and on that it might have been hard for people to keep up."

"Why did they split? Does he say?"

"Charlie claimed they'd just run their course but, at the time, Lucy suggested Charlie didn't take kindly to Angela's flirtatious character." Eric pointed at the photo. "Let's face it, she's really attractive and, seemingly, she was well aware of her effect on men."

"Not victim blaming, I hope, Eric?" Cassie said, under her breath. Eric knew she was joking and ignored the comment.

"Charlie was dropped as a suspect as soon as they zeroed in on Crake. As far as I can tell, Charlie Babcock didn't have an alibi for the Saturday night of Angela's disappearance. He was also there at the circus at the same time as Angela and Lucy, although they were never placed together."

"The circus?" Tamara asked.

Eric nodded. "Oh yes, the circus was in town and that's where Angela had been that evening, to see the performance. Lucy explained that they'd been hanging out with the performers for much of the day. Angela, in particular, was quite fascinated by the lifestyle."

"And the circus folk were interviewed at the time?" Tamara asked.

"Yep," Eric said.

Tom stood up. "Is this the same circus that is coming to town this weekend?"

"I should imagine so," Eric said. "They come around twice a year, have done since I was a kid. I expect some of the performers change over time, but it's the same operation, I'm sure."

"We'll have to speak to them again," Tamara said, "see if the same players are coming."

"Terrific," Cassie muttered under her breath. "Travellers. My fave."

"They're performers, Cassie," Eric said quietly. "Skilled entertainers."

"Skilled travellers… are still travellers, Eric," she said without looking up. "And I wouldn't trust them as far as I can throw them."

"That reminds me, Cassandra," Tom said. "I've got you booked on that *Equality and Diversity*

Training course next month. Perhaps you can get a head start on some of the modules?"

Cassie glanced up and smiled. "Point taken. I'll rein it in."

"Excellent, DS Knight, and I'll be sure to monitor progress."

Cassie's neck and cheeks reddened, acknowledging the unspoken chastisement.

"The other thing to note about dropping Charlie as a suspect is that there wasn't footage of him pursuing Angela out into the night," Eric said. "He did state he was with his friend, Micky George, for all of that Saturday night and into the early hours. However, when George was questioned, he confirmed what Charlie said and then quickly withdrew it after he realised it was a murder investigation."

"So, likely that Charlie was fibbing and expecting his mate to back him up," Tamara said.

"Only for said friend to get cold feet when facing an accessory to murder charge," Tom added. "Do we know where Micky George is now?"

Eric shook his head. "He's bounced around several addresses in the last few years. No reason to doubt he's not still around here somewhere, just not listed on the electoral roll. I'll keep digging."

Tamara sighed. "Any other suspects, besides Ben Crake?"

Eric shook his head.

"It was a short list they had back then," she said. "What about Crake himself?"

"I took that one on," Tom said, walking to the front of the room, notebook in hand. "I read through the transcripts of the interviews with Crake, and then I found the video footage in the archives, and I have to admit it made for interesting viewing. I can see why the focus was so hot on Crake. If he came across to the investigating officers in every interaction as he does in the interviews, I can completely understand their approach."

"Was it that bad?" Tamara asked.

"Crake came across as arrogant, bordering on belligerent," Tom said. "Initially, he declined legal representation and every question that was put to him, he sneered at and batted away using minimal words. His responses only seemed to antagonise the interviewer, no matter who was taking the lead in the interviews. He really didn't do himself any favours. And then there was the confession."

"He confessed to killing Angela?"

"After a fashion, yes."

Cassie sneered mockingly. "How can you confess *after a fashion*?"

Tom smiled. "He was under pressure and he threw it at them that he'd done it. I think it was a way of trying to gain some control of the interview. Up until that point, he'd been repeatedly cornered. I think he was looking for breathing space."

"One hell of a way to go about it," Cassie said, shaking her head.

"In the next interview he had legal representation and immediately withdrew the confession, but it was already on tape. Two days of the trial were dominated by the debate around his intention when confessing."

Tamara sucked air through her teeth. "You can take his performance in interview in one of two ways; either he's angry at being caught or he's frustrated at being accused. You've seen the tapes. What do you think?"

Tom thought on it before shaking his head. "Without the trace evidence they found on his clothing, along with the footage, proving they were together that night, I'd not know which side to come down on. With that in mind," he shrugged, "it doesn't look good for Crake, I have to say. The confession, whether he meant it or not, put a nail in his coffin."

"How many cases go to trial based on speculative forensic evidence and try to secure a conviction?" Tamara said, thoughtfully.

"Too many," Tom said. "But we all know that forensic evidence carries weight with a jury. It's almost achieved godlike status in modern policing."

"Yes, that's true. And we are all guilty of filling in the gaps to make the conclusion fit the evidence."

"Hang on!" Cassie said. "It sounds like the two of you have already decided that Ben Crake isn't guilty. With hindsight, we can all second guess the jurors' motivations and any possible lapses in investigation procedure, but let's not forget Crake was with her that night, had a history of showering Angela with unrequited shows of affection, and was sent down for murdering her."

Tamara offered a measured response. "He was obsessive?"

Cassie shrugged. "That's what Lucy and Jack thought, yes. Crake used to stare at her in class, puppy-dog eyes, I think one of them said. Maybe that obsession grew and one night, he—"

"You're missing one thing, Cass," Tamara said. "Dr Williams registers the decomposition as no more than six months. Ben Crake has been in prison for the last five years, so unless you're suggesting he has an accomplice, or he had some kind of supernatural powers at play, then he couldn't have killed her."

"Damn…" Cassie said, deflated. "Missed that." She fixed her eye on Tamara. "Do you think I'm over promoted?"

Eric silently raised his hand to cast his vote. Cassie offered him a backhanded swipe which the detective constable swerved and batted away with ease, a half-smile crossing his lips.

"So, once the forensic evidence and CCTV came

to light, they focussed squarely on Ben Crake and let everything else drift away?" Tamara asked no one in particular.

"More than that, I think," Tom said. "I remember the case made national news and the outcry from the public to make progress was intense. I dare say that could have played in the minds of the lead investigators no end. Particularly bearing in mind who the SIO was."

Tamara inclined her head. Chief Superintendent Watts was a man for the limelight, almost to the point of craving it, but only when it was positive. When the media scrutiny was leaning towards negative coverage, he would simply offer someone else up to the camera, choosing to take the lead only when he looked good. She doubted he was all that different five or six years ago.

"What about your predecessor, Tom, DI Reynolds wasn't it?"

Tom nodded. "I never knew him. We had a handover meeting when I joined but I picked up a case on my first day, so we had to do it over the phone. It was brief."

"Where is he now? Still in the job?" she asked.

"Yes. He's a DCI in Suffolk Police now. Shall I speak to him?"

She shook her head. "No, leave it to me. I'd like to keep it quiet, so I'll speak to him out of hours."

"Watts?" Tom asked.

Tamara didn't want to deal with him right now. "Let's leave that conversation until we know what we're dealing with."

"I think we all know what we're dealing with, though," Cassie said. She looked around the small group, arching her eyebrows. "I mean, don't we? We're reinvestigating the Angela Dale murder. Only this time, it's not speculation, because we have a body. Most of it, anyway. And it is a mess."

Tom nodded his agreement, glancing sideways at Tamara. "And with Ben Crake's release, there will be an inquiry getting underway to examine the investigation, trial and no doubt, the behaviour of the officers involved. We're going to be—"

"Slap bang in the middle of it," Tamara said, finishing Tom's line. She shook her head. "We can't worry about that. We need to crack on with our investigation and see where it leads. If events catch up or even overtake us, then so be it. But we're going to approach this with a fresh pair of eyes and start from scratch."

Tom bit his lower lip. "We have to visit the Dales and let them know we think we've found their daughter."

"I think there's someone else you need to call in on too."

"Who's that?"

"Ben Crake." Tamara ran a hand through her hair. "When word gets around that he's back, I wouldn't be surprised if some vigilante heroes have a pop at him."

"You think he's in danger?"

Tamara shrugged. "I hope not. Maybe it'll be a gang of teenagers lobbing dog shit at his house, but you never know."

"Are we still treating him as a suspect?" Tom asked.

"Everyone is still a suspect," Tamara said flatly, "until we can prove otherwise."

CHAPTER SIX

Henry and Marie Dale lived at an address in Titchwell on the Norfolk coast. The A149 ran straight through the little village with Titchwell Marsh, a nature reserve reputable for its wild bird population, separating the village from the sea. Slowing the car, Tom searched for numbers on the properties, a mixture of brick-built semi-detached houses, constructed for and traditionally occupied by local farm workers along with older, brick and flint properties which no doubt catered for fishermen as well.

"That one," Eric said, pointing to a row of terraced houses, "on the end."

Tom turned into the drive and switched the engine off. "I'm not sure how this is going to go, Eric.

They're already going to be animated over Ben Crake's release and are probably struggling to process it all. We're about to rip open old wounds."

"Understood," Eric said.

They got out and approached the house, their feet crunching on the gravel drive. A net curtain twitched. Someone had noted their arrival. Tom cast an eye over the two cars in the drive. Neither was particularly new but looked clean and well maintained. An old fishing boat, two-tone paintwork of white above a red hull, was resting on a trailer in a dilapidated cart lodge. The tyres of the trailer were flat and the wheels rusted. The boat hadn't seen the water in years.

It made Tom think about his own boat and how little he'd taken it out this past year. He should probably sell it, but the thought didn't sit well with him and he pushed it aside.

They were met at the front door by Marie Dale. She looked Tom up and down, but there was no sign of the anger and frustration she'd exhibited in front of him when they'd spoken earlier in the day.

"Hello, Mrs Dale," Tom said. Introducing Eric, the detective constable smiled. "This is DC Collet."

"Please, do come in, Inspector," she said, stepping back and welcoming them inside. She directed them into the front sitting room where a man was sitting at a small dining table nestled in one corner.

He was reading the paper. He glanced up at Tom and acknowledged their arrival with a curt nod.

"About time you showed up," he muttered.

Tom took his measure. He was in his fifties, heavy-set and balding. His fair hair was greying and the stronger growth was clumped around the ears and at the top of his neck. Although likely to still be quite a powerful man, he was arguably well past his prime. Twenty years ago, he may well have been a physical match for Tom himself. Setting the newspaper down, Tom noted the rough edge to his hands. You only got those from a lifetime of physically demanding work.

"Henry," Marie said, "this is Detective Inspector Janssen and…" she'd not taken in Eric's introduction, which was quite understandable.

"DC Collet," Eric said, smiling. "But please do call me Eric."

"Yes, well," Henry Dale said, rising from his chair and begrudgingly extending his hand towards Tom, who took it, "as I said, about time you lot showed up. I gather Gary has cleared off?"

"Gary?" Tom asked.

"DI Reynolds," Marie said.

"Yes, he's a DCI with Suffolk now," Tom said.

"Got a nice promotion off the back of my dead daughter, didn't he."

"Henry!" Marie exclaimed.

Tom reassured her. "It's okay, Mrs Dale." Turning to Henry, Tom tried to keep his tone neutral. "I'm sure no one wanted to personally profit from your loss, Mr Dale."

"Yeah, well… looks like he cocked it up, doesn't it?" Henry said. Reading Tom's expression as not understanding, he continued, "Screwed the investigation up, so a guilty man gets off. Free to walk among us again. How long until that animal does it again, huh?"

"Henry, please!" Marie said, stepping between her husband and Tom, placing a gentle hand on his chest and guiding Henry back into his seat before drawing out another chair to sit alongside him. "Henry, you promised."

She turned to Tom and Eric and gestured for them to sit down on a sofa against the far wall. The room wasn't large and there seemed to be far too much furniture shoehorned into it for it to be comfortable.

"I know," Henry grumbled. "I'm sorry, Inspector."

Tom shook his head. "There's no need, Mr Dale. I suspect this has all come as quite a shock to you."

"That my daughter's killer bumps into my missus walking down the street, bold as brass?" He nodded. "Oh yes, quite a shock. It's a good job it wasn't me he bumped into, I can tell you that. I'd swing for that man."

"Probably best if I don't hear comments like that, Mr Dale," Tom said. "Taking matters into your own hands won't do anyone any good."

"Oh, Henry is just sounding off, Inspector," said Marie. "He'd never do anything like that, would you love? Not really."

Henry was staring at Tom but averted his eyes and mumbled something inaudible. Tom was struck by the change in Marie from their earlier meeting at the station. She had been the emotionally aggressive one, whereas now she seemed more rational and pragmatic, whereas her husband was bordering on exploding. Maybe the shock had brought out an instinctive reaction and now it had sunk in, she was trying to keep her husband calm.

"I can appreciate this wasn't the ideal way for you to find out about Ben Crake's release, Mr Dale," Tom said. "But I can assure you that we were none the wiser either."

"You mean you don't talk to one another, the police and the prison service?" Henry said, clearly finding the concept hard to believe.

"I'm afraid not," Tom said. "The probation service, prison boards and even the courts are under no obligation to convey their findings to us. Mad as it sounds, we were surprised as well."

Henry exhaled and his anger appeared to subside, if only a little. "So, what's this visit then? An apology call? If so, it's a bit late."

"No, we're here about your daughter, Angela."

At mention of her name, both parents went quiet and were attentive. Marie spoke.

"Will there be a new investigation now that Ben has been cleared—?"

"He's not been *cleared*, love," Henry said dismissively. "The police and the CPS cocked up the investigation." He looked at Tom, fixing him with a stare. "There will be a new trial, won't there? His conviction has been judged as unsafe, but that doesn't mean he'll get away with it, does it?"

Tom felt Eric shift nervously in his seat. Henry noticed too.

"Just what are you here for, Inspector?" Henry asked, narrowing his eyes.

"There will be an inquiry into the handling of your daughter's case, Ben Crake's conviction and a review of all of the evidence. That will no doubt be carried out by another force—"

"Because you lot can't be trusted?" Henry asked.

Tom didn't rise to the accusation. After all, he wasn't involved in the initial investigation and he could appreciate the man's frustration.

"Because, where an investigation has question marks over it, it is deemed for the benefit of transparency and to avoid doubt, another force should come and look at it. This is common practice and done to try and offer reassurance to families, as well as the public—"

"Because you lot can't be trusted," Henry repeated.

"Oh Henry, for heaven's sake, let the man speak!" Marie snapped. Henry bristled but didn't say anything further. "Please, go on, Inspector."

"As I say, we're not a part of the inquiry into the initial investigation of your daughter's disappearance," Tom said. Marie's gaze flitted momentarily to her husband and then back to Tom. "However, the storm yesterday has unearthed… human remains and we are of the belief that there is a strong likelihood that they belong to your daughter, Angela."

Marie's mouth fell open and she stared at Tom, unmoving. Henry, sitting beside his wife, appeared unfazed. He stared at Tom with the same stoic expression he'd had since Marie begged him to keep quiet although the muscles in his face twitched with controlled tension.

"Now, we have taken a DNA sample for comparison, and we are waiting for the results to come back before we can be absolutely certain but, as I say, we are confident, otherwise we wouldn't be here."

The front door opened and two figures bundled in sharing a joke about something. The entrance hall was barely a metre square and so the newcomers were visible as well as audible to those in the room, and vice versa. Jack Dale entered the room, smiling. The smiled faded as he clocked the presence of Tom and Eric along with his parents' expressions.

"What is it?" Jack asked. "What's happened?"

Marie looked up at her son, tears welling. "They think they've found Angela."

Jack stood open mouthed. The young woman behind him reached out and gripped his forearm supportively. He glanced back at her, appreciating the gesture. Tom rose.

"Hello again, Jack," he said, shaking hands with him. "I'm sorry to meet you again so soon under these circumstances. Tom smiled at Jack's companion and she returned it, nervously.

"I'm Susan," she said, releasing her grip on Jack's arm and shaking Tom's hand. "I'm Jack's…" she hesitated, glancing at him, but Jack was already crossing the room to hug his mother "…Jack's friend," she said.

"Susan Brock?" Tom asked.

"Yes, that's right." She was taken aback.

"I'm sorry," Tom said. "Your name came up in the case file around… Angela—"

"Yes, Jack and I were dating back then," she said, lowering her voice, but no one, aside from Henry, was paying attention to their conversation.

Tom sat back down, while Jack positioned himself next to his mother, a gentle, supportive hand on her shoulder. She sat forward on her chair, eager to hear more news.

"You said you've found her. Where is she? Can I see her?" she asked excitedly.

Tom and Eric exchanged a quick glance. "I don't think that will be possible, Mrs Dale," Tom said. The woman looked deflated. "I was hoping, bearing in mind the DNA test could take a couple of days, that there might be some distinctive markings on Angela's body that you could describe to help us to identify her more conclusively."

"If there are identifiable markings on her body, why can't we see her?" Marie asked, confused.

Jack momentarily looked at his father, his brow creasing. "Angie's been missing for six years or so, Inspector. How are there going to be distinguishing marks on her body? Surely that's not possible?"

Tom didn't want to fall foul of giving them false information, but as Jack rightly pointed out, a body left in the ground for that length of time would have decomposed to the point of being unidentifiable without DNA or an assemblage of personal effects to aid identification.

"We still have much work to do, but this particular woman may well have passed away more recently than six years ago."

The family gasped in unison, apart from Henry who remained stoic.

Tom continued, "Therefore, identifiable marks are visible."

"Then… where has she been? What did that monster do with her?" Marie asked looking between those around her. "And… I still… don't understand why I can't see her."

Henry met his son's eye, exhaling and lowering his gaze to the floor at his feet. "Because he said they've found her remains, Marie… he didn't say a body."

Marie stared at her husband and then her eyes flitted to her son and then Tom.

"What does he mean, Inspector? I don't understand."

"You daft woman," Henry said, shaking his head.

"I'm afraid, the body we found is not… intact," Tom said as delicately as he could, not that he was able to sugar coat such news. *Complete* might have been a better choice of word, but it was too late now and in reality probably wouldn't have made much of a difference.

"And when you say not…" Henry said, pausing, "…how much of my daughter is… missing?"

Tom pursed his lips, reluctant to say.

"Please, Inspector," Marie said, her voice cracking, "We need to know." She glanced at her husband and son. "And I would rather hear it from you than read it in the newspaper or hear it on the television."

Jack nodded his agreement and Henry looked up at Tom, his eyes watering.

"Very well," Tom said. "We have teams scouring the area as we speak, but as of now, we have…" he took a deep breath "a torso, legs… and an arm."

Marie gasped, doubling over and letting out a shriek that would have befitted the most realistic of horror films. Eric lowered his head. Susan Brock began to cry and Jack put an arm around his mother, blinking back tears. Henry Dale maintained his stare, fixated on Tom, scowling.

"And you let that little bastard out of prison?" Henry said through gritted teeth. "And then you come here and tell us this… You've got some bloody nerve."

Tom half expected a reaction like this, and he was prepared for it. To argue was pointless. To defend the police position would be in bad taste. Sometimes in life, you just had to sit there and accept the criticism, even if it was unjust.

It was Jack who spoke, still comforting his mother, sobbing in his arms. "You asked for distinguishing marks. Angie had a tattoo on the small of her back. It was a custom design that she came up with and had a local artist recreate it for her. There won't be another one like it."

"Would you recognise the design if you saw it, Jack?" Tom asked.

He nodded.

Tom looked at Eric who reached into a folder he'd brought with him. He took out a clutch of photographs taken of the tattoo from various angles. Jack drew his arm away from his mother. Marie reluctantly released her grip on his hand. Henry remained where he was. Eric stood and, with Jack coming alongside him, passed the pictures across. Jack flipped through them, nodding solemnly.

"That's Angie's tattoo."

"You're certain?"

He nodded again. "Absolutely. She was my sister. I knew her better than anyone," he said, glancing at Susan who wiped the tears from her eyes with the back of her hand. Jack looked at the pictures again and something in his expression caught Tom's eye, but he didn't say anything.

"So, it's your turn now then, is it?" Henry said.

Tom met his eye. "Excuse me?"

"It's your turn to try and prove what Reynolds and that other spiv couldn't."

"We are going to investigate, yes."

"Won't they take it out of your hands and give it to… what did you say, another force to look at?"

Tom splayed his hands wide. "That's not my

call, Mr Dale. However, until such a decision is made, I will try to solve this case and bring justice to your daughter. To Angela."

Henry stared into Tom's eyes. He had the feeling Henry was gauging Tom's credibility. After a tense few seconds, Henry relented, glancing at his wife beside him and reaching out to take her hand in his. She squeezed his hand so tightly that the whites of her knuckles showed. Henry lifted her hand and she looked up at her husband and he forced a smile. She returned it with one of her own.

"I've always prided myself on being a fair man, Inspector," Henry said. "And a decent judge of a man's character. Don't make a fool out of me, will you?"

Tom acknowledged the comment. "I'll give your family my very best, Mr Dale. I can assure you of that."

Tom rose and Eric led them to the front door. Susan stepped aside, averting her eyes from them as they passed. Was she embarrassed about crying or was it more? Tom couldn't be sure. Jack followed them, escorting them outside and onto the drive.

There was a nearly new Mercedes A Class parked alongside Tom's Volvo. He figured that was Susan's car, seeing as she'd been holding car keys when they entered the sitting room. Jack eased the front door almost closed behind him, before hurrying to catch up with Tom.

"Please forgive my father, Inspector," Jack said. "He's finding all of this… well, we all are, to be fair, but it's tough, you know?"

"No need to apologise. I know it's easily said, but I do understand what you're going through. As much as I can at any rate."

Jack appreciated the sentiment.

"May I ask you something?"

"Yes, of course."

"The pictures you just showed me, of Angie?" Jack asked. "They looked… recent. Like… Angie went missing years ago and… do you know what I mean?"

Tom nodded. "I do. I would like to say more, but until the pathologist has carried out his examination, I fear my answers may only lead to more questions and confusion for you."

Jack listened intently, slowly nodding.

"I see."

He was disappointed, which was understandable.

"You used to live over in Burnham Thorpe, didn't you?" Tom asked, looking around at the nearby farmland.

"Yeah, that's right. We lived out that way." Jack sniffed. "After Angie… after what happened, Dad struggled with it. He was always pretty tight with her, you know? Father, daughter, connection sort of thing. Anyway, things got on top of him and he couldn't cope. Work suffered… I tried to step in but I was at college, and truth be told, I was never really cut out to be a farmer. Long and the short of it… we lost the farm."

"I'm sorry to hear that, Jack. I really am."

"Ah… there are more important things in life. And you can't live in the past. Sometimes I just wish the past would let us go."

"What does your father do now?"

Jack rocked his head from side to side. "Some of the locals throw him a bit of work from time to time, but it's usually seasonal, harvest time and all that. To be honest, it's a bit beneath him… labouring mainly, but he does it and he doesn't complain… much. Truth be told, it's tough on the land these days. Costs are high and farmers are either laying people off or just not hiring if they can help it, scaling back planting, that sort of thing. I don't know what the future holds, but I get the impression Dad's not bothered."

Tom took a deep breath. This experience was all too common. After a murder comes the grief, a police investigation and hopefully a trial. With sentencing most people imagine a degree of closure but, in reality, that was never the case. People move on. The news cycle moves on, but the family are left with a gaping hole in their lives; every room, every family event, wherever they go there is always a shadow, and it never goes away.

"Listen, I know I have no right to ask this of you, but you seem a sensible man," Tom said. Jack met his eye, nodding. "This is going to be quite a story, and I think you've already experienced what it's like when the press gears up."

"Yes, I do remember. Unfortunately."

"We need to keep this under wraps for as long as possible, which means keeping word out of the press. Do you think you could help us with that?"

Jack looked back at the house. "You mean my mum and dad, don't you?"

Tom tilted his head to one side. "Among others, yes. We just need a bit of space to do our jobs."

Jack's gaze narrowed. "You know, another detective once said something similar to me and, after the fact, it didn't turn out too well at all."

Tom sucked on his bottom lip, nodding slowly. "I understand, but anything you could do would be appreciated."

"No promises, Inspector," Jack said. "But I'll try."

"Thank you. I can ask no more. And I don't think I should have to remind you to stay away from Ben Crake, do I?"

Jack bowed his head under Tom's scrutiny, absently tapping at a larger than average stone at his feet. "As I said, I'll try."

"I know it's all a bit much right now," Tom said, "but at some point soon, I would like to hear about

Angela from you, and your parents if they feel up to it. It will help us and it might help all of you. Would that be all right?"

Jack nodded. "Yes, of course. I'll handle Mum and Dad, don't worry."

CHAPTER SEVEN

THE PROPERTY WAS A BUNGALOW, nineteen-sixties style, plain, red brick with what looked like single-glazed, metal-framed windows. Tom parked the car on the drive. Looking around, the place looked semi-derelict. The driveway angled down and wrapped around into the front of the house. It was a tar and chip driveway but weather beaten over the years; it had cracked in many places with vegetation growing through.

Tom eyed the gardens as he got out of the car. They were extensive and must have once required a great deal of tending to but now everything had been allowed to spread and it was hard to determine where bushes, plants and trees were meant to end and the lawn begin. The perimeter fencing was concrete post and chain link, although much of the wire had rusted through or buckled under the pressure of the foliage.

The bungalow itself fared little better. Tiles had slipped on the roof and, as such, there appeared to be water damage around the eaves where a flashing had failed.

"Are you sure this is the right place?" Eric asked.

"It's the address we were given, and it matches his mother's home where he was registered before he went to prison."

They both looked at Ben Crake's home. It was in darkness. There was no car parked out front and the garage door was warped and twisted in such a way as to mean it wouldn't open; at least, not without a concerted effort. Each window was obscured by thick net curtains, stained brown by dirt and time.

They approached the front door and Tom rang the bell. A shrill sound came from within. They waited but there was no movement or further sound from within. Tom rang the bell again and rapped his knuckles on the glass door. The frame was silver aluminium, probably first generation when they began to be fitted in the UK in the late seventies or early eighties. Tom looked to his left as movement caught. The nets definitely moved but was it by hand or just a draught? He wasn't sure.

Crouching down, he lifted the letterbox cover.

There was no draught excluder, just a boxed view of a nondescript interior hall running towards the back of the house with various dark wooden doors off it to either side.

"Police, Mr Crake. We would like a word."

Rising again, Tom took out his wallet containing his warrant card, stretching out his arm towards the window on his left, he brandished it.

"Is someone in there?" Eric asked.

"We'll soon know."

Moments later a figure appeared on the other side of the obscured glass, unlocked the door and it creaked open on old hinges. Two wide eyes peered out at them, nervous, flitting between Tom and Eric.

"Ben Crake?" Tom asked.

"Who's asking?"

"DI Janssen," Tom said, holding his warrant card aloft once more. He nodded to Eric. "This is DC Collet. Are you Ben Crake?"

"Yeah, that's me," he said, still clinging onto the edge of the door as if letting go would see him fall over. He was not what Tom had expected at all. In the interview recordings, Ben Crake was athletically built. Not muscular or stocky by any means, but his frame suggested he possessed strength in abundance. He was angular in jaw, sharp-eyed with a crewcut hairstyle. The man standing before them now was almost the polar opposite. He was hunched forward, much like a man of far greater years. His face looked gaunt, eyes protruding from their sockets, which were all of his features that could be seen in detail for his face was largely hidden by a dark beard that was poorly maintained, thicker in some places than others, and straggly or patchy in others. He wore a baseball cap pulled down over his forehead. It was tatty and had holes in the material lining, with years of grime built up along the edge of the rim.

Despite him wearing what looked like oversized combat trousers and a baggy green field jacket, Tom could see he was skeletally thin beneath the clothing. His appearance was shabby. He could easily pass for a homeless man, if seen in the street.

"May we come in, Ben?" Tom asked.

Crake eyed them suspiciously but slowly nodded, stepping back to give them room to enter. He led them to the rear of the property and into what was the dining room. Floral-print wallpaper lined each face with a serving hatch into the little kitchen in the next room, and the carpet bore a strikingly colourful pattern that clashed horribly with the walls. The dining table was a deep-brown wooden affair and the seat cushions were red and gold striped. Tom figured whoever styled it may well have been colour blind or shouldn't have been allowed to make furnishing choices.

The sun had long since fallen below the horizon

and what little light came in from outside, due to the thick cloud cover, offered only the barest illumination.

"Can we put a light on?" Eric asked.

"Lights out at nine," Crake replied.

Tom glanced through the serving hatch into the kitchen. It was a mess. The plastic bowl in the sink was full of crockery and water was overflowing. The nearby worktops were also cluttered with more cups, plates and food packaging.

"Do you live here alone, Ben?"

He nodded solemnly. "My mother died while I was inside."

"I'm sorry to hear that."

Crake offered a curt nod in acknowledgment.

"Two years ago. Heart attack, they told me." He sniffed hard, lifting his baseball cap off his head and running a hand through a thick, unwashed mass of dark hair, before putting it back on. "They wouldn't let me go to the funeral, you know?" His voice was just above a whisper, measured, not bitter. "Can you believe that?"

"Did they say why not?"

"I was supposed to, but I was stopped at the last minute. They'll find a reason if they want to, won't they?"

Tom cocked his head. "I guess so. How long have you been home?"

"A few days," Crake said. "I don't remember really. Does it matter?"

"No, I suppose not. Is anyone…" Tom glanced at Eric, "looking out for you?"

"Like who? Family?"

"Yes, family or friends."

He shook his head, his eyes fixed on Tom. "Don't have any family, not any more."

"Your file says you have a brother," Tom said. "Have you spoken with him?"

Again, Crake shook his head. "Nah. He lives in Australia. Haven't spoken to him in years. Definitely not since I went to prison."

The silence in between conversation hung heavily in the air.

"What are your plans, Ben, now that you're home?"

Crake pulled a face. "Don't have any." Then his expression clouded and he stared at Tom. "I knew you would be coming."

"Why's that?"

"You're not going to leave me alone, are you? Now I'm home, it'll be me you come to first as soon as anything happens around here. I've been warned about you."

"Who's warned you, Ben?" Eric asked.

Crake eyed Eric warily, then shook his head. "Doesn't really matter, does it? She was right."

"Has anyone been harassing you since you came home?" Tom asked.

He scoffed. "Only a matter of time. But I'll save you the trouble. Whatever it was, I didn't do it. All right?"

There was the same hostility, the arrogance that was on show in the police interviews again. Tom figured this guy was argumentative by nature and could probably start a heated confrontation standing in an empty room.

"Are you going to ask me about Angela?"

Tom met his eye. Was it fear he saw in Crake's expression or something else entirely. "Do you want to speak about Angela, Ben?"

He shrugged. "Do I need a solicitor?"

"You didn't request one before. Why was that?"

"I hadn't done anything wrong. I didn't think I needed one," Crake said. "But then I lost five years of my life as a result of trusting in people like you to do your jobs right."

"I can understand the sentiment, Ben, believe me. What brought you home? I figured with everything that's gone on, you'd steer clear, particularly if you've no family left in the area."

A flicker of passion showed in Crake's eyes, the first sign that he had something about him that Tom had seen since their arrival.

"This is my home!" he hissed. "This is the house

I was born in. The house my mother died in. Why the hell shouldn't I be here?"

Tom shrugged. "Life might not be easy for you, for a while at least."

"You say that like it should mean something," he countered. "What do you think the people here can do to me now? Point fingers? *Gossip* behind my back? As if they weren't doing that every day of my life as it is. Always have. Always will. Screw them. My life here will be a breeze compared to what I put up with the last few years. You know I spent only two days on the induction wing when I went away? Two poxy days! Then they put me in a cell with a psychotic Scotsman who hated sex offenders. Now, they're not supposed to do that, are they?"

"No, they're not," Tom said, silently struggling to believe that it was an accidental error.

"I mean, no inmate likes sex offenders. That's why they get put in their own section of the prison with all the nonces and rapists. But me… stick the murderer of a young woman in a cell with a two-hundred-and-fifty-pound meathead for fourteen hours. *That'll be a laugh.*"

"What happened?"

"What do you bloody well think happened, Sherlock?" Crake said. His eyes were wild, his stance aggressive. The doorbell rang. Crake looked at Tom, his expression softening, before striding out of the room. He walked with a hunch, lurching forward in bounding strides.

Eric silently mouthed the word 'wow' once they were alone and Tom arched his eyebrows in agreement of the sentiment. He heard a female voice and soon enough the two of them came back into the dining room.

The newcomer was in her thirties, blonde hair tied back away from her forehead. She was only five foot three and Tom towered above her.

"Interviewing Ben without his solicitor present. That's brave," she said, looking between them and quickly assessing Tom as the senior rank. Something about her stance and the way she addressed them seemed familiar to him but Tom was sure they hadn't met before.

"DI Tom Janssen," he said, smiling. "And you are?"

"Olivia Goldman."

"Nice to meet you, Olivia. How do you know Ben?"

She bristled, drawing herself up to her full height. "Well, that's not really any of your business, is it Detective Inspector?"

Tom's smile widened. "No, I suppose it isn't. If you don't wish to share, that's fine."

"I think you and your colleague should leave now, Inspector, unless you want charges filed related to intimidation brought before your superiors tomorrow morning."

"Above all else we're here to see how Ben is doing."

She fixed her eye on him, no doubt weighing his sincerity.

"Nothing more?"

He shook his head.

"So, you're not on the case reviewing his conviction?'

"No, just a local officer checking in on Ben's welfare. Nothing more than that. I take it we have you to thank for giving Ben the heads-up that we would come calling?"

"I've enough experience to expect it, yes. I doubt you'll be the last. Getting Ben out of prison was only the start, Inspector. There's still a journey to travel."

"And you'll be at his side?"

"Every step of the way," she said, smiling. It was artificial. "As I said, I think you should leave now. Ben has suffered enough around police officers for a while."

Tom pursed his lips and nodded. Turning to Crake, he met his eye.

"Do you have any friends to call upon in town, Ben?"

Crake snorted. "Not anymore, no."

Tom opened his wallet and took out one of his

contact cards. He extended his hand towards Crake, nodding at the card. "Just in case you need to call on a friend for help. I'll be here."

Crake looked at the card but didn't take it. Tom inclined his head, leaning over and putting the card down on the dining table. He smiled at Crake. "Just in case, Ben. Just in case."

Without another word, Tom and Eric made their way into the hall. Neither Crake or Olivia followed them and they let themselves out. Once the door was closed, and they were on the way to the car, Tom glanced sideways at Eric.

"Find out everything you can on Olivia Goldman, would you?"

Eric nodded. "Sure. Where should I start?"

"With the police, Eric. Start with the police."

Tom unlocked the car and got in.

"You think she has a record?" Eric said as he got in on the passenger side and reached for his seatbelt.

"No Eric, I think she was a police officer."

CHAPTER EIGHT

THE DOOR OPENED at the third attempt to rouse the inhabitants. A woman in her mid to late twenties greeted Eric with a smile. She wore her hair long, past her shoulders and it was wavy as if she'd spent time styling it. Her make-up was immaculate, if overdone for Eric's taste, but she still made an impression on him.

"Sorry. I didn't think you'd be here early," she said. "Can you hang on just a minute?"

"Erm…"

Before Eric had a chance to form a proper reply, the door closed again. The dull thud, thud, thud of dance music playing inside the apartment continued. The front door to the neighbouring apartment opened and an elderly lady emerged, a wheeled shopping basket in tow. She glanced at Eric and he smiled. Her look was impassive, although her gaze lingered on Eric before she shuffled away towards the stairwell.

Eric checked his watch. It was nine in the morning. He probably wouldn't be too happy if he had neighbours playing loud dance music at this time on a Friday morning either. In fact, any morning, for that matter.

A shape appeared behind the door and it swung open again. Eric was surprised by who was standing in front of him.

"Susan?" he asked. She was bidding farewell to the woman who'd first opened the door to him, and the smile faded as she also recognised him.

"Detective Constable…"

"Collet," he said, smiling. He gestured to the apartment. "Do you live here as well?"

"I do, yes. Well… from time to time." She smiled sheepishly. "I still live at home with my parents but if I stay out, then I'll tend to stay here. Lucy is a great pal of mine." She stepped past Eric and onto the landing, glancing over the brick wall and into the street below. "I have to get to work. If you don't mind?"

Eric shook his head. "Of course not. Please don't let me keep you."

Susan Brock smiled awkwardly, said goodbye and walked away. Eric found it to be a curious exchange. Movement in the hallway in front of him caught his attention. She was back, only now she was no longer wrapped in her satin kimono but was fully dressed in a black one-piece dress with an oversized red belt which matched the colour of her lipstick.

"Are you coming in, or what?"

Eric frowned. Taking out his identification, he showed her his warrant card as he heard footsteps mounting the concrete steps from the lower level, off to his left.

"DC Collet, Norfolk Police. I'm looking for Lucy Minors. Is that you?"

A man rounded the corner just as Eric identified himself. Eric glanced at him and the man hesitated before turning around and heading back down the stairs, the same way he'd just come up.

"Oh, yes of course. I should have known." She smiled warmly. "Yes, I'm Lucy. Come on in."

Eric returned her smile and entered, glancing at the empty walkway behind him as he closed the door. He was grateful the music was off. He'd woken with a headache and loud music was the last thing he wanted to hear right now.

Lucy led him into a room at the back of the apartment, casually closing the door to her bedroom as she walked by it. The living room was tidy. Far tidier than any of those occupied by his single friends, which was most of them. He looked around.

"Nice place," he said. "Tidy."

"Do you think so?" Lucy countered.

"Susan is always telling me I'm a bit of a slob. You saw Susan, right?"

"Yes, I did. She was in a bit of a hurry. On her way to work."

Lucy chuckled, plumping the standalone cushions on the sofa and gesturing for Eric to sit down, which he did.

"Work. If you can call it such a thing, what she does."

"What does she do?" Eric asked, curious.

"Oh… some admin thing." Lucy waved the question away. "At least, that's what the paperwork says."

Eric didn't understand the intimation but didn't pursue it.

"Susan is dating Jack Dale, isn't she?"

"Oh… that was a while back. Although, she has been with him a fair bit recently, so you never know. Playing her cards close to her chest at the moment."

He pushed aside any further thoughts about Susan Brock. He wasn't here to talk about her.

"Forgive me if this comes out of the blue, Miss Minors, but we understand you were good friends with Angela Dale."

Lucy was surprised. "Yes, that's correct. But you

already knew that. I spoke to the police quite a bit after… well, afterwards."

"Before my time, I'm afraid," Eric said. He angled his head to one side. "I can read the statements, but it's always better to hear it from the horse's mouth."

Lucy raised her eyebrows and smiled. "Well, I've never been called a horse before… you old charmer, you."

Eric flushed. "No, no… I didn't mean—"

Lucy laughed. "I'm only messing with you. Sorry." She straightened up in her seat and lost the smile. "Right, adult face. What is it you want to know, DC Collet?"

"I'm looking to build a picture of Angela and what she was like. How she lived her life and what she was up to around the time of her disappearance. What we have at the moment, aside from what was in the official files, comes from background reading in the media and online. That sort of hearsay isn't very useful."

Lucy held Eric's gaze. "Have you spoken to the family; her parents or Jack?"

Eric pursed his lips. "We will spend a bit of time with them in the coming days."

He felt awkward under her scrutiny. She was reading his expression, he could tell.

"What's going on? Susan said the police had been out at Angie's parents' place… but she didn't say why. Is it because that weirdo Ben is back in town?"

"You know Ben?"

"Everyone knows Ben," she said, shaking her head dismissively. "He's demented. Always has been. I'll bet a few years locked up in prison will have done him the world of good."

"Do you think?"

Lucy laughed, looking at her feet. Eric had missed her sarcasm. He felt himself flushing once more.

"Ah… I get it," he said. "You're not a fan then?"

"Oh, to be fair, I never really had a problem with Ben. He was an oddball, that's true enough, but I didn't see him as capable of… well, you know, what he did?"

"You think he was innocent?"

She emphatically shook her head. "Convicted, wasn't he? Besides, there was all that evidence of him being with her… and he confessed. Makes me sick to my stomach that I ever…"

"That you what?"

She dismissed the question with a flick of the hand. "So, what do you want to know?"

A mobile phone buzzed on the table next to her and Lucy glanced at it but didn't pick it up to check the message.

"Tell me about Angela," Eric said. "I understand you and her were very tight, so what was she was really like away from her parents. I guess that's what I want to know. We all present ourselves differently to the rest of the world than we do to them."

"I certainly do," Lucy said. She sat back in her chair, concentrating. "Let me think now. Angie was a great laugh, I mean, I know we all laugh with our friends but she was something else. Everyone enjoyed her company. She was so outgoing and fun to be around. Like I say, everyone loved her. I miss her to this day."

"Was she popular with people romantically?" Eric asked, and something in his tone conveyed the question he was really asking.

"Did she sleep around?"

Eric cleared his throat. "Was she promiscuous, yes?"

Lucy looked irritated. "What difference does that make? Do you think she deserved what happened to her? Is that it?"

Eric held up his hand by way of apology. "No, sorry, that was clumsy. What I'm getting at is that she had a boyfriend, on and off, and if she was really popular – and she was a pretty girl – then it stands to reason she would have had suitors. No?"

Lucy smiled. "Sorry. Yes, I see what you mean. The likelihood of jealousy and all that type of thing?"

"Yes, exactly," Eric said. "People can do crazy things in the name of love."

"Most days," Lucy said, smiling. "Angie was attractive. I mean *really* attractive. I'd kill to have cheekbones like hers, you know? Not literally, obviously."

Eric smiled.

"And she got a lot of attention from guys, that's true. She was seeing Charlie. Charlie Babcock. You know him, right?"

Eric nodded. "Yes. There seems to be a disparity among Angela's circle as to the status of their relationship when she disappeared."

She scoffed. "Not as far as he was concerned there wasn't."

Eric took out his notebook and held his pen poised over it, fixing Lucy with a keen eye. "Are you telling me he thought they were still an item?"

"Hell yes! Angie had tried to kick him into touch a couple of times in the weeks leading up to her disappearance, but he always managed to wheedle his way back in and talk her round. It was horrible to watch."

"Was she easily coerced?"

Lucy thought about it. "I wouldn't say so. She wasn't naive or anything. It's just Charlie. He had the gift of the gab, you know? He would talk her round and then within a couple of days she'd be asking my advice on how to get shot of him for the umpteenth time."

"And what did you say?"

"I told her to ghost him completely… then he'd get the message, but I guess that's easier said than done in a small town like Hunstanton. Everyone knows everyone around here. Well, not quite, but near as."

"Do you know if she split with him before she disappeared… or in the run up to it?"

Lucy shook her head. "I'm sure I told you lot this at the time, you know?"

"Humour me?" Eric asked, smiling.

"I think they'd split a few days before, but he'd talked her round… again. So, they were still an item as far as I knew when we went out on the Saturday."

"To the circus?"

She nodded. "The circus was great. The guys were always up for it and we were hanging around with them that afternoon, in between performances."

"They did an afternoon and an evening show, right?"

"Yes, that's right. And in between, we were hanging out, smoking a couple of—"

Eric grinned. "Recreational drugs?"

"Yes… but that's not a major crime, is it?"

Eric shook his head. "I don't think we'll be too concerned. It was a while ago."

She laughed. "Yeah, well, we were hanging out with them *backstage* so to speak, and we talked about meeting a few of them later that night for drinks."

"The performers?"

"Yes. Men and women before you ask. We were having a laugh, getting on. That group hasn't changed in years and they come around twice a year. You get to know people. The circus guys are always up for a laugh. Charlie came to the show. I don't know whether he was looking for Angie or not, I don't know, but he came with his mate, Micky."

"Micky George?"

"Yep. Another proper loser, if you ask me. Charlie wasn't happy about us hanging out with the performers. One of them was really into Angie, and she was quite taken with him."

"How did Charlie take that?"

Lucy smiled. "He wasn't too happy about it, as I'm sure you can imagine."

Eric flicked back through his notes. "Ah, yes. I made a note here. You said in your statement it was a performer called Daniel who Angela was chatting with?"

"DT, yes," she said, nodding. "Daniel Taylor… Turner… something like that."

"Turner," Eric confirmed from his notes.

"He was a knife thrower," Lucy said. "Which would make him good with his hands, I expect." Eric glanced up at her and she winked. He flushed again.

"Um… but you didn't leave together that Saturday evening?"

"No. Angie had somewhere she needed to be, but she said she'd meet us in town later that night…" she looked up as if searching her memory. "said she'd definitely catch up with us for last orders."

Eric looked up again. "But she didn't?"

"No. She didn't."

"Did that concern you?"

She shrugged. "No, why should it? It's not like we're married or anything. I figured she'd just got caught up with whatever she was doing and couldn't make it." She sighed. "It was only when no one had seen her in the next day or so, that we thought something might be up."

Eric cocked his head. "Her mother went to the police the very next day."

"Yeah. Maybe that was a mother's instinct. Not that I'd know about that sort of thing."

"That Saturday night, did you go out with the performers? The ones you were hanging out with during the day?"

"Yes, a few of them but people were coming and

going all night and we used to hit the pubs pretty hard at that time. I couldn't give you names… or times. Sorry."

"And Angela's boyfriend, Charlie. Did you see him being a problem for her?"

"That particular night or in general?"

Eric shrugged. "Either. Both."

"Charlie was a problem that was going to sort itself out soon enough. He had a definitive use-by date."

"Meaning?"

"He was joining the army," Lucy said. "I think he was due to be off in a few months anyway and that would be the end of that. I'm not sure if he'd passed all his panels or what, but the way Angie used to speak about it, it was a foregone conclusion. As far as Angie was concerned anyway. Not that he was suited to it, Charlie, I mean. Angie said so. His heart wasn't in it."

"So why join?"

"Parental expectation… family pressure. Charlie's old man was a retired colonel or something. Charlie was the only son, and there was a lot placed on his shoulders. I'm not sure he was given much of a choice in the matter. Totally dominated by his parents, that one. I guess that was why he sought to dominate Angie the way he did. Trying to get back some control in his life." She laughed. "Picked the wrong girl in Angie, though."

"Going back a bit, to that Saturday when Charlie saw Angie chatting with this knife-throwing character—"

"DT?"

"Yes. How did he react?"

Lucy pulled a mocking face at him. "Do you coppers not read *at all*? You remember DT but not the fracas?"

Eric smiled. "Horse's mouth and all that."

"Okay. Well, yes, it all got a bit heated. Charlie and Angie had words… Charlie got a little heavy-handed. Not that he hit her or anything, but he was keen for her to leave with him and Angie wasn't having it. Charlie wasn't giving up either."

"So, how did it finish?"

"Oh, a couple of the show guys got involved. DT… his sister – I forget her name – and an older guy. He might have been their dad… or uncle or something. I don't really know. Anyway, Micky sort of dragged Charlie away. I think it saved him from a bit of a kicking, to be honest."

"Saved by his mate, huh?" Eric said, jotting down the story in his notebook.

"His mate? Hah!" Lucy said, dismissing Eric's comment.

He looked at her quizzically.

"Micky George was Charlie's mate, true enough. It didn't stop him making a play for Angie when Charlie's back was turned though."

"Did he now?"

She nodded. "It might have been when they were in one of their *off* patches, but I wouldn't swear to it. Micky used to follow Charlie around all the time, licking his boots, but I think he secretly wanted everything Charlie had."

"And that included Angela?"

"Without a shadow of a doubt."

"Was it ever reciprocated?"

"You mean, did Angie ever… go with Micky?"

Eric nodded.

"I couldn't say for sure. Angie was discreet. We were close, but Angie had a way of keeping people at arm's length without causing offence in doing so. I always assumed it was a self-protection mechanism."

"Protection from what?"

Lucy shrugged. "I don't know. Do I look like Sigmund Freud?"

"Did Charlie ever find out about Micky's advances… or that his girlfriend may have responded?"

"I couldn't say for certain, but I wouldn't like to be around Charlie if he did." Lucy glanced at the clock. Eric noticed. It was a quarter to ten now.

"I'm sorry, am I keeping you from your work?"

Lucy smiled. "Actually, yes you are. Time is money and all that."

"I'm terribly sorry," Eric said, quickly rereading

his notes to make sure he'd asked all the questions he'd intended to. "Can I just ask you quickly, whether Angela was a secretive person? You said she was discreet."

Lucy chose her words carefully. "I would say she presented herself differently to different people. Is that the same thing?"

"I suppose," Eric said. "Oh, and one final one. Who was Angela meeting that Saturday night?"

Lucy shook her head. "She never said she was meeting anyone. Only that she had something on."

Eric tapped his pen against his bottom lip.

"And is there any chance she was going to meet Ben Crake?"

Lucy laughed, but this time it seemed artificial as opposed to the other times where she'd seen genuinely amused.

"I can't see why… no."

"Can you be sure? Perhaps Angela was keeping things from you too? Being discreet."

Lucy tilted her head to one side, maintaining her eye contact with Eric.

"I guess that's fair to say. Now, why are you asking about all this again? It must be because Ben has been let out of prison."

"That's a coincidence, I can assure you."

Her expression implied she didn't believe him, but it was the truth. However, he could appreciate the coincidence was hard to trust. Lucy's eyes flitted to the clock again. Eric took the hint.

"Thank you for your time, Miss Minors—"

"Lucy, DC Collet." She smiled warmly. "Please call me Lucy."

He leaned forward, returning her smile. "Eric."

"You have a lovely smile, Eric."

Feeling self-conscious, he looked away, worried that he would redden in embarrassment once again.

"You have a sadness around you, though," she said.

"I do?"

"Yes. You need to let that inner smile out more often, Eric. Free your spirit"

He nodded gently. "I'll… erm… bear that in mind."

"I can help with that."

Eric felt awkward, feeling himself flush. "You can?"

"Give me a call sometime, Detective Constable. We all get lonely."

Eric's mouth ran dry and he cleared his throat, trying to swallow but couldn't. "T–Thank you for your time this morning, Miss… Lucy," he said, forcing a smile and heading out of the room.

"Anything to help the police," she said, smiling warmly. She picked up her mobile phone, unlocked it and began typing as she walked Eric to the front door.

Stepping out onto the walkway, Eric turned and smiled again as he left. Lucy finished typing a text and waved him off. Eric hurried to the stairwell and descending to the first turn, he almost collided with a man coming up. He glanced nervously at Eric as they passed one another and Eric thought he looked remarkably similar to the man he'd seen earlier but didn't give it any more thought as he resumed his course.

CHAPTER NINE

ERIC ENTERED the ops room and Tom beckoned him over as soon as he'd taken off his coat, hanging it up by the entrance. The two met by Eric's desk.

"How did you get on with Lucy Minors?" Tom asked.

"Well. She's… quite a character."

"Made an impression on you then?"

Eric smiled but didn't reply, putting his wallet and keys into the top drawer of his desk.

"Of all the people who were in Angela Dale's circle, I imagine she was her closest friend. That's the impression I got from her, but… even she admitted that Angela wasn't open about her plans. Lucy said she was discreet, but it sounds secretive to me. She shared what she wanted to but not everything by any means. I'm paraphrasing, but that's pretty much what Lucy said."

Tom considered that. He didn't recall reading that description of Angela in the statements obtained around the time of her disappearance. Perhaps it was never implicitly stated, and in that case could have been omitted from the notes. It happened.

"So, the million-dollar question: what was Angela hiding?"

Eric shrugged. "Lucy had no idea, but she reiterated what she said in her original statement. She was expecting to meet Angela in town on that Saturday night, but she never showed. And, seeing as it was a casual arrangement, Lucy didn't think anything of it until Angela failed to turn up in the coming days. She never confided in Lucy where she was going that night. They were together earlier in the day, at the circus, but after that she doesn't know."

"The mystery engagement still lingers," Tom said.

"Yes. She did stress that Angela hadn't made it clear she was meeting someone, though. Only that she had *something on*."

"She didn't hazard a guess?"

Eric shook his head.

"There was one thing that struck me as odd, though," Eric said, his forehead creasing and drawing Tom's full attention. "Seemingly, Charlie Babcock, who we thought might have split from Angela a few days previously, was certain he was still in a relationship with her. According to Lucy anyway. Angela tried repeatedly to end it, but Charlie kept pestering her and talking her round. There was also a bit of a set-to at the circus that evening when Charlie took umbrage with how Angela was flirting with one of the circus performers."

Cassie's ears pricked up at that point, spinning her chair around to face them, but thinking better of making the instinctive, derogatory comment, Tom was sure was primed to cross her lips.

"That wasn't in Lucy's original statement," Tom said. "Angela was flirting with or chatting to Turner but there was no mention of them fighting."

Eric agreed. "She was certain everything she told me was in her statement, but you're right, it's not mentioned."

Tom frowned. "Have either of you found a reference in the case materials to confirm this, conversations with the performers, friends or family?"

Eric and Cassie exchanged looks, but neither could recollect anything. Cassie flicked through her notes.

"There are statements taken from the performers, or some of them at least. Those we thought interacted with Angela. I reread them last night, but they weren't particularly helpful. No one has direct knowledge of Angela."

"See no evil?" Tom asked.

Cassie smiled. "Travellers, Boss. They don't like us, particularly when we're asking questions. Usually means they're guilty of something."

"Well, maybe it's the way you ask them, Cassandra. You'd better dust off your charm book and temper your approach if you're going to get answers."

"You want me to visit the circus?"

He nodded. "We'll both go tomorrow. We can split up and speak to as many of them as we can."

"The nature of that type of work. A lot of the faces will have changed, though. Many of them might not be there any more."

"Maybe the unskilled jobs will be different, but they're a familial group, the travelling community. They keep to themselves and there aren't too many career opportunities for knife throwers and acrobats. I reckon most of them will still be there."

Eric interjected, "And Lucy Minors said they were quite friendly with the performers as they came into town a couple of times a year. It sounded like they socialised more than just on that occasion." He shrugged. "Maybe Angela did as well."

Cassie arched her eyebrows and nodded. "And you think they'll talk to us now, after all this time, where they weren't prepared to before?"

"It's all in how you ask, Cassie," Tom said.

She shot him a dubious look.

"And after that, it's about how much grief you can cause them if they don't cooperate."

She smiled. "Now you're talking."

Tom wagged a finger at her. "But that's the last resort, not the opening salvo."

"You take all the fun out of this job, Tom. You really do."

Tamara entered the room, walking at a brisk pace. She acknowledged the greetings with a smile.

"Where are we with forensics reports?" she asked Tom.

"I'm expecting the crime scene analysis at some point tomorrow morning. Maybe late on today, if I can push them along a little bit, but it's soil toxicology analysis that's slowing it down. We're trying to determine when she was buried and the storm has thrown everything all over the place, so it's tricky."

"Do what you can," Tamara said. "Pathology?"

"Same. Tomorrow is most likely."

"What's wrong with Paxton? Did he only get to squeeze in nine holes this morning?" she asked.

Tom bore a wry smile. "I'm sure he's just being thorough."

Tamara arched her eyebrows in response. "I've arranged a meeting with Gary Reynolds, off the record, over a cup of coffee for later today." She checked her watch. "In fact, I need to head off."

"Where are you meeting?"

"Neutral ground. He's based in Ipswich now, so we're meeting halfway, in Thetford."

"Was he curious as to why you wouldn't speak over the telephone?"

Tamara pursed her lips. "If he was, he didn't say so. The jungle drums must have reached him by now regarding Crake's release. If the chief super knows, then I dare say he'll have given his wing man of the day the heads-up, don't you think?"

"You'd expect so. In which case, he was probably expecting a call from someone."

"Which means he'll be on his guard," Tamara said.

"It's all about how you ask the question," Cassie said dryly. The joke was lost on Tamara but Tom smiled at her.

"Speaking of Watts. Has he been onto you yet?" Tom asked.

Tamara shook her head. "No, but if he comes looking just tell him I had an errand to run."

The gathering broke up and Tom fell into step with Tamara as she made to leave.

"Can we walk and talk?" he asked.

"Yes, of course. What's on your mind?"

"You might want to check how accurate DCI Reynolds is when you speak about the case."

She stopped, turning to face him, likely sensing there was a deeper meaning contained within those words.

"Why? What's going on?"

Tom checked the corridor to make sure they couldn't be overheard. Besides a couple of uniformed officers chatting as they rounded the next corner, the two of them were alone.

"We've come across some discrepancies in the statements. No, sorry. They're not discrepancies, more like omissions. Charlie Babcock may have been distancing himself from Angela when the opposite was true. Lucy Minors, Angela's close friend, says they were very much still an item and he wanted it to remain so. It was Angela who wanted out. Charlie was also at the circus on the Saturday."

"I know. He gave a statement to that effect."

"Except he didn't mention he nearly got into a ruck with some of the performers over Angela." He shook his head. "No one appears to be mentioning that or, more accurately, no officer is recording that. Lucy claims it happened and that she said so at the time, but there's no record of it."

Tamara thought hard, her eyebrows knitting. "What are you suggesting?"

"Only that, at worst, evidence pointing to her boyfriend wasn't followed up or, at best, that they failed to record it."

"Not everything goes into a statement, you know that. It's not taken down word for word."

"Even so," Tom said, looking pained.

"Too focussed on Crake perhaps?"

"Maybe," Tom said. "It just seems odd."

Tamara nodded. "I'll bear it in mind. Have Eric cross reference who carried out which interview. That way we'll have an idea if it's just one copper doing shady work or a deeper malaise at work."

Tom smiled. "Will do."

They parted ways and Tom returned to the ops room. Eric approached him as he entered.

"One thing I forgot to mention."

"What's that?" Tom asked.

"Lucy Minors," Eric said. "I think she might be on the game."

That suggestion caught Tom by surprise. "Really? What makes you say so?"

"I missed it when I was there, but when she opened the door, she apologised because I was early. I guessed she'd mistaken me for someone else, but after I introduced myself… once she was dressed—"

"Once she was dressed?" Cassie asked, a broad smile crossing her face.

Eric glanced over his shoulder at her apologetically. "Not like that… I mean… properly dressed. All made up and that."

Cassie laughed.

"Go on, Eric," Tom said.

"She was playing dance music when I arrived… then when she let me in it was this light, background kind of jazz stuff. Much more…"

"Sensual?" Cassie said, pouting.

"Yes," Eric said, smiling and shaking his head. "Mood music. I think she was expecting a client. Some guy appeared while I was at the door and turned tail when I introduced myself to her. And her flatmate, Susan, was in a hurry to go out." He shook his head. "Maybe I'm overthinking."

Tom was thoughtful. "Do you think it's relevant? Either to her testimony or the case?"

Eric shook his head. "I've no reason to doubt what she told me. I thought she was very genuine."

"Maybe reread the statements and see if any reference to Lucy's work five or six years ago crops up. If Angela was in or around that world, then I guess there's the possibility of her coming into contact with clients."

Cassie spoke up. "Or maybe she was also on the game."

"There's nothing in the files to suggest Angela was a sex worker," Eric said.

"No, that's true," Tom agreed. "At the time, her family were landowners and quite well off, as I understand it. She would certainly be lacking the triggers that often guide people into that world. But, if she was friends with someone who was, then it could have a bearing on the case. Let's just keep it in mind."

"What about Susan Brock?" Eric asked. "She's pally with Lucy even now. Drives a nice car as well. That was her Mercedes parked outside yesterday when we were at the Dales' house."

"You think she might also be..."

"Lucy laughed when I said Susan told me she was in a hurry to get to work. She said it was *funny she called it work* or something like that."

Tom raised his eyebrows. "Okay. Keep that in mind as well, but let's remember Susan comes from an affluent background as well. Let's not get distracted."

CHAPTER TEN

TAMARA WAITED IN THE CAR. The overnight rain had been heavy but the storm had passed through. The day was overcast and the wind was still buffeting the car, making it rock gently in the strongest gusts, but the only concern now was the odd spatter of rain showers swiftly passing overhead. Thetford Forest Park must be teeming with visitors during the high season or local school holidays, providing the weather was reasonable. In November, the car park was empty aside from the occasional hardy dog walker risking the falling trees. That danger was most likely past now though.

Another vehicle arrived in the car park, slowly circling the virtually empty area, it came to a stop twenty yards from where she was parked. The single, male occupant got out, hurriedly retrieving his coat from the back seat and putting it on. He was a large man. Not similar in size to Tom, but who was? He was six feet tall, in his forties with a paunch and rosy red cheeks against a pale complexion. His mousey brown hair was thinning on top and greying all over, swept away from his forehead into a side parting.

Tamara cracked her door, pushing it open with the aid of her foot as another gust of wind tried to slam it shut on her. Her hair caught on the breeze and whipped across her face and no matter how much she pushed it aside, it soon took on a mind of its own once more. Drawing her coat about her, she thrust her hands into her pockets now she was out of the sanctuary of the warm car.

Approaching the newcomer, she smiled.

"DCI Reynolds?" she asked.

He smiled and nodded, reaching back into the front of his car and coming out with two cups of takeaway coffee in hand. He closed the door with his backside, and stepped forward to meet her, handing one cup over. She accepted it graciously.

"It's a pleasure to meet you, DCI Greave," he said, tipping his cup towards her in a casual salute. "Let's not stand on ceremony. I'm Gary."

"Tamara," she said.

"Sorry about the last-minute change of location," he said, cupping both hands around the warm drink, huddling his arms in close to his body.

"I figured we'd get some shelter from the forest here, but damn... it's still cold."

Tamara smiled. "Sitting behind a desk making you soft, is it?"

"Hah! You and I both know one of the perks of higher rank is you don't *have* to go out in the field as often. I like it when the sun's shining, but on days like this I'm quite happy with a cup of coffee in my office."

"So why the change of meeting place?" Tamara asked, sipping her coffee. It had cow's milk in it which tasted vile after years of drinking oat milk. Not that she would mention it. She didn't want to appear ungrateful.

He shrugged, looking around the virtually empty car park. "You can't be too careful, can you?"

She laughed. "You make it sound like we're up to something."

He looked at her sternly and then his face split into a smile. "Yes, I suppose it does, doesn't it?" He shook his head. "Nothing could be further from the truth; it's just you know how things can be twisted."

"Who are you worried about?"

He pulled a face, as if it was a daft question. "The same people you should be concerned about; the press." He took a mouthful of coffee, then tilted the cup towards her. "And if you're not remotely concerned about that, then you should be. Because they will eat you alive once they get wind of what you're investigating."

Tamara was momentarily concerned. Only the four of them back at Hunstanton knew the identity of their victim, as far as she knew. Reynolds' gaze narrowed, reading her expression.

"I mean, that's why you're here, isn't it? You're carrying out the review into the Crake investigation?"

Tamara moved her hair aside from her face, tilting her head and shifting her stance to try and stop it from blowing across her eyes again.

"Not exactly, no, but it is related."

Reynolds was intrigued. "Sorry. When you called, I figured you were on secondment to look into our handling of the Angela Dale murder and Ben Crake's arrest and trial."

"Ah, sorry. That's probably my fault for not being clear."

Reynolds stiffened, the amicability façade slipping, to be replaced by a stern mask.

"So, what are you here for?"

"I'm actually investigating a murder," she said, choosing her words carefully, "and there is a possibility it is linked to Angela's disappearance and death."

That appeared to pacify Reynolds and he visibly relaxed.

"Oh, right… okay," he said, raising his coffee cup, his eyes scanning the nearby trees. He shook his head. "So, what can I do for you?"

"May I be blunt and save us both a lot of time?"

He fixed her with a stare. "Please do."

"I want to know why you were so focussed on Ben Crake right from the get-go?"

"Were we?" Reynolds asked, averting his eye from Tamara's gaze and casually turning his cup in his hand before taking another sip from it. It was almost as if he was too casual, as if he was conscious of it. If the question fazed him, he didn't show it.

"I thought so," Tamara said, "having reviewed the case file, statements and the interview transcripts."

Reynolds was quiet for a moment, biting his lower lip. Then he looked at Tamara, his expression impassive.

"If you've read the files… then you'll know why we focussed on Crake. Because *he* did it."

Tamara nodded. "Yes, I see that was what you thought."

"And you don't?" The question was hard edged, but whether it was anger, frustration or something else entirely, Tamara couldn't tell.

"You had no doubts… then or now?"

He shook his head. "No. Give me a reason why

I should? Do you even have one or are you just passing judgement on me for some other reason?"

"I'm sorry, I didn't come here to accuse you of anything—"

"Well, that's how it's coming across DCI Greave. I figured a fellow professional would understand how a murder investigation works. How many cases have you handled in your time?"

He was irritated, angry. Perhaps she could have chosen her words differently, because she'd certainly put his back up.

"I've worked a few," she said, keeping her tone neutral.

"And are you going to tell me what you're working right now? Seeing as you're asking an awful lot of questions about my case from six years ago."

She shook her head. "I'm sorry. You know how it is sometimes?"

"Oh yeah, I do," he said, bitterness in his voice. "I'd think that a fellow officer would at least give another the courtesy of a heads-up if there's a train coming at him down the tracks though."

"You think you have something to worry about?" she asked.

"No. Do you?"

That was a roundabout way of gleaning something from her.

"Like I said, that's not my investigation, but if you followed procedure—"

"Procedure? Pah!" he scoffed. "You don't get anywhere following procedure most of the time. Do you know how many villains would still be on the streets if we all followed *procedure*?"

Tamara cocked her head. "I appreciate what you're saying, and maybe we walk close to the line on occasion, and I guess that's fine as long as the result is just."

Reynolds laughed. "As long as it doesn't come back on you, you mean?"

Tamara didn't answer, but she did smile and briefly raise a solitary eyebrow. Conversation died for a few moments and Tamara wondered whether she should call it a day and politely make her excuses, but her fellow DCI made no moves to do likewise.

"You've examined my case?" he asked. "The one I made against Crake?"

Tamara nodded.

"He confessed!"

"You could read that in two ways though," she said evenly.

Reynolds bobbed his head. "Yeah, I know, but we had trace evidence… the CCTV…"

"Which was inconclusive," Tamara countered. She held up her hand. "Not that I'm here to give you a kicking, it's just that it showed someone –

most likely Angela – running off and Crake following."

"Crake *chasing* her."

"Again, open to interpretation. It was chucking it down with rain. She may have been running for cover and he ran to keep up with her."

"Bloody hell… you sound like that Goldman woman."

"Who?" Tamara asked.

Reynolds took a deep breath. "Crake's greatest advocate and the thorn in my side… or the pain in my arse… choose your analogy."

"And she is?"

"Ex copper… Derbyshire… Gloucestershire… I don't know," he said, dismissively waving his hand in the air in a circular motion. "Whichever. Ex-hunter turned gamekeeper, poacher… or something like that. You know what I mean? How she got involved, I don't know, but she's been digging around… hasn't let up in the last two or three years. It was her who found all this nonsense that his defence team has used to get him out. It won't help. Crake belongs inside and he'll be back there soon enough."

"You sound confident of that."

"Because I'm damn sure he did it! That's why."

"There's no doubt in your mind?"

He looked at her, his lips parting, momentarily hesitating.

"No doubt at all."

"But you'd have to say that, wouldn't you? After all, your investigation went after Crake at the expense of all other suspects."

"There you go again," he said, dismissively shaking his head. "All other suspects. What suspects?"

"How about Charlie Babcock?"

"What about him?"

"He lied in his statement."

Tamara focussed on him, watching for any tell to suggest he knew what she was talking about. He was either a good poker player or he had no idea what she knew. He tilted his head to one side, his eyes narrowing.

"W-What about?"

"He said he'd broken up with Angela before her disappearance. He even implied he instigated it."

"So… so what?"

"We have it on good authority that it was the other way around… and that Charlie kicked off on the night she disappeared, almost coming to blows with another man at the circus over Angela."

Reynolds bit his bottom lip and shook his head. "That doesn't ring a bell."

"Well, no, it shouldn't because it's not recorded in any of the official documentation. Why might that be, do you think?"

He shook his head emphatically now. "Couldn't have happened."

"And if it did?"

"It didn't." He hesitated momentarily, thinking on it. "If it did, then people didn't tell us or it would be in the statements. Where are you going with all this? Is it that Goldman woman again? You need to watch her. She has her own agenda against the police. Christ only knows why?"

"I've not come across her," Tamara said.

"Give it time. If you're anywhere near the Angela Dale murder, then it's only a matter of time. She's tried to throw multiple people into the firing line, anyone at all to try and leave a whiff of doubt around Crake's conviction." He shook his head. "I don't know why, but she has a real boner for him."

Tamara arched her eyebrows.

"Sorry," Reynolds said. "Poor choice of phrase, but there's nothing more irritating that an ideological zealot."

"Who has she suggested as potential killers?"

"Charlie… his mate, Micky… even both of them together at one point. She even tried to spin it that it was Crake's employer who killed her."

"He was there that night, wasn't he? In his office?" Tamara asked. "Wasn't he recorded on the gate cameras leaving the site before Angela and Ben Crake were together?"

"Yes, that's right. Coupled with that, he was at a

function that evening as the guest speaker. He was on stage fifteen minutes after leaving the site, witnessed by a hundred guests!" Reynolds shook his head, bewildered. "She then suggested it might be someone from the circus because Angela was flirting with one or two of them, but Angela was a flirt. If we went round focussing on everyone she professed to be interested in then we'd have had a suspect list of half the county! She was that type. Honestly, Olivia Goldman will throw mud at anyone if she thinks it will aid her case."

"What evidence did she find that got Crake's case through to the court of appeal?"

He waved his hand dismissively in the air. "Technicalities… some bull about us withholding information pertinent to the case from the defence team at trial. We were under pressure… short of man hours and working miracles every day. Of course, things might get missed, but she made it out like it was some kind of a grand conspiracy."

"So what was it?" Tamara pressed. "The evidence that you failed to disclose." He glared at her, but she lightened the atmosphere with a smile. "Accidentally."

Exhaling, Reynolds shook his head. "A delivery driver dropped off a package at the main site entrance. Crake signed for it."

"So?" Tamara asked.

"So, he was in the guard room ten minutes after

the CCTV has him running after Angela. After a month we managed to speak to the delivery driver and, from memory, he described Crake as calm, clean – albeit damp – and acting normally. They were familiar with each other. He recalled discussing the weather with Crake along with some football result that afternoon."

"And the defence said that cast doubt on him having just killed Angela?"

He nodded. "Yes. That's exactly what it did. The driver was on site offloading and loading for twenty minutes. He claimed Crake was acting normally. It's hardly earth-shattering evidence of his innocence though is it?"

"But it breaks the timeline of a ruthless killer busy disposing of the body."

"Yeah… but that was the time he could have been erasing the CCTV footage that was accidentally *lost* from the system that night."

"Was it just that night's data that was corrupted?"

"Multiple days' worth. It must have been a blanket wipe of the system. Probably quicker and less incriminating than doing only that evening."

"But not the footage of him running after Angela? Seems odd."

"Different system. That part of the site was on an old network and hadn't been integrated. It was due for demolition and rebuilding in some expansion plans the company had, so the owner told me anyway. So, they didn't feel the need. The area was disused anyway. That's why we theorised that he took her there, so he could dispose of the body later when he got the chance. I guessed he didn't know about that particular camera or system, which was why he hadn't got rid of that footage. She broke free of him and made a dash for it. It's a shame she wasn't a faster runner." Reynolds shrugged. "Without that footage, would we have even considered him as the killer? Maybe not. The thing is, if the truth be told, without the body we were playing on the jurors' emotions to get the conviction. The CPS weren't keen to prosecute… but we were all under a lot of pressure to get a result.

"That's a tough position to be in."

He nodded. "Tell me about it. Not that it changes one iota for me. Crake did it. I'm as sure now as I was then. There should be a retrial and he'll go back where he belongs." He frowned deeply. "Look, Ben Crake may play this dopey, thicko, but he's arrogant… calculating and downright dangerous. His home computer had a history of viewing masochistic pornography, violent sexual encounters… and his obsession with Angela while they were at school together was well known among their peers. I wouldn't be surprised if he saw an opportunity and tried his luck, only for her to reject him and he couldn't take no for an answer." He scoffed. "What was Crake's defence? That she came onto him. Angela could have had her pick of the town and she'd come on to someone like Ben Crake. Pull the other one. It was a pathetic defence, but the best he could come up with and that parasite, Olivia Goldman, can sling as much mud as she likes at whomever she likes, but it won't change my mind that we got the right man. It's a travesty that he is out walking the streets."

Tamara took a deep breath, allowing the moment to settle. This case had Reynolds worked up. To be fair, if she was working the case of a murdered teenager, she'd probably feel the same.

"What did he do with the body?" she asked.

"Say again?"

"The body. Angela. What did Crake do with the body? You must have had thoughts on it."

Reynolds exhaled heavily. "That was the problem with our case, right from the off. We couldn't identify the kill site, let alone the disposal location. We had dogs out but the handlers reckon the rain washed away any traces of the scent trail. The company Crake worked for had a sprawling range of sites at that time. He would have been familiar with them and many of these had outbuildings that were seldom used. He could easily have stored her in one of these, popped back during the subsequent nights once he'd figured out how he was going to get rid of her. He had access to small fishing boats, owned by friends, or family friends, that he could have borrowed and rowed out into The Wash. If you time it right with the currents, the body will end up coming ashore on the continent, if ever."

He sighed, running a hand through his hair.

"If only we could have found her body. Then it might have been different."

"But you're sure she was dead?"

He looked at her quizzically.

"Yes, of course. Why would you think differently?"

"I don't know," she said, shrugging. "You said it yourself. You couldn't find the kill site or the body. Surely, you considered the possibility that Angela was still alive?"

"Yes, of course we did." He held out his hand, ticking things off on each finger as he went. "Bank account, no activity. Mobile phone, no service after Saturday evening. No pings to network towers. No contact with friends or relatives. No sightings. She vanished that Saturday and the last person she was seen with was Ben Crake." He jabbed his forefinger pointedly into the palm of his left hand. "He was the last person to be with the victim, and nine times out of ten, that's the person that kills them. Right or wrong?"

Tamara had to agree. "Right."

"Thank you," he said, his shoulders sagging ever so slightly.

"But one in ten times, it's someone else, and we just haven't identified them yet."

Reynolds cocked his head. "True."

"And without a body, that leaves the question open."

"Also true," Reynolds said, begrudgingly. "But we were right. I was right."

CHAPTER ELEVEN

Tamara arrived back at the station later than expected. Getting in and out of Norfolk, let alone cutting across it, was a nightmare on a Friday afternoon with people finishing early from work and heading away for their weekend plans. It's far worse in the spring and summertime, but it was difficult to get anywhere fast in rural Norfolk.

Glancing into the refectory on her way to ops, she saw Tom, Eric and Cassie inside getting something to eat. She went in to join them. A handful of officers working the late shift were inside chatting over their evening meal, but the kitchen was now closed and everything had been cleared away. She must have missed a hot meal by less than a quarter of an hour.

It would be vending machine food or a takeaway for her. Neither was particularly appealing and sometimes she thought choosing a vegan diet was just more hassle than it was worth. She dismissed that thought. Of course it wasn't, but it was a pain when trying to eat on the go.

They all greeted her as she pulled out a chair and sat down, keen to hear what she'd drawn out of DCI Reynolds.

"How did it go?" Tom asked.

Tamara turned the corners of her mouth down, exaggerating the expression.

"I dare say he believes they got the right man."

"Can't have," Eric said through a mouthful of shepherd's pie. "We've got his victim in the morgue and she died while Crake was banged up."

Cassie held a flat palm up in front of Eric's mouth, barely two inches from his lips.

"Say it, don't spray it, Eric!"

"Sorry," he said, repeating the error.

Cassie tutted him. "I hope you'll teach little George not to speak with his mouth full."

"Do as I say, not as I do," Eric said, smiling. "That's what my mum always said to me."

"Hypocrite, is she?" Cassie countered. Eric frowned.

Tom hushed them. "Did you tell him we've found Angela?"

Tamara shook her head. "We've not had it confirmed yet. Not that I'd have told him anyway. I told him we had a related case and needed to verify their investigation was accurate. Stuff like that." She eyed Eric's food alongside Tom and Cassie's empty plates. "I'm hungry."

"You should have called," Cassie said. "I'd have got you something."

"Thanks, Cass."

"Yeah," Eric said, finishing his last mouthful. "You're a great person to have around after a crisis."

Cassie put on a childish mock whining expression, much to Eric's amusement.

"He must have known you were up to something, though," Tom said. "He's a DCI, so he'll be savvy."

"No doubt," Tamara agreed. "He thought I was on the team that would be reviewing the investigation and deciding on whether to go for a retrial."

"Ah… that makes sense. Did he give you anything useful?"

"Perhaps. I'm not sure," Tamara said, her eye drifting to the vending machines. "It's no good. I'm going to have to eat." She stood up but turned back as she made to walk away. "I think once we're further along in our investigation, I'll know how much faith I should have in Reynolds… and… you know?"

She was referring to the chief superintendent. Tom stood up, gathered his plate and his rubbish, taking it to the kitchen hatch and putting it on the side to be cleared away. He then went to stand with Tamara as she made her choice from the scant vegan offerings.

"Pom Pom Bears?" Tom asked, as Tamara selected the same item twice, corn snacks shaped like bears.

"They're vegan."

"Are they? Wow. I'd never have thought it."

"You learn something new every day."

"Speaking of which," Tom said. "Forensic analysis of the victim's DNA came back an hour ago."

"And?"

"As we figured. It's Angela."

Tamara took a deep breath. It was what they'd thought, but the confirmation still saddened her. A seventeen-year-old girl had gone missing and turned up dead as a twenty-three-year-old woman. She scratched the side of her head. It was a case like no other she'd worked in her career to date.

"Are you trying to figure it out?" Tom asked.

"Yes… it's a strange one."

"We'll work it out."

"Tamara, Tom…"

They both looked left to see Chief Superintendent Watts standing at the entrance to the refectory. All conversation in the room died, likely as a result of Watts' tone. He pointed at the two of them.

"My office. Now!"

He turned and walked away. Tamara looked at her crisp packets forlornly. Taking them out of the hatch, she put them on the nearest table and indicated for Cassie to take care of them. Cassie nodded. Tamara joined Tom and the two of them headed upstairs.

Cassie rose from her seat and collected Tamara's crisps. Two officers sitting nearby looked at her for an explanation, but she merely shrugged. She didn't know what the chief super was irritated about, but it was likely to be the case. Not that she was going to let on.

PC Kerry Palmer entered the refectory, glancing around to see who was there. She smiled at Cassie and the two acknowledged one another. Kerry then went to get herself a cup of tea from the vending machine and sat down with the two officers near to Cassie. Cassie glanced at Eric who looked away. She saw Kerry also make eye contact with Eric but as soon as Cassie caught her eye, she shifted awkwardly in her seat and then engaged the officer next to her, cracking a joke about something.

Cassie made her way back to their table and sat down. Nodding towards Kerry, she asked, "What's that about then?"

"What's what about?" Eric asked nonchalantly.

"Kerry… back then, ghosting you?"

"Did she? Didn't notice."

"Yeah, you did," Cassie said. "I saw you make eye—"

"Leave it, will you?"

"Leave what? The two of you used to be thick as thieves—"

"I said—" Eric stopped himself and, lowering his voice as the officers at Kerry's table all looked over at them, pleaded, "Leave it. Please."

"Okay, Eric. No problem," she said. Kerry had the hots for Eric. Cassie had had suspicions to that effect from the first time she'd been seconded to CID. And it was safe to say she was certain on the second case they'd all worked together. However, she must have missed something, which was unlike her. "Sorry. I didn't mean to… well… whatever."

Eric smiled at her. "I know. It's just… ah, never mind."

"So, tell me something good about life, Eric," she said, changing the subject. "You haven't mentioned baby George much recently. How is parental life?"

Eric smiled, arching his eyebrows. "When do they stop being considered babies? He seems to be growing so fast…" Eric looked down at the last of the tea in the cup he was nursing, swirling the contents gently. "It's great… getting home and seeing him after work. No matter how rough the day's been, I see him and it's all worthwhile, you know?"

He lifted the cup and drained the contents, but he didn't make eye contact with Cassie.

"Yeah, I can imagine," she said.

"He's ace. He really is," Eric said.

"And how's Becca getting on?"

"Oh, you know? Fine," Eric said, smiling briefly. "She gets a bit stressed with it all, but… new mum and all that."

"How much maternity is she taking?"

"Um… the school had maternity cover in their business plan, so she can take the full year."

"That's great. Forward-thinking employers."

Eric bobbed his head. "Yeah, they've been great." He turned to Cassie, putting his empty cup down. "Hey, you've got siblings with children, don't you?"

"Yes, I've got so many nieces and nephews that I didn't need to bother having my own. I can just timeshare my sisters'. All the benefits of ownership but without the aggravation of the long-term maintenance."

Eric smiled weakly. "Yeah," he said. "Good one."

"Why do you ask?"

"Oh… nothing really. Forget it."

Cassie sensed he was struggling. Reaching out,

she placed a friendly hand on his forearm. "What is it?"

"I was just wondering… if… well, after they had their kids, did they struggle a bit? To get back to normal, I mean?"

Cassie blew out her cheeks. "What's normal?"

Eric nodded, wringing his hands.

"Look, Eric… having a child changes everything. For a woman it changes her mindset, her body… her ambitions… literally, your entire world changes. And so does yours."

He glanced sideways at her and nodded.

"Yeah, I guess so."

"Definitely," Cassie said. "You know, I think both my sisters tried to hang onto their previous lives." She snorted a laugh. "And I know their husbands tried to for far longer. It doesn't work out well if you're not prepared to move into the new phase of life, because babies and… youth culture – I can't believe I just used that phrase, by the way – just don't mix." She squeezed Eric's arm. "The point is, the two of you are on this journey together. The three of you if you include the little man, and you just need to keep talking to one another." She forced him to meet her eye. "Do you know what I mean?"

He rolled his lips together, nodding. "Yeah, yeah. I get it."

He smiled appreciatively and Cassie tapped his

forearm again. "Come on, let's get back upstairs. I'm dying to know what Teflon wanted with Mum and Dad." As an afterthought, she turned and put a restraining hand on Eric's chest. "Have you called home?"

"No, not yet," Eric said.

"Right, well, you do that now. Let Becca know you'll be a bit late. It's the little things that count sometimes, Eric."

"Yeah, I'll do that now," he said, reaching for his mobile. "Have you called Lauren?"

Cassie laughed. "It's Friday. She'll be in the pub with the guys from work. I'll be home before she is!"

Eric hit dial, smiled at Cassie and walked to the other side of the room with his mobile pressed to his ear.

"When were the two of you going to tell me you were investigating the Angela Dale case?" Watts barked at them, the moment Tom closed the door to the chief superintendent's office.

Tamara exchanged a look with Tom but his expression didn't convey that he knew how Watts had found out either.

"To be honest with you, sir, we didn't know

ourselves until… what?" she confirmed with Tom, "an hour ago when the DNA results came back."

Watts stared at her and then shifted his gaze in Tom's direction. He nodded.

"Then why were you questioning Gary Reynolds this afternoon?"

Now they both understood.

Tamara stuck her chest out, confidently. "That was on, what I believed to be at the time, a related case—"

"Don't you dare take me for a fool, Tamara!"

She bit her lip. There was no point in maintaining the charade. "Sir… it's true that we didn't have confirmation until the analysis came through."

"But you suspected?"

She nodded. "Yes, sir. We suspected the remains we found out at Ringstead were Angela Dale's, but we couldn't say until we knew… under the circumstances."

"And I should hear it from Gary Reynolds? Regarding a case happening on my watch, in this very station!"

"I apologise, sir."

"Too bloody right you should, DCI Greave. Who do you think I am?"

His cheeks were flushed and the pronounced vein on the top of his forehead was going into overdrive. For a moment, she actually thought it might explode, but Watts forced himself to calm down and pulled out his chair.

"Although, to be clear, sir. I didn't tell DCI Reynolds what we were investigating."

"He's not a moron, Tamara," Watts countered.

"No, sir. Of course not."

Watts exhaled slowly, gathering himself.

"Tell me where you are," he said, running both hands across his scalp and down to the back of his neck.

"We've had DNA confirmation that the remains found buried in Ringstead are indeed those of Angela Dale, although some key parts are missing. Notably, her head, hands and one arm."

Watts looked horrified. "That's rather disconcerting."

"Yes, sir. We are working on the theory that the body was dismembered in order to aid with disposal."

"Dear Lord." Watts sank back into his chair, raising a balled fist to his mouth. He was momentarily lost in thought. "And… where do you think the rest of the body… Angela is?"

Tamara shook her head, glancing at Tom.

"We have search teams combing the woodland and the grass verges along the Downs at the moment, sir," Tom said. "However, so far we've had no joy."

Watts frowned. "So, she was here all along."

"Well, that might not actually be correct, sir," Tamara said.

He looked up at Tamara and then Tom. "Whatever do you mean?"

"Preliminary examination from the scene suggests that Angela died in the last month to six weeks."

Watts' mouth fell open. "Well, how is that possible?"

"That's what we are endeavouring to find out, sir."

"I… I don't know what to say,' Watts mumbled. "Do you have a potential cause of death."

"No, sir. We're waiting on pathology, which should come back…"

"Tomorrow," Tom said. "Dr Paxton is working on it now. Hopefully, we'll have more answers then, but there is no clear cause of death from the remains that we have. We would be speculating at this point."

"I see."

Watts drifted off, lost in thought. Tamara wondered what was going through his head.

"I think you can understand why we played our cards so close to our chest, sir," Tamara said.

"What's that?" Watts asked, snapping himself out of it.

"Keeping it to ourselves, sir. The last thing we need is a media frenzy to get in our way. We know it's coming, obviously, but I saw no need to speed things up."

"Yes… yes, of course, Tamara," Watts said, quietly. "It was probably for the best."

"So, can we continue with the investigation, sir?"

He looked up, his eyes flitting between the two of them. "Yes, please do. But I want to be kept advised of progress, do you understand?"

"Yes, sir," they both said in unison.

"This case is very close to me… and I don't want to be blindsided again. Is that clear?"

"Crystal clear, sir," Tamara said. Tom concurred.

"Carry on,' Watts said, and they left his office.

Once clear and halfway along the corridor, Tamara allowed herself to breathe.

"Well, that was fun," she said.

"It was always going to happen, I suppose," Tom said. "But it doesn't make it any more pleasant!"

"Let's hope we don't find out he dropped the ball," she said.

"I don't want to contemplate that right now."

Tamara stopped them in the corridor before they reached ops. "Let's keep Teflon's meltdown between us for now, Tom."

He nodded his agreement.

"Tomorrow morning, are you okay to visit the

Dales? You've already met them… I could do it, but familiarity and all that."

"Yes, of course. I'll do it," Tom said.

"And then I want you to stick to the plan; go out and speak to the circus and see what anyone can remember."

"Something tells me that won't be much," Tom said with a wry grin. "Cassie can be a bit of a throwback with some of her attitudes, but something tells me she'll be right on this. They'll have selective memories."

Tamara smiled. "Ask anyway."

"If you've no objection, I might leave visiting the parents until after I've spoken to Dr Paxton. He may have answers to some of their questions. The Dales have waited long enough for answers, and I'd hate to go there without as much information as I can."

"Fair enough," Tamara said. "A few more hours won't make much difference, although I can't begin to imagine what they're going through at this time." Her mobile rang and she reached for it. Glancing at the screen, she saw it was David. She looked at Tom. "I need to take this."

Tom excused himself and walked on towards ops. Tamara answered.

"Hey, what's up?"

"Hi, Tamara."

His tone was strange, but she couldn't work out why.

"What's wrong?"

He sighed quietly. "You forgot, didn't you?"

It came back to her immediately and she grimaced, turning and leaning against the wall, she pressed her free hand against her forehead.

"You know what, I did. Sorry, love. I only got back to the station like twenty minutes ago and I've just been chewed out by the boss."

"You are coming home soon, aren't you?" David asked, all but whispering.

"I can hardly hear you."

Tamara heard voices in the background. Familiar ones.

"Where... are you, David?"

"I'm at *your place*," he said, still whispering, "and I thought you said your folks were *going away*."

"Ah... yes. Change of plans. Beryl had a fall... or something." She bit her lip. "Are you... alone with my parents?"

"Yes!"

He said that too loudly. Tamara heard her mother's voice come close.

"You tell Tammy not to worry about rushing home, David. I can soon rustle you up something to eat."

"Oh, dear god, no," Tamara said to herself.

"What's that?" David asked.

"She's going to make you mac and cheese," Tamara said. "Whatever you do, don't let her serve you mac and cheese..."

"Why not?"

"Because it tastes like feet."

"Oh... when will you be home?"

He sounded desperate now. Tamara checked the time. She should have been home three quarters of an hour ago. As if it wasn't bad enough that David was alone at the mercy of Francesca, he was about to be fed a meal that Tamara had eaten so many times it had driven her to veganism. That wasn't strictly true, but subconsciously it may have played a part.

"I'll be home as soon as I can."

"When?" David hissed.

"Love you!" she said, hanging up. She felt bad, but the thought of David squirming did make her smile. "You're a bad woman, Tamara Greave," she said. "A very bad woman."

She strode into ops, tucking her phone back in her pocket.

"Everything all right?" Tom asked.

"Nothing I won't pay handsomely for later."

CHAPTER TWELVE

TOM AND CASSIE turned off the main road and drove along the short track that wound its way beyond the farm shop, a timber cabin open for a few hours each day to sell local produce. The field at the rear of the property was used periodically throughout the year for a range of functions; a location for a large bonfire and fireworks display in November, the charred ground denoted where the bonfire had been only a couple of weeks ago and, presently, it was the site for the travelling circus. There was enough space for the big top to be erected in the centre of the field, to house all of the vehicles around the boundary as well as the mobile ticket office. There was still space to utilise as a customer car park.

Getting out of the car, Tom looked around. It

was early on a Saturday morning, but the site was prepped and ready for the day. He had seen the performers begin to arrive a couple of days previously with the main group following on yesterday. The big top went up with incredible speed, but they did it almost every week and must therefore be almost second nature. The wind was still gusting much as it had been in previous days. Tom noted multiple flags on poles at the top of the tent denoting the various nationalities represented by the performers; the home nations obviously, but also he saw Brazilian, Portuguese and Hungarian flags fluttering in the breeze.

A pick-up truck was parked in front of the ticket office, hitched to a promotional trailer with posters and a loudspeaker mounted upon it. Two men were chatting, one leaning against the open driver's door of the vehicle. They said farewell and the driver got in, fired up the engine and pulled away, glancing at them as he left the car park. The pre-recorded message began almost immediately, a loud fanfare followed by a traditional ringmaster's call to visit the circus. No doubt the trailer would be doing laps of the area in the coming hours, drumming up more business.

The other man stood with his hands on his hips watching their approach. He was in his sixties. A large man, barrel-chested with thinning hair that had receded from his forehead.

"I'm afraid the ticket office doesn't open until nine," he said.

"That's okay," Tom said, reaching him and taking out his warrant card and displaying it casually to him. "DI Janssen and DS Knight."

The man nodded and smiled. "What can I do for two of Norfolk's finest? No one can be complaining yet, surely? We've only just got here."

Tom laughed, noting a sideways glance from Cassie, almost to say *I told you so.*

"It's nothing like that. Could you point us to the person in charge?"

"Well, that would be me… sort of. Liam Ratcliffe. General Manager and Ringmaster to Arturo's Circus, at your service."

Cassie looked around. "Where's Arturo?"

Ratcliffe spoke from behind his hand, conspiratorially. "Doesn't exist… and never has, but don't tell anyone."

"Have you been with the circus long?" Tom asked.

"Born into it," he said. "It's my life. So, what can I do for you?"

"You recall a case a few years back. A local girl went missing—"

"Angela?"

"You remember."

"Of course, I remember. How could I not?" He shook his head glumly. "Not only the disappearance of the pretty young thing, but I recall your colleagues climbing all over us for nearly a week. We had to cancel an entire town because we weren't allowed to leave."

There was a bitter edge to his tone. He soon shook it off.

"But a bit of inconvenience and some lost revenue were nothing in comparison to what that poor family went through." He looked at Tom, puzzled. "Why on earth do you want to bring all that up again? You caught your man, and he had nothing to do with the circus."

"That's true," Tom said. "And we're not here to cause trouble for you. We just have to speak to anyone who might recall that particular weekend. We'll not disrupt your preparations. That's one reason we came early."

"Ah well, I appreciate that, Inspector. I really do. Anyone who was with us at the time will have some recollection of that weekend. After all, it's more eventful than the usual day, to be sure."

"Do you mind if we wander round, have a chat with your folks?"

"Go ahead," he said, and then hesitated.

"What is it?"

He took a breath, rocking his head from side to side. "Just... bear in mind that not everyone here has had great experiences with the law. You might find some people are… a bit standoffish. It's nothing personal."

"Don't worry," Cassie said, smiling. "We undergo equality and diversity training to overcome our prejudices."

Ratcliffe looked at her sternly, and then smiled. "Good to know."

"How about you, Mr Ratcliffe?" Tom asked. "Do you remember Angela?"

"Not so as you'd mention it, no. I saw her picture in the papers and on flyers and TV in the days after her disappearance. You couldn't miss it." He sighed. "Pretty girl, right enough."

"She frequented your circus," Tom said. "Her and a few friends hung out with some of your performers."

"Aye, so I was told. That's not unusual, you know? To the teenagers we're quite an exciting bunch. Our way of life is… how should I say, appealing in an exotic sort of way."

"Exotic?" Cassie asked, containing a smile.

"Yes, exotic, Detective Sergeant," Ratcliffe said, undeterred. "When you're going to school or to a dead-end job on a daily basis, life on the road, living and working with people from different countries and cultures, the excitement of performing in front of large crowds… the applause… it's fair to say, it's exotic."

Cassie had to concede he made a strong argument. "Yes, if you put it that way, then you have a point."

"I do. Perhaps it doesn't reflect the hard work of setting up in the pissing rain, the constant training, not to mention the hours spent sitting in traffic jams as you move around the country... or the barrage of abuse and suspicion you get from some of the locals every time you stop. I suppose it depends on whether you're a cup half-full kind of person."

Cassie smiled. "I'm definitely a half-full person myself."

Tom glanced sideways at her but said nothing.

"As I say, I never met the girl, but feel free to wander around, but be careful. The acts will be warming up."

"I hope you're going to put on a good show this time around," Tom said.

"Are you thinking of coming along to a performance, Inspector?"

"I have a young lady at home who would be devastated if we didn't."

"Well, I'll see you right for a family ticket before you leave!"

Tom smiled. "Thank you, but there's no need. I'm sure you'll all earn your money, but I appreciate the offer."

"Right you are, Inspector."

Tom excused them and they headed deeper into the site.

Sounds coming from inside the main tent drew their attention. Entering, they found the acrobats practising their trapeze, high-wire routine. Both Tom and Cassie stood in awe as they swung back and forth, flipping from one to the next in almost uniform perfection. The safety net strung out beneath them did little to undo the impressive nature of the performance. It was breath taking.

"Can I help you?" a woman asked, standing off to their right. She was blonde, her hair which would hang past her shoulders were it not tied back. She had piercing blue eyes. Beneath her overcoat, Tom could see she was wearing joggers and a leotard. He wondered if she was one of the performers.

"DI Janssen and DS Knight," Tom said, reaching for his identification.

She waved the movement away. "That's okay. If Liam wasn't okay with you being here, you'd be gone already. I'm Aislene Turner."

She spoke with a lovely lyrical Irish lilt to her voice, but it was tempered with another accent. Perhaps the West Midlands? Tom wasn't sure.

He indicated towards the three acrobats, one woman and two men, sharing the trapeze as they linked legs, the men holding onto their respective swing while the woman was suspended between them, upside down, arms outstretched.

"That's seriously impressive."

Aislene smiled. "I'll pass it on. You should come back and see the main show. It'll really blow you away."

"I intend to," Tom said. "Are you also part of the act?"

She shook her head. "No, I'm very much one to keep my feet on the ground. I tend to be tied up and have things thrown at me."

"I beg your pardon?" Tom asked.

She chuckled. "My man is good with knives and wields the occasional axe. Often from horseback."

Cassie raised her eyebrows. "You must have a lot of trust in him."

Aislene grinned. "I do. Although he cuts it close sometimes."

"No pun intended," Tom added.

She smiled.

The acrobats finished up and descended to the arena floor. Aislene clapped them off and they came over to her.

"The new move at the end really works, Lynsey. It was great," Aislene said, tossing the female acrobat a towel. She dabbed at her face, smiling but breathing hard.

"Thanks. I knew it would work. You can tell Daniel that he was wrong."

"You tell him," Aislene said. "He hates it when I pull him up."

"I will," Lynsey replied. "Where is he anyway? Shouldn't you be getting warmed up?"

"Ah, he's around someplace," Aislene said. "These two are police."

"What do they want?"

Aislene shook her head. "A preview of the show, I reckon because they haven't asked."

The comment was said very tongue in cheek, much to her own amusement.

"I'm sorry," Tom said. "We are looking for people who were with the show a few years back. Specifically, those of you who were around when Angela Dale went missing."

The two women exchanged a look. Behind them, the older of the male acrobats, a muscular man in his late forties, looked over at them from where he was changing his footwear, couple of metres away but well within earshot. The remaining man paid them no attention at all.

"Well," Aislene said, "we were all here back then."

"And you remember Angela?"

She cocked her head. "Now, it'd be incredible if I didn't, wouldn't it?"

"People forget," Tom said.

"You don't forget a girl being murdered."

"Or police digging around your loved ones trying to find someone to pin it on either," Lynsey said.

Tom pursed his lips. "We're not here looking for a sacrificial lamb."

"Then why are you here?" Aislene asked, her prior amicability dissipating as she fixed Tom with a stern look.

"We are looking for confirmation of an altercation that took place between Angela's boyfriend and one or two of your people."

Lynsey nodded. "I remember. That loudmouth guy thought it'd be good to square up to DT. Luckily for him, some of us have a level head."

"DT is Daniel Turner. Is that right?" Tom asked.

"Yes," the man standing nearby, finished tying his laces and came to stand alongside Lynsey, putting an arm across her shoulder. "Danny is my boy. What do you want with him?"

"Is he around?" Tom asked, glancing around the arena. There were a few people on the far side moving things into position.

"Somewhere," the man said.

'Dad," Lynsey elbowed him gently in the ribs, "you don't need to be so antagonistic. They're just doing their job."

"Harassing law-abiding people going about their work," he said.

"I'm sorry, Mr Turner?" Tom asked.

He nodded. "Cory Turner, aye. Danny's my boy and," he hugged Lynsey close into him, "this is my little girl."

"Daniel didn't fancy a life in the air?" Cassie asked, indicating the trapeze with a nod of the head.

"He did, but decided to branch out on his own, carve his own path," Cory said. "Got to respect that."

"So, who took his place in the team?" Tom asked.

The last remaining acrobat, who hadn't yet spoken, realised they were speaking about him. He looked over but his expression remained passive.

"That'll be my husband, Paulo," Lynsey said, smiling. She glanced at him and he smiled, winking at her, and throwing a towel over his shoulder.

"And were any of you involved in the altercation?"

"Only to tell that neanderthal with a posh voice to get lost," Lynsey said. "His mate pulled him away as well, as I recall."

"Do you remember Angela's reaction?"

The women exchanged glances and Lynsey shook her head while Aislene shrugged.

"What about Daniel –DT – how did he react?"

Cory interrupted before anyone else could speak. "My son can speak for himself."

"And we'll be delighted to ask him," Cassie said. "When he shows up."

Lynsey playfully patted her father's chest. "Honestly, Dad, just behave yourself."

Cory sneered, shook his head and harrumphed, turning to walk away.

Lynsey mock grimaced. "Sorry about Dad. He's just very private and… you know?"

"He doesn't like the police," Cassie said.

Lynsey wrinkled her nose and nodded. "I'll tell you what I do remember though. I saw Angela with a guy earlier in the day."

"What?" Tom asked. "Here at the circus?"

She nodded. "Yes, chatting to him in the car park."

"And?" Cassie asked.

She shrugged. "Just a guy… she was really flirty. I mean, I didn't know her well and she was really flirty with," she looked at Aislene, "some of the guys here… and maybe that was just her way around men, but… it caught my eye."

"Can you tell us anything about him?"

Lynsey looked at Aislene again. "You remember, don't you? That guy she was cosying up to?"

Aislene's brow creased, but she shook her head. "Can't say I do, no. Are you sure I was there?"

"Yeah, yeah… you remember… the guy got into a BMW, and we looked at each other…"

Aislene turned the corners of her mouth down. "Nope. You're imagining things again."

Lynsey laughed, swiping a playful hand at her sister-in-law. "Maybe I am. Anyway, she was quite pally with this guy."

"Can you tell us anything about him?" Tom asked.

"Yes, a bit. He was white… older…"

"How old?" Tom asked.

"I dunno… old. Older than me."

Aislene chuckled. "You'll have to forgive her, Inspector. Lynsey doesn't do detail. It's amazing she can hold onto her husband when she's five metres up in the air."

"I'm not that bad," Lynsey countered.

"Okay, what about the car? A BMW you said?"

"Yes, definitely. A sporty one. Red."

"Bright red… dark red?" Cassie clarified.

"Not sure… red, red. I think."

Cassie took a deep breath. "So, it was red, red…"

"Look, it was a long time ago, wasn't it? Can you remember who you saw five or six years ago speaking to one another in passing?"

Cassie inclined her head. "If the girl ended up murdered later, then yeah, I think I might."

"Well," Lynsey said, indignantly, "maybe you're a control freak."

"Excuse me?"

"I saw it once on the TV. If you're overly focussed on details, then you're probably suffering with anxiety, and you need to relax a little bit. Be less uptight, you know?"

Cassie nodded. "Uptight? Right, okay. I'll…

think about that when I get a chance." She looked at Tom. "Maybe I should have a wander around and see if there's anyone else I can chat to. What do you think?"

Tom nodded. Cassie happily excused herself. Tom watched her go before turning back to the two women.

Lynsey exchanged a look with Aislene.

"Definitely uptight," Aislene said, turning to Tom. "Those are the people who get cancer you know?"

Tom frowned, thinking maybe Cassie had got the better end of this particular deal.

CHAPTER THIRTEEN

CASSIE WALKED around the ring to where the men she'd clocked earlier were working, close to the performers' entrance to the main tent. They appeared to be checking the wiring for lights and sound. She hadn't noticed before but there were speakers mounted on poles all around the central ring. Presumably, once the audience were in place and the performances got going the arena would become somewhat raucous.

"Good morning, gents," she said, trying a different approach, seeing as she figured she'd get further with them. Besides, Tom was right, she had to get over her prejudices but she wasn't sure this environment was the best place to test a new approach.

The four men eyed her suspiciously. One of

them looked away and continued with what he was doing. He had a clipboard in his hand, along with a screwdriver, and he paid her no attention at all, casually walking away. It was a curious equipment combination.

"Something I said?" Cassie smiled warmly.

The remaining men stopped and two of them looked to the third, so Cassie guessed he had seniority. He looked Cassie up and down, sighing.

"You're police, right?"

"What gave it away?" Cassie asked, breezily.

He frowned at her. "You have that air of superiority about you."

Normally that would bring about a stinging riposte, but this time Cassie merely tilted her head, maintaining her smile.

"We're not that bad, are we?" she asked. "I usually save that attitude for my boss."

"Oh no, right enough," he said. "Your lot always give us the benefit of the doubt. So, what is it we've done this time? It can't be much because most of us only arrived yesterday."

He looked at his companions who smirked at his shot at humour.

"Can I ask who you are and what your role is here?"

"Ian," he said. Cassie arched her eyebrows, inviting more. "Ian Gallagher." He glanced around. "I'm the jack of all trades around here."

"And also the master of none?" she asked.

Gallagher cocked his head, a fleeting half-smile crossing his face.

"So, some of the lads would say, yes. Although, this place would fall down without me." He glanced up into the roof of the tent. "Literally."

"So, you must be a guy who knows what's going on around here then?"

"Aye, that's fair comment, right enough."

The other two men got on with what they were doing, one nodding at Gallagher before picking up a nearby box, with a grunt, and moving off.

"So, what can I do for the lady in blue?" he asked.

"We're here about a young woman that went missing after visiting your show. It's going back a few years—"

"Angela Dale?"

"You remember?"

He laughed dryly. "As if I'm going to forget that." His expression changed and he fixed her with a stare. "Why are you asking about that? I thought you got a guy for it. Some ex-boyfriend or something."

Cassie briefly rocked her head from side to side. "Not quite, but someone was convicted. He's just been released."

"Has he now?" Gallagher asked, leaning against the railing that separated the audience from the performance arena and folding his arms across his chest. "Already?"

Cassie smiled.

"So, you messed up the investigation or the lawyer messed up the trial?" Gallagher asked.

Cassie shrugged. "Beats me. It was all before my time."

"Yes, the accent doesn't say Norfolk, born and inbred."

Cassie grinned. "That's a bit rich, coming from a traveller, isn't it?"

Now it was Gallagher who returned the grin. "Oh, absolutely," he said with mock sincerity. "We all marry each other. You know, I'm married to my second cousin and her side of the family had to change their name to at least make an effort to appear like we weren't all related."

Cassie wasn't sure if he was joking. He read her mind, laughing.

"You're winding me up, aren't you?" she asked.

He winked.

"Well played, but you had me going."

There was evident humour in his tone and she found both his candour and sense of humour attractive. He was in his mid-thirties, she guessed, with collar-length, wavy brown hair along with several days of stubble growth. Dressed in blue jeans, a checked shirt with a T-shirt underneath, he didn't appear to be feeling the cold. His appearance was rugged but quick with a smile and a natural wit, he came across as charismatic with a hawkish appearance.

"So, what does bring you here? Lost your main suspect and looking for a pikey to pin it on?"

"I'm not looking for a fall guy, if that's genuinely what you're worried about?"

He angled his head to one side, flashing another winning smile. "Tell that to my cousin who spent a day and a bit in a police station accused of burglary when we all knew he'd been working with us at the time he was apparently seen."

"Well, did he do it?"

Gallagher fixed his eye on her, biting his bottom lip. "Well… not that particular one, no."

Cassie smiled. "Angela Dale. What can you tell me?"

He glanced up at the roof, the wind rattling through the canopy and creating a low whistling sound.

"What is it you want to know, Detective Constable?"

"Sergeant," she corrected him.

He bowed theatrically. "My apologies. What would you like to know, Detective *Sergeant*?"

"Anything that you can remember from the day might be helpful. She was here with friends, chatting to some of you—"

He shook his head. "Not with me."

"With your… colleagues. Do you recall her?"

He shook his head again. "Can't say as I do. If I did, I'd be lying."

"And you would never lie to the police, right?"

He held up his left hand in a salute. "Scouts' honour."

"Wrong hand."

He laughed. "I get left and right confused."

"And you're looking after the wiring?" she asked. "Should the audience wear rubber boots?"

"Only after hours," he said, his accompanying expression indicating the double entendre.

"Focus, Mr Gallagher."

"Ian," he said, smiling. "Look, I'm not messing with you. I don't remember much from that day, which is what I told your officers at the time. I didn't have anything to do with Angela." He looked around the tent. "I know she was friendly with some of the people here, men and women before you ask, but I wasn't one of them."

"And yet you have a clear recognition of her name and the case?"

"Yes, of course. I got to know a lot about her after she was reported missing and you all came out asking questions." He shook his head. "I mean, a few of us were asking questions of each other as well, you know?"

"Really?"

Cassie was surprised. Usually, this community

would never break ranks to cast doubt on another in this way. Within their own group certainly, but not to an outsider and especially not to a police officer.

"Yes, really! We're not all at it, you know?"

"You thought one of your people could have done it?"

He laughed. "No, I didn't, but people are going to ask questions, especially when the police come calling. But no, for the record, I didn't think any of us had done it. Not that it didn't stop your colleagues – I know you weren't one of them because I never forget a pretty face – and the girl's family from hanging around and trying to dig up dirt."

"The family… what, Angela Dale's family?"

"Oh aye, yeah. That brother of hers was here… Jack, I think his name was, along with the father, I think. All here, asking questions. Others too."

"Others?"

"Friends of the family, I guess," he said, shrugging. "Not a lot has changed either."

"How do you mean?"

"Well…" he said, "look at you here today, asking the same questions… and the family… it's like Groundhog Day."

Cassie looked at him inquisitively.

"Here, this morning, just like you are now!"

Cassie looked around, half expecting to see familiar faces but there was only Tom.

Gallagher chuckled. "Not here," he said, pointing to outside. "The brother was here… along with some lassie. Then another bloke came and got them." He shook his head. "I don't think he was too keen on their being here, to be honest with you."

"The father, Henry Dale?"

He shook his head, shrugging. "Don't remember the father, so I couldn't say. No idea why they'd be here either. Sorry. I figured I'd pre-empt your next question. Was I wrong?"

"No. You must be familiar with police questioning."

"Well, us gypsies are."

He was mocking her and she knew it.

"This man, the one you said was unhappy they were here, you sure you didn't recognise him?"

He shook his head. "Nope. Can't say I did. He got a stronger reaction from the lass though. Jack, that's his name, right?"

Cassie nodded.

"Yeah, Jack was largely indifferent to whatever the guy was moaning about, but he got in the car as well."

"They were here asking questions?'

"Yes."

"Of whom?"

He shrugged. "Couldn't say."

She had the impression he was now straying

into the attitudes she'd expected to encounter, unlikely to drop anyone's name, regardless of whether he thought they were innocent.

"Would you tell me if you could?"

"I might," he said, smiling.

"Or not."

He nodded, the smile broadening. "Or not," he repeated.

"What car did they get into? Do you remember?"

"A Range Rover. Silver. Nice car. I had one myself… although mine was a Sport. His was a full-fat Range, you know?"

"Circus life pays well then?"

He laughed. "Well, you know our sort… we don't pay any tax, do we?" he said, winking, playing up to the stereotype. Cassie suppressed a smile. Gallagher noticed.

"DS… I never did catch your name?"

"Knight."

He angled his head and smiled.

"Cassie," she added, reluctantly.

"Well, DS Cassie Knight," Gallagher said, "are you going to tell me what brings you here asking the same questions of us today as your colleagues did six years ago?"

"I might," she said, before playfully adding, "or not."

Gallagher took a deep breath. "When something

bad happens when we're around, sooner or later the police come a-calling to find one of us to blame."

Cassie shook her head. "Now, that's not true."

"Isn't it?"

"Well, we didn't blame any of you six years ago."

"And yet, here you are..." he said, pursing his lips.

"You've been helpful, Ian," Cassie said. "Surprisingly."

He grinned. "Always willing to help an officer of the law. Particularly one who isn't wearing a wedding ring," he said, nodding towards her left hand.

"Yes, my mother noticed that too, but she'll be waiting a long time to see one."

"You've not met the right man or has he been and gone?"

Cassie smiled. "You'll be waiting a long time to see me walk down the aisle to meet a man waiting at the end."

"Oh, a woman after my own heart," he said. "Would you like to grab a drink with me one night?"

"I thought you were married to your cousin?"

Gallagher laughed. "Well, my fictitious cousin and I have a fictitious open marriage. And she's not the jealous type."

Cassie smiled. "Aren't you only in town for a few days?"

"But what a whirlwind of a few days it would be!" he said, beaming. "I can picture it clearly in my mind. I know people. I have a knack for reading them."

"Well, I'll mull it over," Cassie said, making to leave.

"Don't take too long about it, DS Cassie… The world keeps turning while we hesitate! And she who hesitates—"

"Is lost," Cassie said over her shoulder. "I get it."

"I'll be seeing you," he called as she walked away.

Glancing back, she shot him a wry smile. He might be able to read people but perhaps not quite as well as he figured. Still, it wouldn't hurt to keep him on the hook, so to speak. After all, you never know when you might need a little bit of information and if someone is playing you, it doesn't hurt to play them at their own game.

Looking over to where Tom was still chatting to the acrobats, she saw a figure in the background. Was he watching or did he just happen to be there? He shared a lot of similarities with Lynsey Turner, the same hair colour, complexion, height and build, although he was more muscular. Guessing it was Daniel Turner, she took a circuitous route rather than walk directly towards him.

She couldn't be certain, but he may well have clocked her approach as he stepped back into the shadows and disappeared from view. Cassie ducked through a flap to her left and hurried around the outer perimeter. Reaching the spot where she'd seen him, she looked around. The fields surrounding the site were grey with a thin mist clinging to the ground. The air was cold and damp, a chill came over her as she scanned the array of mobile homes, caravans and vans parked nearby.

Catching a sign of movement between two nearby camper vans, she hurried around to try and intercept him. They met, startling one another. It wasn't Daniel Turner. The woman eyed Cassie warily, almost as if they were familiar but Cassie was pretty sure they'd never met. Prejudice clouding her judgement or not, there was no way this woman was a member of the circus. The way she was dressed and the way she carried herself indicated she shouldn't be there despite her attempt at looking like she belonged.

"Morning," Cassie said.

"Good morning," she said.

Cassie assessed her. She was blonde, petite and attractive in a stunted, slightly out-of-proportion sort of way. Looking into her eyes, there was an edge there too, Cassie recognised it for she saw it in herself when she looked in the mirror. She took out her identification.

"DS Knight, Norfolk Police." The woman offered a curt nod. "And you are?"

"Minding my own business."

Cassie wasn't surprised to hear the spiky tone.

"What are you up to creeping around the site? You're not with the company, are you?"

The woman averted her gaze from Cassie's scrutiny.

"Olivia?" Tom asked. Both women turned to see Tom standing at the rear corner of the campervan. "Olivia Goldman?"

She smiled at Tom. Was it embarrassment Cassie saw in her expression or something else?

"Who's Olivia Goldman?" Cassie asked as Tom approached.

"The great defender of the maltreated…" Tom said. "Isn't that correct?"

Olivia looked at him, gauging the sincerity, Cassie thought, and then she smiled.

"I think we're here for the same reasons, Detective Inspector."

"Which are?" Cassie asked.

"Answers, DS Knight," she said, looking directly at her. "Isn't that what we do for a living?"

Cassie cocked her head. "It's what I do. I'm not sure about you."

Olivia stared hard at Cassie before turning her attention to Tom. "May I go, Inspector Janssen?"

He revealed an open palm, indicating that she could pass and Olivia did so, moving by him slowly.

"One of these days we will need to talk, Olivia," he said as she passed.

Once beyond him, she stopped, hesitating, but didn't look back.

"I have your number," she said before resuming course.

Tom watched her go. Cassie came to stand alongside him.

"Tell me again who she is," Cassie said, "as well as how she has your number?"

CHAPTER FOURTEEN

GOOD MORNING, TOM," Dr Paxton said, rising from his chair as Tom entered the pathology lab. He glanced at his watch. "I was rather hoping you'd have made it across a little earlier. I was supposed to be teeing off at three o'clock."

"Sorry to have kept you," Tom said, genuinely. "I thought you'd be pressed to finish today, so I didn't hurry."

Paxton affirmed the sentiment with a brief nod.

"Quite understandable, Tom. However," he said, gesturing for him to join him at the stainless-steel table in the centre of the room, "you've left me quite a conundrum with this one."

Tom came to stand opposite him while Dr Paxton uncovered Angela Dale's remains. Laid out was the torso with the four parts of her two legs in situ where they should be if the body was intact. A part of the left arm was also in place, but as Tom already knew, her forearm and hand were missing. It was a macabre sight. One he would no doubt revisit in fitful dreams to come.

Paxton sighed. "I must admit, I thought I'd seen most things in my career." He shook his head. "I once had a fellow in Croydon who'd been decapitated with a samurai sword." He looked at Tom, pursing his lips. "But at least that poor fellow's body came to me complete, albeit in two parts. A flat-pack cabinet, so to speak."

Tom took a breath. Dark humour was one way to cope with this job, but he usually left that to Cassie.

"So, what can you tell me?" Tom asked, scanning the remains.

"Well, DNA analysis has confirmed this to be Angela Dale, as you suspected," Paxton said, scanning the notes on the file in his hands. "We have her genetic sample on the database from the first investigation, and I've double checked to ensure there's no chance of an error on that front." He looked at Tom, peering over the rim of his glasses. "Thank you for the information regarding the tattoo. It pretty much seals it."

"Cause of death?"

Paxton shook his head. "Impossible to say with what you've given me."

Tom was disappointed.

"Although, I can confirm there was no damage to her internal organs. Nothing brutal, by which I mean there are no lacerations, stab or gunshot wounds and no blunt-force traumas, at least not to the core parts of the abdomen... or indeed the portion of the left arm that we see here. Her left leg is broken though. It must have been quite an impact, nasty."

"Cause?"

"It's a blunt-force break... possibly from a fall but more likely one caused by a flat object travelling at speed."

"A car?"

"Quite likely, yes. With a more complete body, particularly the head – no pressure, but it would help if you located one – then a road-traffic collision would be more obvious. People usually hit their heads when they are run over."

"I was thinking it's possible the killer was trying to make identification difficult by removing the head and hands."

Paxton wrinkled his nose, signalling he found it doubtful.

"You disagree?"

"Well, I wouldn't go so far as to say that, Tom, but in my opinion that only presents itself as plausible in a victim who will be difficult to identify in the first place; an immigrant or a runaway… that sort of demographic, if you follow me?"

"With little or no ties to the area they are discovered in, you mean?"

"Exactly that, yes." Paxton shook his head. "In this case, for a time, Angela Dale was a household name and a well-known face once the investigation into her presumed murder got underway. It was obvious we would have her DNA on file and you only need to watch a television show – even the hack ones with unbelievable oddballs as pathologists – to know how effective we are with that." He frowned. "Although, had the killer mutilated her, so to speak, prior to all of the publicity, then maybe he didn't consider that. If the killer was from out of town, for example. He may not have realised."

"Or cared," Tom said. Paxton agreed with a subtle nod. "Dr Williams theorised that Angela had only been dead for a month to six weeks, maximum, prior to being unearthed by the storm. If she's correct, then that would rule out a quick dismemberment, wouldn't it?"

"Oh, indeed it would, Tom yes." Paxton arched his eyebrows displaying a flicker of knowledge that piqued Tom's curiosity. "But she was wrong, there."

Tom looked at him quizzically. Paxton raised a hand.

"Quite understandable under the circumstances, though, I assure you, Tom. I must admit I found it quite a puzzle to decipher myself." He looked over Angela's remains, shaking his head.

Tom caught his eye. "Are you going to share it, or do I have to guess, because you'll not be teeing off any time soon."

Paxton laughed. "Sorry, I was just admiring the process of deduction I went through in figuring it out. You remember the Zodiac killer and the cypher that he supposedly taunted the police with for years?"

"I do."

"Well, you've handed me a similarly-complex puzzle only in biological form."

"Now you've got my attention," Tom said.

"Right, first off, these rather strange abrasions that Fiona observed when you were exhuming her from her unofficial grave," Paxton said, leaning forward and using the tip of his pen to point out the patches of rough skin Dr Williams had noticed.

Tom leaned in. "Yes, have you figured out the cause?"

"How much storage do you have at home, Tom, food wise?"

Tom was puzzled. "The usual, a fridge freezer… cabinets for tins."

"A freezer, Tom," Paxton said, jabbing the end of the pen in his direction. "And have you ever left a slab of meat in the freezer a little too long or not wrapped it properly?"

Tom examined the abrasions again, then looked at the pathologist. "Freezer burn?"

"Freezer burn," Paxton confirmed. "It's difficult to see with the naked eye but it is very apparent the moment you place a slide beneath a microscope. You see, when you freeze meat, a joint of pork for example, the freezing process causes the cells to explode. The effect of this isn't seen until the joint is defrosted and that is why you find the water and the blood seeping out into the bag or onto the plate. The tissue has lost its structure, which is exactly what has occurred in this poor thing."

"She was stored in a freezer? For how long?"

Paxton shook his head. "Very difficult to say. Theoretically, you can keep meat in a freezer indefinitely if the conditions are maintained."

"So you've no idea when she died?"

He shook his head. "Pure speculation, I'm afraid. She was killed, again, I'm speculating, but," he cast an open hand over the remains in a sweeping gesture, "dismemberment implies it, and then placed in a freezer. I suspect she was cut up prior to that happening—"

"Why do you think so?"

Paxton's gaze narrowed. "Have you ever tried cutting up a frozen joint? Nigh on impossible." He appeared thoughtful. "I suppose she could have been defrosted prior to carving, but a human body takes a while to thaw out and who has the luxury of doing so without the body being seen? No, I suspect it was done at the time. Although, I would hazard a strong guess that she'd been dead for a while before she was dismembered and dropped into the freezer for preservation. You see these cuts," he stepped forward and indicated where the legs had been parted at the knee, "were done quite carefully. To me that suggests someone was trying to be as clean as possible."

"Surgical?" Tom asked. "Again, Fiona Williams doesn't believe so."

"And she would be correct there," Paxton agreed, nodding. "When you examine the cuts at the top of the thighs you can see they are much more ragged, and when I say ragged, I'm suggesting the butcher used a mechanical device. A saw of some description. Unlikely to be a circular or a jig; most likely a reciprocating saw. Imprecise, but quick and effective."

"Messy," Tom said.

"You would think so, wouldn't you, Tom? However, you'd be wrong. That's why I said I believe the action was done postmortem, sometime after her death I should imagine. The blood had ceased flowing, so it is likely rigor had been and gone, giving the body the flexibility in the muscles to make it easier to carve."

Working in this field had given Dr Paxton a curious view of the deceased, hence Cassie's nickname for him, *Dr Death*. Tom wondered if he saw these victims as real people or merely puzzles to be solved. Perhaps it was a coping mechanism rather than a callous nature. Everyone in their line of work needed to throw up some barriers to protect their souls. For Tom, it was bringing justice to the victim and their family. He could think of no stronger motivation.

"I think he began with a sharp knife, likely a carving knife or similar due to the length of the strokes," he made a passing movement before him with an imaginary blade, "but either the blade edge wasn't sharp enough or he was under significant time pressure and switched to the more effective, but far rougher implement of the saw."

"Disgraceful treatment of a human being," Tom said quietly.

"Quite so, Tom." Paxton shrugged. "But if you've already crossed the line into taking a life, then your goal compass is somewhat skewed already."

"There are many reasons to kill a person, or situations that it leads to, but to cut someone up like this is…"

"Callous?"

"To say the least."

A moment of reflection crossed the pathologist's face. Tom noticed.

"What is it?"

He glanced at Tom and then back at the remains. "It's funny you should say callous… I mean, you're not wrong, but I had the thought that…" He frowned.

"What?"

"Well, that the killer cared about her."

"He chopped her into pieces."

"Yes, yes, yes, I know," Paxton said, waving away Tom's scepticism. "But these initial cuts were done with care… I can imagine the strokes of the blade were slow, measured. Almost as if he didn't want to… defile her."

Tom looked at the body again, Ben Crake coming to mind.

"Oh well, it's just a thought I had," Paxton said, shaking it off. "He certainly took less care with the subsequent cuts. It does concern me what he did with the head."

"Yes, that has us a little stumped, too," Tom said. "Why only dispose of these parts of the body. Perhaps he is trying to conceal the method of the kill, or to make identification harder. Although, as I said earlier, I do think concealing her identity would be a waste of time."

"Maybe I can help you with that, Tom," Paxton

said. "Perhaps not solve it for you but give you a steer."

Tom was all ears.

"I think Fiona was correct about the poor girl's rate of decomposition, which determined her understandable, if flawed, estimate of the time of death. You see, I think the decomposition process began prior to Angela being frozen. In fact, I suspect the freezing process was undertaken precisely because she was decomposing. That speeds up the time frame regarding the period she spent in the ground, as she will already have *gone off*, so to speak, before the initial storage and the subsequent move to her final burial place." He frowned. "I suppose *burial place* makes it sound more respectful than it was."

"So, she was buried more recently?"

He nodded.

"Not that I wish to tell anyone else how to proceed in their own field of expertise, but I would have your forensic chaps look into the soil around the body if I were you."

Tom thought about the inference. "How long do you think she has been in the ground?"

"You know me, Tom. I deal in the realms of science and not fiction. Although I am partial to a little bit of science fiction in my reading… Forgive me, I digress. It's impossible for me to be certain in any specific time frame but the human body undergoes changes when exposed to the elements, soil, bacterial growth and the like. These changes are notable, and on that basis, I think she's only been in the ground a matter of weeks… perhaps even days."

"Days?" Tom asked, failing to mask his surprise.

"Oh yes, quite possible, Tom." Paxton cast an eye over Angela's remains. "And I would say days rather than weeks, but I must stress that is only my opinion. I think it holds water though."

"Is it possible that she was buried… not buried, but placed in the ground after the tree came down?"

"Now you're thinking along the same lines as me, Tom," Paxton said smiling. "I think that is certainly possible, yes." Paxton looked at him. "Does this help your investigation or hinder it?"

Tom shook his head, exhaling slowly. "At this stage, I've honestly no idea."

CHAPTER FIFTEEN

Tom finished recounting the conversation he'd had with Dr Paxton, summing up with his own suspicion that Angela Dale's remains may have been placed in the crater formed by the uprooted tree coming down in the recent storm.

"Do we know when the tree came down?" Tamara asked him.

Tom shook his head. "I'd assumed it was on Thursday night when the worst of the storm hit us, but we've had high winds in the run up to it and who's to say?"

"So that puts Ben Crake back in the frame, doesn't it?" Eric asked.

Tom inclined his head. "If, and it is only speculation, the body was dumped in the crater, then yes, it could have been Crake. He was back in town by then."

Tamara interceded, closing down that element of the discussion. "I don't want us to get side-tracked by speculation. I think that hampered the initial investigation and their focus narrowed way too much."

"You can't hide from it, though," Cassie said. "Crake comes out of prison and Angela's remains are unearthed within a matter of days… I'm all in favour of a bit of coincidence in life, but that's serendipitous, wouldn't you say?"

Tamara looked at her, concentrating hard. "I'm not hiding from anything… and you're quite right, the timing is gloriously helpful, but to whom?"

Cassie looked confused. "How do you mean?"

"Well, for Angela to reappear shortly after Crake is released could suggest that having never revealed her whereabouts, he is released from prison and the first thing he does is to recover her remains and leave them to be located. Any intelligent person who has anything about them would realise that once the autopsy is carried out, we'll realise she hadn't died recently—"

"We can't be sure about that either," Tom said, apologising for interrupting her. "The freezing of the body massively hampers the time of death analysis. Plausibly, she was killed around the time of her disappearance due to the fact no record of her since has been found, but we cannot be certain that she died prior to Crake's imprisonment… or afterwards, for that matter."

"Which is why such theorising, although not entirely unhelpful, really doesn't advance the investigation at all. It may steer us away from what we should be seeing," Tamara said. "Yes, we have to accept that Crake could have come home and placed Angela somewhere where she would be found sooner or later, but in doing so it would bring about a lot of attention on him." She nodded towards Cassie. "The coincidence you mentioned. Who would believe it was just that. It's more likely to make us focus on him again."

"I take your point," Cassie said. "Can we ask who knew Crake was coming home or, perhaps, not coming home necessarily, but that he was being released? After all, the discovery of her body may well do exactly what you say and the killer, if not Crake, might look to exploit his homecoming."

Tamara agreed. "By all means. It wasn't well publicised that Crake's appeal had been successful, so there's an argument there to look into it. At any rate, I doubt the killer would volunteer their knowledge of his release, but we can keep it in mind."

Eric raised his hand. Tamara pointed to him. "Go on, Eric."

"Hypothetically speaking, where would Crake

have been able to store Angela's remains until he was released where we wouldn't find her? I mean, his home and workplace were well searched. If he had a deep freeze someplace, it'd be surprising that investigators didn't find it."

"True," Tom said. "Maybe you could, if you've no objections?" Tom said, looking at Tamara who gestured for him to finish what he was about to say, "carry out a search for properties related to Crake and his family or close friends that he may have had access to: grandparents' home, second homes, or a weekend getaway place… that type of thing."

Cassie scoffed. Tom looked at her and she turned the sound into a cough, shaking her head. "Sorry… it's just the Crakes… aren't really rolling in money are they?"

Tamara frowned. Cassie had a point, but so did Eric and Tom.

"It won't hurt to look into it. I would say I'd be surprised if the original investigation didn't look into the possibility but, then again, they didn't appear to do things by the book. Check it out, but don't take too long on it."

Eric nodded, making a note.

"It'd be a hell of a risk for him, though, wouldn't it?" Tom asked.

Tamara agreed. "Conceivably. The light would be on him and to do this under everyone's nose would indeed be taking a massive gamble. When was he released? What was the actual date?"

"Good question," Tom said. "I'll find out."

"Right, next steps," Tamara said, briefly glancing at the information boards. "Let's go back to the beginning and reinterview all those close to Angela who gave statements at the time of her disappearance."

"Well, I was due to speak with the Dales family tomorrow," Tom said, "but I've brought it forward to tonight. They're keen to know what progress we are making."

"Will you be seeing the son, Jack?" Cassie asked.

"I would presume so, yes."

"Ask him why he was at the circus this morning?"

"I will," Tom said. "I think there's more going on among that group than we're aware of." Cassie made to speak, but Tom held up his hand. "No pejoratives required on this occasion."

"As if I would!" Cassie said, feigning offence. "I did make an interesting friend earlier, though. Ian Gallagher. I'm not sure what he does for the show, but the way the others deferred to him made me think he carried some clout among them. He seemed quite keen to get to know me."

Eric smiled. "Can't know you well enough then."

"Thank you for the vote of confidence, Eric," she said. "He was the one who told me Jack was there today, along with a woman - I presumed that was his girlfriend – and another man, older, driving a silver Range Rover."

Tamara was curious. "But he didn't say what they were doing there?"

Cassie shook her head. "Claimed not to know, but he was lying."

"You always think they're lying," Eric said, chuckling.

"Because they usually are," Cassie protested. "Besides, cynicism serves you well in this job."

"Yeah, I need a bit of that," Eric said.

"Right… assignments," she glanced at the clock on the wall; it was after 7 pm, "starting from tomorrow morning," Tamara said. "Cassie, I want you to find Charlie Babcock, Angela's on-off boyfriend. Put him under a bit of pressure regarding the state of their relationship when Angela went missing. And find out what he's been up to these past few months and years. Eric, similarly, track down Charlie's old wingman, Micky George. If he had the hots for Angela then he should be forthcoming with information to find her killer. If he clams up, it'll sound an alarm." She looked sideways at a smiling photograph of Angela, reminding herself of who they were looking to find justice for. "Let's stay focussed and put this thing to bed before everyone figures out what we're working on and all hell breaks loose."

The meeting broke up and everyone began gathering their things. Tom came to stand alongside Tamara.

"What are your plans?" he asked.

"I have some grovelling to do."

He smiled.

"Sounds intriguing."

"I abandoned David to an evening with the folks last night," she said, grimacing.

"Ah… a fate worse than death."

"Not even that good," she said. "My mum cooked for him."

"A fate worse, than a fate worse than death…"

Now Tamara smiled. "And I have a lot of ground to make up."

"How is it going with the two of you?" he asked.

"Pretty well, I think. He's divorced, already has a couple of kids, so there's no pressure on me to move in with him or anything like that, so that's nice. He could do with being a bit more athletic… but all men can't be–" she looked at Tom, momentarily casting an eye up and down him before quickly breaking off "- you know?" If Tom noticed, he didn't react. "He talks about his work a lot, though."

"Criminology?"

"Hah! No, that would be interesting. It's more the politics of the university. That type of thing."

"Hmm… maybe you could compare notes?"

"Oh, we do, Tom. Believe me. I like him. He's nice."

"Nice! A ringing endorsement, if ever I heard one. Exactly what every man wants to hear."

She laughed. "How are the wedding plans coming along?"

"I'm the wrong person to ask," he said. "Alice has all of that in hand."

Tamara finished gathering her things and the two of them left together bidding Eric and Cassie goodnight.

"Set a date yet?"

"Yes, late summer next year. Local venues have been booked out for some time, and I think we were lucky to get what we did for next year."

"Brings me out in hives thinking about all of that," Tamara said, recollecting her engagement to her long-time partner Richard before she broke it off. "Rather you than me."

Tom laughed. "It's been a long time coming, but we've made the right decision."

Tamara stopped them, reaching out to touch his forearm affectionately. "I'm pleased for you, Tom. You and Alice are good together."

"Thank you."

"And besides," she said, setting off again.

"Safety in numbers. Saffy will be running rings around the pair of you in the decade to come."

Tom smiled wryly. "You're not wrong there."

CASSIE SAID goodbye and watched Tom and Tamara leave ops, turning back to her desk and putting her things in her bag.

"Any chance of a lift home?" Eric asked.

"Yes, of course. Where's your car?"

"Oh, Becca needed it today, so I got here under my own steam."

"You should get yourself a bike, Eric. Good exercise." She smiled. "It'll help shake off the middle-age paunch you're working on."

He nodded glumly. Usually, Eric could be relied upon to bite under her gentle teasing.

"Everything all right?" she asked.

"Yes, of course. Just been a long day."

"True," Cassie said, slipping her bag over her shoulder. "You ready?"

"Yep," he said.

The two of them made their way to the front of the station where Cassie's car was parked. Eric was noticeably quiet. He was very quiet and largely monosyllabic when responding to conversation. He seemed very preoccupied with his own thoughts. The house Eric shared with Becca was only a short drive away in a new-build estate on the edge of town not far from the lighthouse, on the road to Old Hunstanton.

Pulling up to the kerb, Cassie glanced at Eric as he got out, checking he'd picked up his mobile and fishing his keys out of his pocket.

"Can I come in and say hello to Becca?" she asked, leaning across the passenger seat so they could see one another. "I've not seen her or baby George for a while."

"Um…" Eric frowned, looking at the house. Cassie followed his eye line and saw the house was in darkness. "Looks like they're asleep. George has had a touch of colic recently… might be best not to disturb them."

"Yeah, of course," she said. "You're probably right."

"Sorry," Eric said. "Another time, though, yeah."

She offered him a casual thumbs-up. "Night Eric. See you bright and early."

"Thanks for the lift," he said, closing the door.

Eric slid his key into the lock and cracked the door open, waving to her as he went inside and flicked the hallway light on. Cassie spun the car around and drove away. Only at this point did it cross her mind that Eric's car wasn't parked in the drive.

CHAPTER SIXTEEN

Tom rang the bell and didn't have to wait long for the door to open. An ashen-faced Marie Dale stood before him. She looked exhausted, the skin around her eyes was puffy and she appeared to have been crying.

"Mrs Dale," Tom said, forcing a smile. He knew why he was there, and so did she, to confirm what they'd already suspected: the fate of their daughter, Angela. "May I come in?"

She nodded, stepping back and opening the door. "Please do. Henry is in the kitchen, through that way," she said, pointing along the hall.

Tom waited, allowing her to take the lead and they walked through to the rear of the house. Henry looked up from the table where he was sitting, in a chair with his back to the garden. He'd been staring at the surface, as if reading the paper but nothing lay in front of him. He nodded a greeting to Tom as Marie offered him a seat. He pulled out a chair. Marie sat down beside her husband.

"There's no easy way to say this, so I'll just be straight," Tom said. "The DNA analysis has confirmed that we've found Angela."

Marie gripped her husband's upper arm, leaning into him. He tilted his head in towards hers and kissed the top of her head as she rested on his arm. Tears flowed unbidden from both her's and Henry's eyes as he looked up at Tom.

"Do you know how she died?"

Tom shook his head. Henry looked despairingly at him.

"Will you do better than the last lot who tried to find out what happened to her?"

"We are working very hard, Mr Dale," Tom said.

"That's what the last lot said as well."

Marie withdrew from her husband, but maintained a hold on Henry, moving her left hand down to where his rested on the table. He took her hand in his, smiling at her weakly.

"My husband doesn't mean to be rude, Inspector Janssen."

"There's no need to apologise," Tom said. "I'm

sorry that we couldn't have found your daughter sooner."

"Where has she been, Inspector?" Marie asked, desperation in her expression. "When you were here last, you said she may have been alive until recently. The thought of her being out there... all alone, when we were here... it's unbearable."

Tom saw Henry squeeze his wife's hand in support.

"Having spoken with our forensics team, as well as the pathologist, they are in agreement that we can't be sure of when Angela passed away. However, it is my opinion that she did die close to the time of her disappearance."

Henry's gaze focussed on Tom, his eyes narrowing. "But you said... there were distinguishing marks that were... the photographs you showed our Jack."

Tom held up a hand, nodding slowly. "I know it is confusing... and I'll be straight with you. We are working on the basis that Angela was murdered around the time of her disappearance and then subsequently her body was... stored in a preserved state until more recently when she was buried."

"Stored?" Marie asked, looking between Tom and her husband. "Whatever do you mean?"

"The pathologist found evidence that Angela had been frozen."

Henry let go of his wife's hand, balling his into

a fist. He let out a guttural, agonising scream and thumped the table.

"I'll swing for that bastard!"

Tom remained calm. Henry's reaction was perfectly understandable. It was better to allow him to let off steam, as long as that was all it was.

Marie looked at Henry, eyes wide. "Henry… what did… what did he do?"

"He kept our daughter in a bloody freezer, Marie," he barked. "A bloody freezer!"

He stood up from the table and paced the room. Marie put a hand to her mouth, shell-shocked. She looked at Tom for confirmation and he nodded. She lowered her arm, clasping her hands together in her lap.

"I appreciate this is a difficult time, I really do," Tom said, "but I would like to ask you about Angela, if I may?"

Marie met his eye and silently nodded. Henry continued his pacing, his expression a picture of seething rage.

"What is it you would like to know?" Marie asked.

"Around the time prior to her disappearance, did you have any concerns about her, about how she was living her life?"

Marie seemed taken aback. Tom glanced at Henry, who appeared to have calmed down a little, and the man returned to his seat. He took a deep breath and rested his hands on the table as he sat down. It rather looked like he was bracing himself.

It was Henry who spoke first.

"We knew Angela… enjoyed a night out. She'd always been the same, loved being the centre of attention and she played up to it. Even as a child, I mean really young, five or six years old. That was her."

"She was an entertainer," Marie said. "People loved her spirit. She could raise the mood in a room just by walking into it. She had something about her."

Tom's thoughts drifted to Saffy. He could relate.

"Not that there was anything wrong in that, you understand," Henry said, sitting forward and imploring Tom. "I mean, she was just a fun sort of person, you know?"

"I do," Tom said. "And I know there's often a move to blame the victim in these cases, as if they somehow got themselves into this situation and what happened to them could've been avoided if only they'd changed their behaviour."

Marie was disheartened. Tom forced eye contact with both of them.

"But I can assure you that is not the feeling of me or anyone else on my team. The only person to blame for what happened to Angela is the person who attacked her, and no one else."

Henry took in a deep breath. "Thank you, Inspector. It is good to hear you say so. You know, I'm not…" he looked at his wife, smiling weakly, "we're not on social media. A lot of our friends are, but it's just not us, but you wouldn't believe the things that were aimed at Jack on his… saying the vilest of things about Angela, us as parents… all sorts of things."

Marie nodded. "He came off it in the end, couldn't bear it anymore."

"Were there aspects of Angela's lifestyle you were unhappy about?" Tom asked.

The parents exchanged a glance, and both looked awkward.

"What is it?" Tom asked.

"Well…" Marie said, shifting in her seat, "we did worry about everything she seemed to have… material things. Didn't we, Henry?"

He nodded, frowning. "She was forever coming back with stuff… new phones… clothes and things like that. More than she ever could have afforded through a part-time job or her allowance. I mean, we were doing quite well back then, and the allowance we gave her was pretty… generous, if that's the right word? But, even so…"

"She said she was borrowing off her friends, trying on each other's clothes and so on, but often I'd see the labels. They were brand new."

"Where do you think the money came from?" Tom asked.

Marie looked down at the table and Henry was decidedly uncomfortable. After an awkward silence, Tom asked the question in a different way.

"How do you think she got hold of those things?"

Marie shook her head. "I really don't know, Inspector."

Henry agreed. "It's true." He shook his head. "I asked... I was worried... but she fobbed me off every time and... I'm her dad. I was too soft on her."

"What about her friends? Have they ever said anything?"

"No, not to us," Henry said. "Maybe they said something to Jack, but if they have, then he didn't tell us."

"Would he keep things from you – Jack?"

"Maybe," Henry said, glancing sideways at his wife. "If he thought it would hurt us, then I suppose he might."

"He has always tried to protect us, hasn't he, Henry?" Marie said. "He didn't tell us about all the abuse we were getting on social media for fear that we'd be upset."

"He was right, too," Henry said.

"Do you think that might be related? That the things people were saying might be true?"

Tom was at a loss. He hadn't read any reports or

accusations regarding Angela's private life from the time. "What were people saying?"

"That she was... taking money..." Henry said, stiltedly.

"From men," Marie finished.

"I see. Jack was close to her, wasn't he? Did he comment on it?"

"Comment on what?" Jack asked, standing at the entrance to the kitchen. How long he'd been there, Tom didn't know.

Tom turned to face him. "Hello, Jack. Your parents and I are talking about Angela's lifestyle running up to her disappearance. They said you and your family received a lot of abuse via social media afterwards—"

"Scum with nothing better to do than slag off people they've never met," Jack retorted. "Abusing people for kicks... should be illegal."

"So you're aware of the allegations about where Angela got her money from?"

"Lies," Jack said. "All of it, patent lies."

"You were close to your sister, weren't you?" Tom asked.

"Yes, I was. And that's why I'd know if there was any truth to all of that stuff. Angela liked a drink, enjoyed a party..." he inclined his head, "maybe too much on occasion, but she wasn't selling herself. I'd know."

His expression was determined, focussed.

"You're sure?" Tom asked, holding eye contact.

"I'd know," Jack repeated.

The doorbell rang and Marie rose, hurrying past her son and into the hall. Jack folded his arms across his chest, a defiant expression on his face. Henry appeared lost in thought. Voices carried from the front door, all female to Tom's ear. Marie reappeared moments later with Susan Brock, who slipped an arm around Jack's waist, and another, older woman, in front of her exchanging words with Marie.

The newcomer looked at Tom, smiling a greeting.

"This is Marsha, a good friend of the family," Marie said. "Marsha, this is DI Janssen. He's looking into… well…"

"I know," Marsha said, stepping forward and offering Tom her hand as he rose to greet her. "Marsha Brock."

"Tom Janssen," he said, glancing at Susan, standing beside Jack. "You're Susan's—"

"Mother. Yes, that's correct." She looked at Marie, smiling. "We go back quite a way, the two families."

"That's right," Henry said, sitting back in his seat and coming back to life. "Greg and I used to be business partners… way back."

"Greg is my husband, Inspector," Marsha said.

"And a very shrewd businessman, as well," Henry added, jabbing a finger in the air pointedly.

"Oh Henry," Marie said. "You do go on."

Marsha Brock smiled at Tom. "Greg wasn't one for working on the land. That was his father and his grandfather's life, but Greg wanted to take his career a different way once he'd been to university. After his father's passing, he took on the farm for his mother's sake, but once she died, he only ever wanted to get on to something else."

"Our fathers shared the load," Henry said. "Once Greg made it clear he wanted out, I bought his share. Good price as well."

Marie slipped her arm through Marsha's, steering her into the kitchen. "Honestly, if Henry's told this story once then he's told it a thousand times."

"If not more," Jack said.

"How are you all?" Marsha asked. "Did I come at a bad time?"

"There isn't a good time at the moment," Marie said.

"I'm so sorry," Marsha said. "These trials are sent to test us. We have to be strong in the face of them."

Jack scoffed, turning and leaving the room. Susan looked embarrassed but she followed him.

"You'll have to forgive our son, Inspector,"

Henry said. "He doesn't share our faith in the Lord's plan."

"He used to," Marie said. "We have always taken our children to Sunday school and Jack was quite keen... but after what happened to Angela... his heart was no longer in it."

Marsha laid a supportive hand on Marie's arm. "He'll come around. I'm sure."

"May I use your bathroom?" Tom asked.

Marie directed him back into the hall and the door to the right of the entrance. Tom found the front door was ajar, and he opened it to find Jack and Susan leaning against Susan's Mercedes. Jack was taking a steep draw on a cigarette. Susan reacted to Tom's approach, shifting her weight between her feet. Jack was the opposite, training his eyes on Tom with an impassive expression.

"Come to ask me again if my sister was a prostitute?"

Tom angled his head. "I'm sorry, but it's my job to ask the uncomfortable questions."

"Well, she wasn't. All right?"

Tom pursed his lips, glancing over his shoulder at the house. "Your parents aren't so sure."

Jack rolled his eyes. "They've got all that Bible stuff running through them. Clouds the mind. No offence to Susan's parents," he said, looking at her apologetically, "but Greg and Marsha have too much faith in the power of the Almighty."

Tom looked at Susan and she smiled sheepishly.

"My father's a Lay Preacher… it's true, they are pretty full on a lot of the time."

"I see," Tom said. "So, where do you think your sister was getting her money from?"

He shrugged.

"You must have some idea, particularly seeing as you were so close."

"Yes, we were close, Angela and me," Jack said, "but we didn't live in each other's pockets. I really wouldn't know. I guessed she was picking up extra shifts from work and that."

"Fair enough," Tom said. He looked between the two of them. "Why were you both at the circus this morning?"

Jack and Susan exchanged a brief look. Something odd struck him about Susan's expression. Was it fear in her eyes or something else entirely? Her expression shifted and she adopted a similar surprised look to mirror Jack's.

"Who's to say we were?" Jack asked.

Tom wondered why he was evasive. Usually it signified having something to hide.

"Are you saying you weren't?"

Jack sighed, averting his eyes from Tom's. It was Susan who broke the awkward moment.

"We were probably asking people the same questions as you were."

"Go on," he said.

Susan looked to Jack for support and he relented.

"You told us, on your last visit, that Angela was likely killed recently, right?" Jack asked.

"That's true, yes, but—"

"So that means Ben Crake couldn't have done it, so… that got me thinking. Before Angela showed up with Ben Crake the night she disappeared, she was there at the circus earlier on that day," Jack said. "Someone there must know something about what she was up to or who she was meeting. She'd been in and around that group for a couple of days, hanging out with them. Then she vanishes."

"Why do you think the circus folk would know? She didn't even tell her closest friends."

"That's exactly why they must know," Jack countered. "I trust her friends. If they knew then they would have said. Angela," he shook his head, "was hanging around those people, the ones at the circus. Someone knows. They have to. And let's face it, they're a community who live by their own codes of conduct. I bet they wouldn't volunteer anything to the police unless they had to."

"Okay," Tom said, "so who were you speaking to?"

Jack ruminated on his answer. The more he hesitated, the greater Susan's angst appeared to be.

"We wanted to speak to Danny."

"Daniel Turner?" Tom asked.

Jack nodded.

"Why him?"

"Because Angela was flirting with him… he was the draw for her. He was what took her back there time and again."

"He's married to his co-performer, Aislene."

"Not back then he wasn't," Jack said.

"Do you know anything about a spat that Charlie Babcock had with some of the guys from the circus on the day your sister went missing?"

"Yeah, I remember," Jack said.

"Me too," Susan said. "It was looking like it might turn nasty for a moment."

Jack sneered. "More handbags at five paces, if you ask me. Charlie fancied himself as a bit of a tough guy but he'd have been rinsed in seconds. You don't mess with those guys, you know?"

"Who did he square up to?" Tom asked.

"DT," Jack said, nodding as he spoke. Tom raised an eyebrow in query. "Danny, Daniel Turner. A couple of others were sounding off as well. Charlie's mate dragged him away before he got himself in too deep."

"Micky George?"

Jack confirmed it with a curt nod. "Why do you ask?"

Tom shrugged. "Just background information on the day."

"Well, I don't know about the others necessarily

but, like I said, Danny knows something… and he's not talking."

"What makes you so sure?" Jack pursed his lips, clearly annoyed. *What did he think he was going to do, carry out some sort of private investigation*. "You don't trust the police, do you, Jack?" Tom asked.

"Give me one reason why I should?"

"Jack, he's doing his job," Susan said. Jack glared at her but didn't speak.

"If you know something, then you should tell me, Jack. If you really want closure on this, then you need to help me to find it."

Jack took a deep breath. "Okay. Look, I didn't say anything before because… because I don't have any actual evidence. It's just… when I spoke to Danny, after Angela went missing, he said something that got me thinking."

"Which was?"

"He told me I didn't know what was *really* going on in my own family, or with my own family," Jack said, exhaling heavily. "You see, it's nothing. Not really. When Ben was arrested, I didn't think much more about it because the police said they had him. They'd caught him and he'd go to prison. That was it over. Now… now I'm not so sure."

Tom thought about the comment. "Did he say in or with?"

Jack looked at him curiously. "What do you

mean?"

"Well, a single word can change the intention of the comment quite significantly."

Jack shrugged. "I…I don't remember."

"So what do you think he meant when he said it?"

Jack shook his head. "That's why I wanted to ask him today."

"And?"

Jack met Tom's gaze.

"He denied it. He said he couldn't remember saying anything of the sort… but he's lying." He glanced at Susan. "You were there that day. You remember."

"Absolutely. He definitely said something like it… but like you, I can't remember the exact phrase, sorry. He meant it though. He was almost gleeful, dismissive, when he said the words. It felt really odd at the time."

"Did you report this to the police?"

Jack shook his head. "I would have, but they were already onto Ben Crake and let's face it, Ben's a bit of a nutter at the best of times. It sort of fitted… what with the CCTV and all."

"But now you're not so sure?" Tom asked.

Jack shook his head. "My sister was a lot of things, Inspector, but she wasn't what you're getting at. Anyone who knows her, would say the same. Right, Susan?" he asked, glancing at her.

She hesitated but then nodded emphatically. "It wasn't Angela's style. Like Jack says, she was a bit of a party girl… but she'd have had nothing to do with that sort of thing."

Tom felt he needed to set something straight. "Look, I don't know how long the two of you were there listening to me speaking to your parents, but you should know that our initial assessment of the time frame was incorrect."

"What do you mean?" Jack asked.

"Forgive my bluntness, but there really is no other way. We believe that whoever abducted or attacked your sister stored her body in a freezer, only putting her remains in the ground recently."

Jack's expression hardened. "And when you say recently, how recent do you mean?"

"That's impossible to answer definitively. The forensic analysis indicates that Angela's body… likely began decomposition prior to her being put into a freezer. That's what has skewed our assessment of the timings."

Jack scoffed, shaking his head. "So… Crake could have done it after all," he said, looking at Susan who exhibited a pained expression. "And here was me feeling bad for hating him all these years."

"Let me say this, Jack…" Tom addressed both of them with a stern look, "we are investigating this with every resource available… and we will make sense of it. I don't need a part-time vigilante tearing up the town while I'm at it. Do you understand?"

Jack stared hard at him. "I just want to know what happened to my sister."

"We all want the same thing, Jack. I can assure you." Tom glanced back at the house to see Marie appearing on the porch. Tom lowered his voice so she couldn't hear him. "And the last thing your parents need is for you to get yourself in trouble."

Jack held Tom's gaze. Susan reached out a supportive hand, but he slowly pushed it aside. "I think I'll be the judge of what my family needs, Inspector."

He walked past Tom, brushing his shoulder against Tom's arm. Not enough for them to collide in any meaningful way, but just enough to let Tom know he'd no intention of heeding the warning.

Susan looked at Tom, apologetically. "He's not usually so aggressive, Detective Inspector… it's just…"

Tom smiled. "I know. Try and talk some sense into him though, would you? For his own sake if not for anyone else's."

She nodded and followed Jack into the house. The young man was a variable in this investigation Tom didn't want to have to deal with. He was bright, passionate and focussed. These were all positive traits, but he also gave off signals that he could be a loose cannon and that, Tom could do without.

CHAPTER SEVENTEEN

Cassie sounded the horn, two sharp blasts followed by a third for good measure. The front door opened and Eric hurried out, one arm in his coat, tripping on the step as he tried to close the door behind him. Cassie sounded the horn again. Eric glared at her, waving his free hand and urging her to keep the noise down.

An upstairs curtain twitched in the neighbouring house. Cassie smiled as Eric yanked open the passenger door and got in, slamming it shut.

"What are you doing?" he hissed at her. "It's a Sunday."

She indicated the digital clock in the centre of the dashboard.

"It's eight o'clock."

"Yes, on a Sunday," Eric stressed, realising he

was sitting on his coat and that's why he couldn't draw it about him.

Cassie shrugged.

"Your neighbours must love you," Eric said.

"Not much… but Lauren makes up for it. She's the social animal and everyone loves her. We balance each other out. She's the Ying to my Yang." She looked thoughtful. "Or I'm the Ying to her Yang. One way or another."

"Does it matter which way round it goes?"

"I've no idea… but I've always seen myself as a bit of a *yang master*."

Eric stared at her; his mouth open.

"What are you on this morning?" he asked.

"High on life, Eric. High on life."

"No one's this happy, this early on a Sunday." Eric clicked his seatbelt into place, leaned forward and peered out, casting an eye over the surrounding neighbours. "Can we go now, before you make my life even harder around these people?"

"What's that?" Cassie asked, putting the car into gear and reversing into the street.

"You!" Eric barked. "With… all the bibbing. It sounded like downtown Delhi with all that going on. You could've just been like a normal person and come to the door."

"It's cold, Eric," she said, looking at her display. "Five degrees… I'll stay in the car thank you very much. Besides, I said eight when you texted to ask if you could cadge a lift."

He seemed oblivious to what she'd just said, shaking his head.

"That'll have wound the neighbours right up."

Cassie accelerated away and Eric sat back in his seat, settling his head against the rest, closing his eyes and exhaling. She glanced sideways at him. He looked a bit of a state, even if you gave him a bit of leeway for her rushing him out of the door.

He hadn't combed his hair or shaved, which was becoming more of a regular feature for Eric and she was pretty sure he wasn't trying to execute some attempt at designer stubble. Despite the rings denoting a father of a young child's lack of sleep, Eric still had the baby face of someone much younger than his twenty-something years, although even by recent standards, he looked dreadful. He didn't smell a whole lot better either.

"Everything all right?" she asked casually, taking the next turning on the right onto Westgate and driving down the hill, skirting Hunstanton High Street and rounding the corner past the new library that appeared to have been under construction for years without much progress.

He looked over at her.

"Yes. Why?"

His eyes were bloodshot and he didn't sound convincing.

"You don't seem your usual self at the moment, that's all."

He sneered, dismissing the suggestion. Cassie knew better than to push it. The road wrapped around to the right at the foot of Westgate and Cassie turned left as if she was going towards the swimming pool and the amusements on the seafront. The road narrowed here and she slowed to pass a larger oncoming vehicle.

The car dealership was all locked up and beyond that was a line of Victorian terraced, two-up, two-down, houses with their front doors opening out almost directly onto the pavement, directly opposite a car park used for the coaches that bused tourists into the town during the spring and summer seasons. They were so close to the through road leading out to several holiday parks and a large supermarket that the front of the houses and their windows were visibly stained with grime thrown up by passing vehicles. The windows were mostly shrouded by thick net curtains to stop passers-by being able to see inside. Privacy in the front living rooms must be hard to come by here.

Cassie pulled the car into the kerb, pointing at one of the mid-terraced properties.

"That one," she said.

Eric followed her eye. Nothing was stirring. The curtains were all drawn and there were a couple of bin bags in what passed for the front garden, barely eight feet wide and two deep. The house looked uncared for. Cassie glanced at Eric, who must have been thinking similarly.

"What is it?" he asked defensively, catching sight of her staring at him.

"You, Eric!" she said as if it was the most obvious answer in the world.

"What?"

"Back there, at your house."

He looked at her, frowning, then shrugged. "I don't understand."

"You were worried about waking up the neighbours."

He looked puzzled. "And? So what?"

"You weren't worried about me waking George or Becca."

The harshness in Eric's tone and expression ebbed away, and he bit his lower lip.

Cassie softened her tone. "What's going on, Eric?"

He shook his head, averting his eyes from her gaze. "Becca…" he said, shrugging, "has gone to stay with her mum for a few days." He looked up at Cassie. "That's all. Just for a few days, you know, to find her feet a bit. I'm working this case and all that, so… probably makes sense, for a… you know?"

"For a few days," she said.

He nodded. "Yeah, just a few days."

Cassie held his eye, seeing something unsaid in his eyes. She reached over and patted his forearm. "Come on, let's go and shake up Charlie Babcock. It'll make you feel better."

The storm had now passed but the tail end of the weather front was still buffeting them as it made landfall, ensuring the day felt even colder than it was.

Cassie rang the doorbell, the same pattern as she'd done outside Eric's house in the car, although she followed it up by banging her closed fist on the door. She stopped for a moment, saw and heard no sign of movement and repeated the process.

"All right, all right! For crying out loud!"

The door flew open and they were greeted by a man in his boxer shorts and a pink dressing gown, which he pulled tightly around him as soon as he felt the outside air pass over his skin. He was athletically built, with several days of beard growth and straight dark hair that flopped down across his face. Bleary-eyed and impatient, he glared at them both. "What's the bloody problem?"

"Mr Babcock?" Cassie asked.

"Who's asking?"

"Police," she said, holding her warrant card up to him. Babcock's eyes widened ever so slightly and his aggressive stance softened a little.

"Okay. What do you want?" He looked up and down the street, then directly at Cassie, squinting in the daylight. He must have just woken up. "Are you sure you've got the right house?"

"You're Charlie Babcock, aren't you?" Cassie said.

He nodded.

"Then we've got the right house." She cast an eye over him, indicating towards the dressing gown. "Suits your eyes."

Babcock shot her an inquisitive look, then realised what he was wearing.

"Ah bloody hell," he said, stepping back away from the door. "It's my girlfriend's."

"That's what they all say," Cassie replied, smiling. "May we come in?"

"Yeah, sure… whatever. I'm going to put something else on."

Cassie and Eric entered, Babcock pointing towards the front room. "Wait in there and I'll be back in a minute."

He hurried upstairs while Eric and Cassie exchanged glances. The hallway was incredibly narrow with two doors off it. Cassie quickly ducked her head through the second door into the rear reception room. It would have been designed as a formal dining room, and there was a table and two chairs pushed up against a boarded-over fireplace, but the room was full of clutter. Papers, magazines and assorted odds and ends were piled up on top of one another. There was a passageway through to the kitchen beyond but you wouldn't choose to spend much time in here. The dog-leg kitchen was tacked onto the rear as was common in these types of houses.

She joined Eric back at the front of the house and they went into the front room. Eric drew back the curtains and the room was illuminated by the dullish grey light from the overcast day outside. The air in the room was stale and laden with the smell of cigarettes. Cassie inspected an ashtray on the coffee table and found it spilling over onto the surface. Beyond the filter-tipped butts, she found hand-rolled smokes with homemade cardboard filters. Picking up an empty packet of cigarette papers, she saw the flap was torn with centimetre-wide rectangular segments ripped out.

"Someone got a bit stoned last night," she said, nodding at it to make Eric aware.

There were also empty beer cans on a side table with a couple lying on their sides on the floor. Eric picked one up and shook it, but it was empty. He sniffed the can, scrunching up his nose.

"These have been here for a few days," he said. "They're bone dry."

Cassie arched her eyebrows, hearing creaking floorboards above as their host headed back downstairs.

"He's living the life," she said quietly.

Charlie Babcock entered the room, tucking a

shirt into his jeans. His belly overhung the top of his trousers slightly, pronounced by the light-coloured shirt he'd thrown on. Drawing his hair away from his face, he ran a hand through it, sweeping it up and away from his forehead.

"Better?" Cassie asked, smiling. "I hope we didn't wake your partner as well?"

"She doesn't live here," he said absently, looking around and spotting a packet of cigarettes on the sofa nearby. He reached for it, took one out, putting it to his lips and frowned as he couldn't see his lighter. "Either of you have a light?" he asked.

"Sorry," Cassie said. "Don't smoke."

"What do you want?" Babcock said, searching for a lighter. He triumphantly found a box of matches, his eyes flitting between the two of them as he struck one against the box and lit his cigarette. "Must be important," he said, taking a steep draw and exhaling it away from them, "to have sent the two of you."

"Familiar with the police, are you, Mr Babcock?"

"No," he said sarcastically, "I'm just a genius."

"Is that so?" Eric asked.

He stared at Eric. "An IQ of one hundred and forty-one," he said, smiling. "That's considered genius level on most scales."

Cassie glanced around. "And you're making use of it, I see."

If the comment offended him, then Babcock didn't show it. He just smiled at her before sinking down onto the sofa.

"What can I do for you?" he asked politely before taking a steep draw on his cigarette.

"We wanted to ask you about your relationship with Angela Dale, Charlie. Is that okay?"

He looked surprised. "Angela?" He raised his eyebrows, tilting his head to one side. "That's a name I've not heard in a while. I suppose I should have expected you now that weirdo is out and about again."

Eric looked at him. "Ben Crake?"

Babcock nodded. "Is it true what people are saying?"

"That depends," Cassie said. "What are they saying?"

"That you lot screwed up and that's what got him out of jail."

Cassie smiled. "Before my time here, so I couldn't say. We've been reviewing the case file, witness statements and the like, speaking to people again. That sort of thing."

"Right. What is it you want to know?"

He seemed very at ease with himself.

"When was the last time you saw Angela before she disappeared?"

"Oh, that's easy. It was the Saturday afternoon… I don't remember the date."

"At the circus?"

"That's right," he said, sitting forward and tapping the end of his cigarette over the ashtray. "Around 4 pm, I think." He sat back again. "But it was a long time ago now."

Cassie nodded, glancing at Eric who had his notebook in hand. Babcock eyed Eric.

"I've got something in the kitchen that might take the edge off for you," he said.

"Excuse me?" Eric replied.

"The hangover. I make a brilliant pick-me-up cure for the morning after."

Eric shook his head. "No, I'm perfectly fine, thanks."

"Ah… you say that now, but in a couple of hours around half-ten, eleven you're going to feel like death warmed up."

Eric's cheeks reddened.

"What was the nature of your relationship with Angela?" Cassie asked, ignoring the tangent he'd gone off on with Eric. He looked at her.

"The nature?"

"Yes," Cassie said, rocking her head from side to side, "On, off… good terms, arguing… the nature of your relationship."

"Angela was great," he said, cupping his hands, smoke from the cigarette swirling up past his face as he stared straight ahead. He broke into a cough, racking and deep from within his chest. Whatever he coughed up, he forced himself to swallow before inhaling another drag. "We were great."

"Yes, you said in your statement at the time that you were still in a relationship."

His head came up and he looked at Cassie warily. "That's right. If you have my statement, why ask?"

"As you said, it's been a long time. Sometimes the memory plays tricks on you."

"Not mine," he said.

"Right. Would you say you've got a good memory?"

"I would."

Cassie frowned, glancing at Eric. "What was it that happened that day… there was an altercation, wasn't there?"

Eric nodded, flicking back through his notes, focussing. "Yes, between you," he said, gesturing to Babcock with his pen, "and Daniel Turner, who worked at the circus."

Babcock sighed, sitting back and shaking his head. Cassie arched her eyebrows.

"Does your memory recall that event, Mr Babcock?"

He exhaled the last draw of his cigarette, leaning over and stubbing it out aggressively in the pile of ash already in the tray, disturbing it and sending more falling to the surface. He was burning through the cigarette in record time.

"Yeah," he said, "what of it?"

"What was it about?"

He shrugged. "I don't remember. Probably nothing, looking back."

Eric read from his notes again. "Your friend Micky had to pull you away."

"Hah! Yeah, right."

"Is that not true?" Cassie pressed. "Because a number of people witnessed it and they thought he saved you from a bit of a pasting."

Babcock glared at her. "I can take care of myself, love. Don't worry about that."

"Micky – are the two of you still friends?" Cassie asked.

"I see him around from time to time, but that's about it."

Cassie nodded. "So what was it about, the fight, I mean? Angela?"

Babcock reached for the cigarette packet again.

"Do you mind if you don't," Cassie said. The air was still thick with the smoke from his last cigarette. "You might not care about your lungs, but I do mine."

Babcock took out another cigarette anyway, playfully bouncing it in the palm of his hand before tucking it behind his right ear.

"Look," he said earnestly, "I took exception to that guy."

"Daniel Turner?"

"DT, yeah." He shook his head. "Well, not to him but something he said. He was disrespectful... and I couldn't let it pass." He spread his hands wide. "Sometimes you have to fight your corner, don't you?"

"Was the fight about Angela?"

He shook his head. "No."

"But you don't remember what it was about?"

"Like I said, no, I don't. If it had been over Angela, then I would. Especially after everything that followed."

Cassie didn't believe him. "Can you tell me why all of this was missing from your original statement?"

He looked confused. "Say again?"

"Your version of the altercation with Daniel Turner. It is not in your statement."

He frowned and then shrugged. "I... guess it wasn't relevant."

"Really? Your girlfriend was known to be flirting with another man who you then proceeded to call out... and it isn't relevant?"

Babcock shook his head. "What do you want me to say?" He casually threw a hand dismissively in air. "Ask whoever wrote it down, because I didn't, and how the hell would I know why it wasn't written down?"

"I will ask, don't worry." Cassie's brow creased in thought. "Another thing. We've heard that Angela had broken it off with you in the days leading up to her disappearance."

Babcock's lips parted. He was nervous.

"But in your statement, you said you were happy together. In fact, you just confirmed it to us a few minutes ago. Why the disparity?"

He stared at her, and then glanced at Eric, sniffing loudly.

"Yeah… well, relationships have rocky patches, don't they? We'd had words… but we were still together. Whoever told you otherwise… probably just got the wrong end of the stick."

"It'd annoy you that Angela was chatting up another bloke though, right? I mean, the big man locally and all that. These gyppos come in… and your girlfriend takes a shine to one of them. It's got to hurt, right?"

He glared at her, the muscles in his face tensing.

"I don't remember anything like that happening."

"Because you *would* remember," Cassie said, "a man with your memory?"

"Yeah," he said, aiming a look of daggers at her. "I would remember."

"I thought so," she said, holding the eye contact. "You left town soon after Angela's disappearance, didn't you?"

"It was hardly like that. I joined the army so, yes, I left town soon after."

"You went to the Royal Military Academy at Sandhurst," Cassie said. "Officer's Commission."

"That's right…" he straightened his back, puffing out his chest with pride, "sponsored by the AGC."

"AGC?" Cassie asked.

"The Adjutant General's Corps," Eric clarified, tapping his knowledge of the military.

"And yet," Cassie looked around, "here you are. It's not quite the Officers' Mess, is it?"

Babcock sniffed, wiping the end of his nose with the back of his hand. "Didn't work out."

"Why not?"

"I got injured."

"Oh, what happened?"

"I fell thirty feet in an abseiling exercise… busted my shoulder and three vertebrae. I spent six months in recovery. I was deemed unfit to continue service." A dejected expression crossed his face. It was fleeting and he shrugged it off. "Things happen."

"And what do you do now?"

"I work at one of the gaming arcades… on the seafront."

Cassie inclined her head. "That's a bit of a change. Something of a step down."

He smiled wryly. "Yeah, isn't it? It's a lot safer, though, that's for sure."

He looked up at the two of them in turn,

spreading his hands wide. "Anything else depressing you'd like to discuss from my past or can we call it a day there?"

Cassie and Eric exchanged a look. Eric offered her an almost imperceptible micro-shrug to say he didn't have anything to ask. She had nothing further either.

"Yes, I think we can leave it there for now, Mr Babcock," she said. "But you might be speaking to us again."

"I'll look forward to it. Nothing quite like waking up after a long night and digging over the abject horrors from your earlier life."

"Well, to some extent we are the masters of our own destiny," Cassie said smiling. "But how we behave in life comes back on us sometimes, don't you think?"

"Are you talking about karma?" Babcock said.

"I suppose that works," Cassie replied. "Oh, while I think about it, what did you make of your friend Micky hitting on your girlfriend?"

Momentarily he looked confused, but a veil soon descended, and his face was unreadable. "What are you talking about?"

"Your best mate, Micky George. He had the hots for Angela while the two of you were together. I just wondered what you thought about that. It seems to have been common knowledge among Angela's circle of friends."

He shrugged. "You shouldn't listen to idle gossip. It's largely rubbish, particularly from that bunch of slappers."

Cassie nodded. "Yeah… and also that Angela might have welcomed the advance… Got to sting a bit, wouldn't you say, Detective Constable Collet?"

"Oh, I would think so," Eric said flatly. "Any man with an ounce of self-respect would struggle with that level of betrayal. I know I would."

"Are you insinuating something?" Babcock asked, looking between them. "Because it sounds like there's a bit of something in there."

"Take it however you like, Mr Babcock."

Charlie Babcock fixed her with a dark expression. "You should be careful, Detective Sergeant Knight. One day you may not realise just who you're talking to."

Cassie found the riposte curious, but she didn't press it. Instead, she smiled.

"Thank you for your time, Mr Babcock. I'll look forward to calling in again soon."

Charlie Babcock closed the door on them so quickly, and forcefully, that it almost caught Eric's heel as he left the house. They walked the short distance back to the car in silence. When they reached it, Cassie rested her hands on the roof, toying with the key fob in her hand as she looked back at the house.

"Contact the Ministry of Defence, would you, Eric?"

"Get a copy of his file?"

She nodded. "Let's double check what he just said."

"You doubt him, don't you?"

She grinned. "There's something wrong about that guy."

"Wrong? How do you mean?"

She shook her head. "I don't know, but he just feels—"

"Wrong?" Eric said.

She smiled. "Oh, and I doubt everyone, Eric. You should know that by now," she said, unlocking the car and opening the door.

He raised his eyebrows. "Yeah, you do."

Cassie got in, speaking as she disappeared from view. "Apart from you, Eric. I'd trust you with my life."

She didn't get to see his smile as he got in. Fixing his seatbelt, he looked across at her. "On to Micky George?"

She nodded. "Micky George."

CHAPTER EIGHTEEN

CASSIE GLANCED sideways at Eric as they climbed the stairs at the rear of the shop fronts up to the row of flats above. The concrete walkway leading to the front doors was narrow, barely wide enough for two adults to walk side by side, so Eric slotted in behind Cassie. Their footfalls bounced off the brick walls of the buildings across the alleyway, echoing about them.

"It doesn't look like people are early risers here either," she said.

The sound of the daily life getting under way carried from the street at the front, but it was Sunday morning and, if the weather wasn't great, people were seldom drawn into the town this early.

"Number four," Eric said.

They came to stand before a white UPVC door.

A small casement window was off to their right and Cassie peered through the net curtains and into the kitchen. It was small, dated and cluttered.

Eric raised the knocker and gave it two blasts. The sound carried. With no sign of movement from within, Eric knocked again. The door to the neighbouring flat opened and a child emerged, followed by his mother levering a pushchair, with another child harnessed in, over the lip of the frame, encouraging her son to get a move on as he was blocking her path. It was difficult for them to navigate past Eric and Cassie and she pulled up. Cassie nodded towards the flat.

"Have you seen Micky?" she asked.

If the woman was perturbed by their presence, she didn't show it. Peering over the balustrade, she looked the length of the alley.

"His van's there, so he'll likely be in."

Cassie followed her eyeline and saw an old, white Transit van parked up against the side of the building. The side panels were dented with rust visible around the wheel arches.

"Who does he work for?" Cassie asked.

"One of them courier firms… delivering online shopping and that," the woman said. "He's out all hours. I'm surprised he's home, even on a Sunday."

Cassie thanked her and they squeezed in as best they could to enable the family to pass. Turning back to the door, Cassie raised a balled fist, only for the door to open before her. A bleary-eyed figure blinked out at her, squinting and shielding his eyes against the brightness of the daylight even though it was overcast. Cassie noticed his pupils were dilated.

"Micky George?" she asked, lifting her warrant card and presenting it right to his face. He shied away from it as a vampire might a crucifix, before frowning and cocking his head, looking past it at her.

"Whatever it was, I didn't do it," he said flatly.

"We'd like a word, please."

He sighed, nodded and stepped back from the door, beckoning them to enter.

Once inside the narrow hall, Eric closed the door. The air inside was stale and the odour reminiscent of that which accompanied student digs. Micky George ran a hand through his collar-length brown hair, eyeing them warily. He had a thin, hawkish face with dark circles around his eyes.

"What can I do for you?" he asked, stifling a yawn.

"Up late last night, were you?" Cassie asked.

"Yeah… I didn't get home from work until gone half-ten," he said, yawning through the words and, this time, making no effort to hide it.

Cassie looked around, spying the living room, which was still in darkness, curtains closed, with takeaway cartons on a small table next to the sofa.

"What work do you do, Mr George?"

He sniffed. "Deliveries… and that."

"They keep you working late then?"

"I'm self-employed. The more packages I deliver, the more I get paid." He followed her gaze into the living room. "And it's not like I have a lot going on here."

"You live alone?" Eric asked.

"Yeah, can't you tell?"

Cassie smirked, glancing into the kitchen. "You make enough mess for a family of four."

George frowned. "Do I have to pay extra for the lifestyle critique or what?"

"No, that's gratis," Cassie said with a wink.

He sighed. "What *do* you want?"

"To ask you about Angela Dale… your relationship with her, her ex-boyfriend… and what her reaction was when you tried it on," Cassie said, smiling sweetly. "For starters, anyway. After that, we can just freewheel."

Micky George stood with his mouth open, almost dumbfounded.

"Good. I have your attention," Cassie said. "Let's start with you and Charlie. You were friends, weren't you? Inseparable, we hear," she said, glancing at Eric who nodded.

"W-well… we were once, yes. That's true. Long time ago, mind you."

"So what happened? I know he wasn't aware of

you hitting on Angela… you should have seen the surprise on his face this morning."

"Yes," Eric said, nodding sagely, "he didn't take it well at all."

Micky George put his hands up to his face, drawing them slowly down his cheeks, stretching his eyelids down and letting out a low moan.

"Seriously… I've not had enough sleep to go into all of this."

"Unfortunately, we can't schedule our investigation around your use of recreational substances, Micky," Cassie said, bluntly.

George shook his head, sighing. "He'll go ape at me, he really will."

"Even after all this time?" Eric asked, surprised. "How often do you see one another?"

He shook his head. "Not often. I don't go to the same places as he does, but even so. This is a small town. I'll see him soon enough, especially if he's looking for me."

"Likely to bear a grudge, is he?" Cassie asked.

"Oh yeah… like you wouldn't believe. Charlie isn't one to let things go. Certainly not if he thinks he's been wronged. Petty bugger, he is."

"Like he couldn't let go of Angela?" Eric asked.

He met Eric's eye, a fleeting look of sadness crossing his face.

"Yeah. She tried to dump him loads of times, but Charlie had a way of getting into her head… as you say, not letting her go. It was some talent he had."

"Talent?" Eric asked. "Sounds like coercive control to me."

George snapped his fingers, pointing at Eric. "That's exactly what it was."

"And you? What was your relationship with Angela like?" Cassie asked.

He leant back against the wall, folding his arms across his chest, his face set in a deep frown.

"I liked her." He glanced up at Cassie, forcing a smile. It seemed genuine enough. "I liked her a lot. She was fun… didn't deserve to be treated like that by Charlie, or anyone else for that matter."

Something in his tone piqued Cassie's curiosity. "Who else?"

"What?"

"She didn't deserve to be treated like that by Charlie or *anyone else*. Who else?"

He shook his head. "Anyone, like, you know? Blokes." Shrugging, he averted his eyes from Cassie's gaze. "You know what I mean?"

"Angela's friends seem to think she was seeing someone else at the time she went missing. What do you make of that suggestion?"

He shrugged but said nothing.

"Was it you?" Eric asked.

"No!"

"Well, that was emphatic," Eric said. "If not you, then who?"

"How would I know?" George said, agonised. "If I knew, then I'd have said so back then, wouldn't I?"

Cassie shrugged. "Would you? People seem to like keeping secrets in this case… bodies stored in freezers… secret liaisons…"

"What do you mean… bodies kept in freezers?"

He sounded slightly alarmed. Cassie looked past him, down the length of the hall. There were two doors off it, presumably a bathroom and a bedroom.

"Do you have a freezer, Micky?"

"Do I have… a…" he glanced over his shoulder. "I don't have one big enough to keep a body in, if that's what you're asking… no!"

"Oh, we're just looking for parts at this time," Cassie said, nonchalantly.

"I-I… I don't know what to say to that."

"I'm sure that's true," Cassie said. "Didn't you know, whoever killed Angela chopped her into pieces and kept her in the freezer? Not that we've found all of her. We're still trying to find the missing bits—"

"I-I think I'm going to be sick…" Micky said. He was definitely looking nauseous.

"Oh no…" Cassie said, deliberately overdoing the sincerity. "Was it something you ate?"

Micky George hurried along the corridor and into the first door on the right. Cassie indicated for Eric to supervise while she had a nose around the living room. Eric's brow creased, and he whispered, "I get all the good jobs around here, don't I?"

Cassie smiled. "You need to take a significant collar and get yourself promoted, Eric."

"If you don't get me sacked first," he grumbled, following Micky into the bathroom. "That's it, get it all out," Cassie heard him say.

Walking into the living room, she screwed up her nose at the smell. The previous night's meal, a mixture of curry dishes, now largely unidentifiable. The dregs of the meal were currently solidifying in foil cartons. Crossing the room, she pulled back the curtains to allow some natural light in. On the table beside the leftovers were three remote controls, all lined up beside each other pointing at the television, satellite television box and a DVD player. She hadn't seen a DVD player in years.

"You live a wild life, Micky, you really do," she said quietly.

By the looks of it, he'd spent the night on the sofa. A tartan throw was pushed to one side as if it'd been used as a blanket. Movement in the corner of her eye made her turn. Micky had entered the room, looking pale and more than a bit sheepish. She felt sorry for him then, wondering if she should have gone in so hard on him. The thought passed when she remembered his record.

"Three years ago, you were arrested for assaulting a sex worker," she said flatly.

Micky sank down onto the sofa, nodding glumly. "Yeah, I was."

She'd expected more of a protest, a defiance, that it was a misunderstanding, but he didn't say any such thing.

"Tell me about it."

He looked up at her, shaking his head. "It'll sound like I'm making excuses."

"Try me."

Taking a deep breath, Micky nodded solemnly. "I didn't know she was a sex worker at the time, honestly. I pegged her for a lass out on the town and tried my luck. I guess that doesn't make any difference when all is said and done." He shrugged. "I thought she was interested in me… I was wasted that night, I really was. I was different back then, such a mess."

Cassie glanced around. If this was what together looked like, then he must have been in a proper state. He noticed her looking.

"Yeah, I know what you're thinking, but I was in a real spiral back then… booze, drugs… being out on the rob most of the time."

Cassie inclined her head.

Micky held a hand up. "Yeah… I'm not proud

of myself. I was going one way and that was down. I was headed… well, I'd have ended up in prison or dead."

"So?"

"I turned it around." He smiled when Cassie arched her eyebrows, glancing at Eric. "This…" he said, holding his arms out wide, "all that you see… isn't much, but it's honest. I work hard and I try to be a decent person. I'm not that guy any more."

"What guy were you when Angela went missing?" Eric asked.

Micky looked up at him. "Selfish… arrogant. Entitled. I didn't care much for myself, let alone anyone else."

"How did Angela respond to your attention?"

He bit his lower lip, avoiding eye contact. "Angela was special… to her friends… and to me."

"So how did you feel when she gave you the old heave-ho?" Cassie asked. "It must have stung… I mean really cut deep if you're this selfish, arrogant… what was the other one?" she asked Eric.

"Entitled."

"Yes, entitled. How dare she do that to you, of all people!"

Micky shook his head. "It wasn't like that… it really wasn't."

"Then what was it like, Micky?" Cassie asked. "Tell us."

He laughed. "You're just like the others, you

know?" He glanced at both of them in turn, smiling. "You guys really need to be more original with your questions."

"You've heard all this before?" Cassie asked. He nodded. "From whom?"

"Your colleagues. Six years ago… or is it five? I'm not sure. Like I said, I was drinking a lot more back then. They came at me with this rubbish as well." He fixed his gaze on Cassie. "I'm a lot of things, but I don't kill women… and certainly not someone I care about. Even if I was a bit of a dick back then, it doesn't make me a murderer."

"Then who did? Because we don't have many suspects to choose from—"

"Ah… this is what it's all about, isn't it?" Micky said, wagging a knowing finger at her. "You sent an innocent guy to prison and now he's out and you're looking to round up the old names, hoping to pin it on one of them."

Cassie cocked her head. "You've heard about Ben Crake's release?"

"Yes, of course. Word is spreading. Like I said, small town, and where there's scandal, there's rumour and no shortage of narrow minds to feed it."

Cassie observed him. He was remarkably erudite for a delivery driver.

"Ben Crake isn't clear of this yet," she said. "Everything is still on the table."

"Including Charlie this time?" Micky said,

glaring at her with a passion that thus far had been lacking in his responses. "Or does he get a free pass… again?"

"What are you talking about?" Cassie asked, her eyes narrowing. "Charlie is just as much a suspect as—"

Micky burst out laughing, running a hand through his lank hair. "Yeah, right."

"I'm serious," she said, finding his reaction irritating.

"Like last time?" Micky said, looking her up and down.

"What are you saying, Micky?"

"Charlie… used to rough Angela up… claimed she liked it, but she didn't. I know she didn't."

"You're the one who was arrested for assaulting a sex worker."

"Oh please!" he protested, waving her accusation away. "I was hammered… and couldn't even string a sentence together at the time. It is hardly the premeditated actions of a murderer. I was drunk… and out of order, and the arresting officers let me know about it once I was back in the station, if you know what I mean?"

"They beat you up?" she asked. "Is that what you're alleging?"

"Yeah…" he said, sitting forward. "And I deserved it too. She never pressed charges and they let me go the next day." He sat back. "I've been clean ever since. But Charlie… I wanted to have it out with him – after Angela told me what he'd do to her – but she wouldn't let me, made me promise not to say anything."

"Why would she do that?"

Micky shrugged. "At the time I figured she didn't want him to get hurt but, looking back, I suppose it was me she was worried about."

"She thought Charlie would hurt you?"

"I guess so," he said, sighing. "To be fair, she was right. Charlie would've kicked my arse." He pursed his lips, brow furrowing. "So, you're here trawling over my past. What about his? What about Charlie?"

Cassie saw the gleam in his eye. She was curious. Moving to the armchair opposite him, she sat down, looking him squarely in the eye.

"What about him?"

"Have you asked him why he left Sandhurst?"

"We spoke about it," Cassie said. "He had an accident on a training exercise."

Micky threw his head back, laughing. "Is he still flogging that old guff."

"You know differently?"

"Yeah, I do," Micky said, grinning.

"Enlighten me."

He shook his head. "Do your own work. I'm underpaid for the work I do, so I'm sure as hell not going to do yours for nothing."

"Is that how it is?" she asked.

He nodded. "It is. You'll find it interesting though, I'm sure. Unless, of course, Charlie picks up the phone like he did last time to take the heat off himself."

"Picks up the phone to whom?"

"You really don't know, do you?"

Cassie's irritation was growing. Micky was enjoying this. She could tell.

"Be careful," he said to her first before glancing up at Eric, his grin broadening, "what you wish for."

CHAPTER NINETEEN

Tom Janssen turned to see Cassie and Eric entering the ops room. Cassie bounded into the room like she was a woman on a mission, making a beeline for him.

"What is it we don't know about Charlie Babcock?" she asked.

Eric hurried to join them, gathering his breath. Cassie must have set a blistering pace upstairs. Tom's eyes flitted between them.

"Good morning to you, too," he said, smiling.

Cassie mock grimaced, frowning. "Yes, morning. Of course, sorry."

Tom took a breath. "Right, what's Charlie said that's rattled you so much?"

Cassie shook her head. "Not that I didn't find him to be a loathsome creature and all, but it was more his old mate, Micky. He was hinting…" she glanced at Eric "no, not hinting… what would you say, Eric?"

"Gloating, I'd say."

Tom was taken aback, but Cassie nodded.

"Yes, he was almost gleeful that he knew something we didn't," Cassie said, "which was altogether odd bearing in mind there doesn't appear to be much love lost between the two of them. They're not exactly friends anymore."

Eric's eyebrows knitted together. "And then Charlie pretty much threatened you."

"Threatened you?" Tom asked.

Cassie blew it off with an exhale through pursed lips and a flick of the hand. "Water off a duck's back, but he was confident. I asked him why there were things left out of his statement…"

"And?" Tom asked. "What did he have to say for himself?"

She shrugged. "He wasn't bothered, either about the apparent omissions or his inaccuracy regarding the status of his relationship with Angela. I had the feeling we were in the dark with him as well. He almost seemed to enjoy our visit. He's hiding something."

"What?" Tom asked.

"I don't know, but I'm going to kick over some rocks today and see if I can find out. Eric's going to get onto the MOD and see what he can find out from Charlie's brief stint in the army. I'll see what I can find out locally."

Tom's mobile rang and he took it out of his pocket. It was an unknown number. He nodded at Cassie, raising his eyebrows as he made to walk away and answer the call. "See what you can find out. I don't like being in the dark. You always come across unexpected things when you can't see anything and we don't need any surprises right now."

She nodded and Tom turned his attention to the call, entering his office and closing the door as he tapped the green answer button.

"DI Janssen," he said, heading for his desk.

"Detective Inspector, it's Olivia."

"Olivia?" he asked, momentarily confused and then it clicked as she further identified herself.

"Goldman—"

"Yes, of course. What can I do for you, Miss Goldman?"

"Very formal, DI Janssen," she said, and noted a playful turn in her voice. "Is that an everyday occurrence, just on the weekends or have you saved it for me?"

"I play things by the book."

"Yes, I've heard that about you… unless you have an extenuating need to cross the line."

He perched himself on the end of his desk, glancing out of the window overlooking the car park. "I take it you've been doing your research."

"One should always analyse the opposition, Inspector. It makes good sense, wouldn't you say?"

"You make it sound like we are enemies, Miss Goldman—"

"Olivia, please," she said. "Miss Goldman makes me sound like an old spinster with a large collection of cats."

"We're not enemies, Olivia. We all want the same thing here."

"Are you sure about that, Tom?"

The move to first name terms didn't bother him. He preferred it. Olivia Goldman was seemingly the driving force behind Ben Crake's release from prison. Whether that turned out to be judicious or misguided, only time would tell. However, he was keen to avoid her becoming a thorn in his side.

"I can speak for myself and my team," he said.

"You have a very small team, Tom."

He wondered how much research she'd undertaken and if she'd already scrutinised his CID team, then what else did she already know about other suspects or lines of inquiry? After all, she'd been working this case for several years as opposed to his several days. "But they're good at what they do."

"Your record is decent, I have to say."

The exchange was light-hearted and playful but he found his irritation growing.

"What can I do for you, Olivia?"

"You said we would need to speak one day."

"Yes, I did. What have you got in mind?"

"Meet me for coffee this morning?"

Tom checked his watch. They had a briefing scheduled for midday, but he had time.

"Sure. Where would you like to meet?"

"On the promenade," she said and he heard the sound of gulls in the background along with the whistle of the wind through the mouthpiece. "I'll meet you at… lateral mark eleven."

He figured she'd just checked her surroundings. From memory that put her close to the Oasis Leisure Centre. "I can be there in about fifteen minutes?"

"How do you take your coffee?" she asked. "Like all coppers, NATO Standard?"

"NATO Standard?"

"Milk and two sugars."

"Milk, no sugar."

"See you soon."

Picking up his jacket, he passed through ops. "I'll be back in time for the briefing," he said. Cassie nodded and if she wondered where he was off to, she didn't ask.

It was a short drive across town to the seafront. The curious little one-way system that the council imposed a few years previously meant he had to circumvent a large car park that was in the process of being split in two with half of it being turned over to residential development. It was an odd decision bearing in mind how many tourists descended on the town in the holiday season. Parking always seemed limited and yet here they were, handing more of it to developers.

Pulling into the smaller car park and drawing up to the sea wall, he switched off the engine and scanned the markers a hundred feet or so out into the water. The tide was on its way in but much of the beach was still accessible with combers picking their way through the sand and stones, hunting fossils while a few hardy children examined small rock pools, no doubt in search of crabs. Lateral mark eleven was close to where he'd imagined it to be and he slipped through the nearest opening in the sea wall and walked onto the promenade.

The promenade was clear now, but for the spring, summer and early autumn there were a multitude of mobile food and drink vendors plying their trade on the three-metre wide sea defences that stopped the tide from tearing the town away like it did in the unprotected areas beyond the town limits. The small businesses left again once the tourists dried up, pitching up at private venues and festivals instead during the offseason.

Olivia Goldman was standing with her back to him, facing the sea. A camel long coat was wrapped around her and she stood in dark trousers and black boots, her shoulder-length blonde hair extended out behind her in the stiff ocean breeze. Seeing his approach in the corner of her eye, rather than hearing him, such was the noise of the wind, she turned and offered him a warm smile. He returned it with one of his own as she handed him a takeaway cup of coffee which he accepted gratefully.

"Milk, no sugar," she said, using her free hand to move hair away from her face now that she'd turned side on to the wind.

"Thank you."

"It's beautiful here," she said, looking back at the sea. Two children shrieked their delight at finding something in the sand nearby, calling for their mother to come and see.

"Yes, it is," Tom said. "As beautiful as the Derbyshire peaks or Greater Manchester?"

Olivia's lips split as a smile crept across her face and she cocked her head, looking at Tom. "I see someone else has been doing some research of their own."

Tom raised his eyebrows. "It pays to analyse the opposition."

"Touché." She laughed. "But we're not enemies," she said, sipping at her drink.

"Not as far as I'm concerned." He tasted his coffee. It was cool enough to drink. "Care to walk with me?"

She nodded and they set off in the direction of

the funfair. The gulls were aware of their presence, circling overhead and dropping down closer in the hope they might drop some scraps for them to fight over. Undaunted by the lack of visible food, they remained close, keeping a watchful eye nonetheless.

"So what made you go over to the dark side?" Tom asked as they walked. She was a fair bit shorter than he was, although that could be said about almost anyone bearing in mind his height and frame.

"Is that what you see the private sector as?" she asked, without any hint of judgement. "That's a tortured analogy. I'm hardly working for the forces of darkness, Tom. I haven't changed. I still want to see the guilty behind bars… but we should ensure the right people are there. Don't you agree?"

He inclined his head, sipping at his drink. "Undoubtedly. Ben Crake was convicted by a jury of his peers."

"By the use of dubious and misleading evidence."

"That's quite a statement," he said, his eyes widening.

"A coerced confession and inconclusive CCTV footage," she said, stopping and turning to face Tom.

"Coerced is a strong word."

"Have you watched the interview tapes yet?"

"No, I haven't," he said, feeling guilty, although knowing he hadn't had the time yet. "I've read the transcripts, though. Ben didn't do himself any favours under questioning."

She scoffed. "If you were being unjustly accused of murdering someone you cared about, I'll bet you'd be pretty indignant about it too."

"Fair point."

"And if the officers at the time had bothered to do some proper policing, then maybe we wouldn't be here right now. Ben found her standing in the rain, soaked to the skin in a skimpy top and shorts, and offered his friend shelter. Do you know what the newspapers christened him for that act of kindness or how he was vilified?"

"I do," Tom said. "They called him the Angel of Death. You're adamant that Ben is innocent, aren't you?"

She hesitated before nodding, only for a moment, but it was enough to pique Tom's curiosity.

"One hundred percent?" he asked.

She averted her eyes from his. "As sure as I can be."

"What kind of an answer is that? Either you think he's innocent or he isn't."

"I think he didn't get a fair trial," she said, fixing him with a stern look. "And a fair trial is what everyone should have, especially if they are facing spending most, if not all, of their lives in a prison cell. I don't think that's unreasonable."

"And you have doubts about the conviction?"

She laughed but it was a bitter, contemptible sound. "Don't you? The lad knows her, is attracted to her and is seen running after her on grainy camera footage and he gets sent down for life. Any prospect of parole is extinguished unless he gives up where the body is buried, which is impossible to do if you don't know where it's buried because you *didn't* actually kill her. Without me, Ben Crake would be spending at least another fifteen to twenty years at one of His Majesty's Hiltons."

"How do you account for her DNA being found on his clothes?"

"I don't have to," she hit back. "Ben covered that himself."

"Ah, right. She came onto him," Tom said, before draining the remainder of his coffee. "Although she'd never shown any interest in him previously in that way, and she'd never mentioned him to any of those within her inner circle of friends."

"It doesn't mean he's not telling the truth."

"No, right enough," he said, indicating his empty cup and pointing at hers. She finished her own and handed the cup to him. Tom crossed to one of the many green bins positioned along the promenade and tossed the empty cups into it before turning back to her and gesturing for them to resume their walk. "But it does stretch his credibility… along with him being the last person to see her alive."

She nodded, smiling. "Apart from her killer, obviously."

Tom returned her smile. "Speaking of whom, who do you think killed her, if not your client?"

She sighed. "If I knew that, then I'd be golden, wouldn't I?"

"You must have an idea… thought about it."

"I think there are gaps in the investigation… witnesses were allowed to drift away, suspects not pursued… others ignored altogether."

"Such as?"

She turned to face him once more. "You're a decent copper, from what I've been able to find out about you at any rate. Don't tell me you're not having doubts."

"Are we about to disappear down a rabbit hole of conspiracy theories?"

"You're referring to Charlie Babcock, aren't you?" she asked.

Tom smiled but didn't confirm anything. He was curious to know what she knew about the man.

"I take it you've looked at Charlie?"

"Too right."

"What do you know?"

"That he was booted out of Sandhurst, for one."

"Emotive term, *booted out,*" he said.

She smiled knowingly. "The army will happily cover up the misdemeanours of their soldiers when they're out in the field, but they tend not to turn a blind eye when you screw up in public."

Tom tilted his head knowingly to one side despite having no idea what she was talking about. "There is that," he said.

"And his uncle wasn't able to smooth that one over for him. It was too much of a stretch back then… maybe now it might be different, but we'll never know."

Tom's gaze narrowed and he caught her eyeing him.

"You do know, don't you?"

On this occasion, Tom had to come clean, shaking his head. Olivia chuckled.

"You really are out of the loop, Tom. You're bumbling around in the dark," she said shaking her head. "Charlie Babcock's uncle was the supervising officer in the original investigation."

Tom stopped, turned to face her with a deep frown. "Watts?"

She nodded. "Your chief superintendent got a decent step up in his career by nailing Ben Crake… and at the same time kept his nephew away from scrutiny."

Tom sucked air through his teeth. Olivia laughed again.

"You really didn't know, did you?"

He shook his head, feeling a growing sense of embarrassment.

"As far as I can determine, he never disclosed that information, either to the CPS or to Ben's defence team. Whether he brought it up with his colleagues, I have no idea."

"That would explain…"

She looked at him, waiting for him to finish the comment but he didn't.

"The gaps in his witness statement?" she asked. Tom met her eye but he didn't comment. "Because there are glaring errors in Charlie Babcock's statements. It's almost as if they were screened prior to submission."

Tom raised a pointed finger. "Now that is straying into conspiracy and conjecture. Not that I'm dismissing anything."

"I should hope not, Tom," she said. "Otherwise you'd not be the detective that I'm hoping you are."

"It doesn't mean that the investigation was corrupt."

"No," Olivia said, conceding the point, "but if they thought they had their man in Ben Crake, then there is every reason to believe that they didn't look beyond what they already had. They zeroed in on Ben very early on in the investigation and any other suspects were passed over, if they were even looked at at all. I've been sitting on that familial connection. I didn't want to use it if I didn't have to when Ben's case came before the court of appeal."

Tom rubbed a hand against his chin, thinking hard.

"You mean you wanted to keep it in reserve in case the case stalled."

Olivia smiled and then winked. She was only confirming his own suspicions in relation to how the investigation was carried out, but it left Tom with an uneasy feeling.

"So the question, Tom Janssen, becomes: are you going to carry out a proper investigation or take the short cuts like your predecessors did?"

Tom pursed his lips, matching her stern gaze with one of his own. "In all honesty, I don't know how long I'll have to solve this case."

"They're bringing in another team?"

"I'm not a party to it, but I should imagine so. Particularly once it gets around that we've found Angela's body."

"You've what?" she asked. It was her turn to be surprised.

He nodded. "The body that's been uncovered out at Ringstead. It's been confirmed, but we haven't made it public yet. I probably shouldn't be telling you."

"So why did you?"

He held her eye. “Because we both want the same thing, wherever it leads. Can I trust you to be discreet?”

She frowned. “Yes, I’ll keep it to myself but you won’t be able to sit on it for long.”

He nodded vigorously. “We know that. Which is why it’s only my team, my DCI… and now you, who are aware of this besides the family.”

“Do you think you’ll be able to solve it before the cavalry arrive?”

He smiled. “I’m not one to overpromise.”

She smiled. “Is there anything I can do to help?”

He looked at her, assessing her sincerity. “What if it starts to look like they got the right guy in the first place?”

“Then I’ll help you put him away, Tom.” She shook her head. “I’m not in this to beast the police or the CPS. I just want the truth, but I want it done right.”

They turned to head back the way they’d come. They walked in silence for a couple of minutes before Tom glanced sideways at her.

“Tell me why you quit the force,” he said. “If you’re so keen on putting the right people away, why did you give up on it?”

“Now that’s not an easy question to answer. I got tired of the politics… tired of dealing with fragile men’s egos,” she looked at him, “present company excluded, obviously.”

"Naturally," he said.

"I just wanted to nick the villains… and the higher I rose in the force, the bigger the villains were but also the chase got tougher. Too many obstacles."

"They're called codes of practice."

"No, that's not what I meant at all," she said, waving away his comment. "I have no problem with the rules, but so few people were following them. The lines were getting blurred and I wondered whose side everyone was on."

Tom was intrigued. "Give me a specific."

She looked at him and seemed comfortable that his interest was genuine. "Okay, I'll give you a for-instance. Years back, I'm fresh out of training and in my first week – it doesn't matter where, could have been anywhere – but I'm out with my supervisor, first week on the street. We see a car drive past us, three guys inside it: two black and one white. He tells me to pull them over."

"What for?" Tom asked.

She shrugged. "That's what I said and he told me a phrase that was drummed into me that first week, *black and white, stop on sight*."

She looked at Tom and he cocked his head.

"As far as my lead was concerned, a white man had no business with a black man, unless it was for something criminal."

It wasn't a phrase he'd come across during his

time in the Metropolitan Police, but he had no reason to doubt her memory was accurate.

"So you pulled them?" he asked.

She nodded. "We did."

"And?"

She smiled wryly. "They had a shed load of drugs in the car along with an illegal firearm that was matched to a robbery three months previously. It was quite a result in my first week… but the result doesn't make it right. We could have done that ten times and got nothing. We should have had a reason to stop them." She shook her head. "My supervisor said it was instinct. It wasn't instinct. Not in my mind. Anyway," she frowned, "I started to think I could achieve more on the outside than I could from within."

"I find that hard to believe," Tom said. "We're not perfect, but without us – the police, I mean – it would be bedlam. Even out here in beautiful Norfolk."

She laughed, arching her eyebrows momentarily. "I don't doubt that for a second." She turned to face him. "You asked why I left?"

"I did."

"Well, after a decade working in London, I nicked a lot of bad guys… but sometimes I found it hard to look myself in the mirror."

"Those rules you spoke of?"

She nodded. "If you can bend, flex and circumvent them enough times, then you start to think they don't apply to you anymore, only to the bad guys. Do the ends justify the means? I got used to thinking they did… and that was when I had to do something different. I know you might see me as puritanical and rigid, but that's only because I know what it looks like from the other side of the line, Tom, and I don't ever want to go back there again."

He took a deep breath and nodded slowly. "I understand."

"If I can offer you a little advice?"

He tilted his head quizzically and nodded.

"As much as I think Charlie Babcock is worth looking at, there are others."

"Care to name one or two?"

She thought about it for a moment. Tom was sure she'd already assembled likely suspects, so he found her momentary hesitation curious to say the least.

"The circus folk know more than they're letting on. I'm quite sure of that."

Tom's expression cut a wry smile. "They tend not to like speaking to the authorities at the best of times. It doesn't necessarily mean anything."

"Yes, I know," she said, angling her head to one side thoughtfully, "but it's more than that."

"Anyone else?"

"I always saw Greg as too good to be true."

"Greg Brock, Ben Crake's employer?" Tom struggled to keep the scepticism from his tone.

"Don't be so quick to dismiss him, Tom," she said, shaking her head. "He was there that night... and if Ben didn't erase the security footage, then someone else with access did."

Tom shook his head. "I understand that Brock has a watertight alibi for that night."

Olivia smiled. "I remember someone said the Titanic was watertight once upon a time."

CHAPTER TWENTY

TOM PULLED up before the metal entrance gates and reached through his open window to press the button on the intercom. While he waited, he observed a lot of activity to the eastern side of the property as a mini dumper came into view, operated by a grizzled-looking man sporting an orange high-viz vest, combat trousers and muck-covered boots. The vehicle began beeping as he threw it into reverse momentarily, allowing him to make his turn before heading back out of sight. The sound of machine tools came to him on the breeze but were drowned out by the crackle of the intercom.

"It's Detective Inspector Janssen from Norfolk police for Greg Brock," he said in response to the greeting. "I believe he is expecting me."

A buzzer sounded and the electronic gates

shuddered as they slowly opened. Tom passed through them and made his way up the shingle driveway that wound its way in a curve through mature trees, a mix of beech, oak and ash as far as Tom could tell. Parking in front of a cart lodge, he got out and spied a silver Range Rover parked in the second of three open bays. A sports car was under cover in the leftmost bay and the final slot was empty, although there were double doors to an adjoining garage which were closed.

The sound of workmen was louder now and Tom found himself contemplating how much they'd be earning what with working on a Sunday. Tamara had called to cancel the midday briefing, just as he left Olivia on the promenade, but she didn't give a reason as to why, only telling him they'd speak later. He took the opportunity to have a word with Ben Crake's former employer, Olivia Goldman's suspicions still fresh in his mind.

The front door opened and a man stepped out from under a leaded canopy that adorned the front of the brick and flint farmhouse that the Brock family resided in. He was in his fifties, angular of face, lean and tall – by most people's standards but not Tom's – with greying hair that was swept back from his forehead. It was thinning, revealing a tanned scalp that matched the complexion of his face and exposed arms beneath rolled-up sleeves. Either Greg Brock had been away to sunnier climes recently or he tanned from a bottle.

"DI Janssen?" he asked, extending his hand as Tom approached. They shook and Tom silently acknowledged the firm grip and rough skin of the man's hand. Evidently, Greg Brock had a strength belied by his slender frame.

"Thank you for seeing me on such short notice, Mr Brock, but I was in the area."

He waved away the comment and ushered Tom towards the house.

"No matter, Detective Inspector. I'm just home and the family are out and about doing their thing, so I was just catching up on some paperwork."

The beeping of another vehicle grew louder as it rounded the side of the house, the amber light flashing as it made the turn.

"You have a lot going on here today," Tom said.

Greg laughed as he closed the front door behind them, gesturing towards a room to their immediate left overlooking the front of the house. It was a study and Tom led the way, Greg a step behind him.

"Yes, this infernal extension that appears to be taking forever and a day to complete." Greg gathered a chair from against the wall on the far side of the study and set it down in front of his desk, offering it to Tom as he hustled around to seat himself. "I must admit it's been a nightmare," he said, sighing as he sank into a leather-lined captain's chair. "We had something of a ramshackle old timber-framed barn, a twentieth century addition to the farm, and I'd been avoiding replacing it for fear of the bureaucracy that I'd have to wade through."

Tom looked at him quizzically and Greg explained.

"The house is Grade II listed, but that particular barn is not, but in order to replace it—"

"You need permission."

"In a nutshell," he said, touching the tips of his fingers to his temples and mimicking an explosion outwards. "From the planners, English Heritage... the bloody neighbours..." he cocked his head. "To be fair, the latter have been pretty decent putting up with the noise and the heavy plant running back and forth." He threw his hands in the air. "I'd have quite happily left it but Marsha, my wife, feared it was going to fall down and we had so much stuff in it – a lifetime's worth of memories stuffed into cardboard boxes – that she kept on at me to sort it." He inhaled deeply, glancing out of the window as if he could see the construction works. "Now I'm just hoping it will all be done before winter kicks in, hence the activity you mentioned."

"Must be costing you a fortune in weekend payments."

Greg laughed. "Not me, the main contractor. I'm not daft, I set penalty clauses for missing completion dates. I'm amazed he agreed to them, seeing as builders are in such short supply around here these days." He turned to Tom. "So, what can I do for you today, Inspector? I must admit I was surprised to get your call."

"Yes, thank you again for seeing me, Mr Brock—"

"Greg, please."

Tom nodded gratefully. "I wanted to speak to you about Ben Crake."

"Ben?" he said, looking surprised. "Of course… but I've not seen or spoken to him since," he intimated with a flick of his head and a frown, "all of that nasty business with Angela. Poor girl."

"You're aware Ben has been released from prison?"

"Oh yes, of course I am." His forehead creased and he leaned forward, elbows on his desk and pitching a tent with his fingers. "Word travels fast as I'm sure you know."

"I do," Tom said smiling.

"Nasty business… and I thought that was all behind us," Greg said, glancing at a framed photograph on his desk. He picked it up, taking a deep breath as he looked at it before slowly placing it down so that Tom could see it. Tom looked at it and saw a family shot of Greg, his wife Marsha, who Tom had met briefly at the Dales' home, both standing behind a young woman, Greg with his hands on her shoulders. It was Susan, Jack Dale's girlfriend.

Greg looked at Tom, shaking his head. "This whole business broke that poor family… and nearly mine too, if you take into account how entwined Susan was with young Jack."

"How well do you know the family?"

"Very well," he said, tapping the desk twice with his fore and index fingers. "Henry and I go way, way back."

"You were in business together, weren't you?"

"Yes, that's right," Greg said. "I sold out to Henry. Farming was more his thing than mine. I wanted to be more of a middleman. Less risk, more opportunity. For a time, I thought our Susan might end up marrying young Jack, but the pressure of it all… you know, when Angela went missing, put too much strain on everyone close to her and… well… extraordinary events."

"They broke up, Susan and Jack?"

"Oh yes," Greg said, sitting back in his chair and looking thoughtful. "They drifted apart from one another. That whole family turned in on itself for a while. They couldn't trust anyone, you see? They just relied upon one another. Poor Henry never recovered from losing his daughter like that." He looked at the picture again, no doubt viewing his own daughter who was a similar age. Tom thought of Saffy. "Maybe if they'd had some measure of closure, but without the…" he sighed "without actually being able to lay her to rest, I guess closure is nigh on impossible."

"Do you speak with the family now?"

He thought about it for a moment. "Marsha is still friendly with the family, and I offered the support and services of the church, to try to offer comfort where possible, but when Henry's business failed… he withdrew even further." He smiled, but it was accompanied by a sad expression. "When a man loses his faith, he is prone to lashing out at those who preach."

Tom's gaze narrowed. "Are you referring to yourself?"

"Yes, well, metaphorically speaking," Greg said, seeking to clarify. "Henry has never been the violent sort. At least, not in my experience," he said, touching one hand to his chest. "In times of strife many people find comfort in the house of the Lord but others fail to understand His plan and attack the faith."

"You're a believer, I take it?" Tom asked.

Greg smiled, warmly this time. "Yes, I'm a Licensed Lay Minister. Didn't you know?"

Tom recalled Susan telling him.

"I came to it late in life. I'm a reader, preaching on occasion in the local parishes, what with congregations not being quite what they once were there are fewer resident vicars these days." He picked up another photograph on his desk and leaned forward to pass it to Tom, who took it and examined the picture. Greg was in a barren landscape with two young boys standing to either side of him, smiling at the camera. "I also join the Mission in Tanzania whenever work permits me the time to travel for a few weeks."

"Been there recently?"

Greg grinned. "How can you tell? I had to come back to get this building work moving, otherwise I'd happily stay out there."

"Your wife doesn't mind?"

He waved away the suggestion. "If it weren't for everything she is involved in locally, then I'm sure she would join me."

"Who runs your business while you're away?" Tom asked, handing the photograph back.

"Oh, I have managers who are more than capable," Greg said. "In all honesty I've been scaling back my workload for the past couple of years." He tapped his heart with the flat of his hand. "A little scare a while back. It starts you thinking. Why should I be at the office until all hours? What's it all for?"

Tom sought to move past the small-talk and the last comment provided a neat segue. "You were at the office that night, weren't you? The night Angela disappeared?"

Greg's expression turned glum, and he nodded.

"Yes, I was. Marsha was out for the day with friends… golfing followed by an evening meal. I knew she would be back late. I had a function on later that evening and rather than kicking my heels around the house all day by myself, I figured I'd come into the office, while it was quiet, and get a few things tied off." He shook his head gravely. "You have no idea how many times I've played that night over and over in my mind. What if I'd left ten minutes later or come across Angela myself instead of Ben? How things might be different now?"

"You believed that Ben was guilty then?"

Greg exhaled through pursed lips, shaking his head. "To be honest," he said, splaying his hands wide as he met Tom's eye, "no, I didn't. I was so surprised when you, well, not you, but your colleagues, arrested Ben. It didn't sit well with me at the time; everything they said he did… it didn't sound like the Ben that I'd had working for me for a year, or the child I watched grow to adulthood."

"You knew him well then?"

"Yes, very well! He is a similar age to my daughter… classmates of Angela and close in age to Jack Dale as well. They attended the same birthday parties as children, school events and whatnot… so yes, I've known that lad for years. Most of his life, in fact. It was devastating to find someone in your midst who could do such a thing." Greg arched his eyebrows before frowning deeply. "Like many others around these parts, I really don't know what to think. For many months I refused to believe that Ben could do such a thing to a friend of his. I spoke up for him at his trial, at great personal cost I should add."

"The Dales?"

Greg nodded forcefully. "Which I could understand… but after he was convicted… seeing the evidence presented at the trial."

"The CCTV from your site?"

Greg dismissed that with a flick of his hand. "That was rubbish… the camera footage and what the police said about it." He raised a hand apologetically. "I don't mean to belittle your profession, Detective Inspector, but I told your colleagues at the time."

"Ben was seen running after Angela."

"Yes, yes, yes, I know, but I'm referring to the suggestion that Ben wiped the other footage."

"You don't believe he did?"

Greg scoffed. "We are an agri-foods processing business, Inspector. I employed minimal security guards at the time. Primarily, they were there to stop our machinery from being stolen on a Friday and shipped to the continent over the weekend to be sold on a Monday before we even knew it was missing. Believe me, security was minimal and," he tilted his head to one side and grimaced, "the equipment was largely low-paid staff and a torch."

"What about the cameras around the site, and the recordings?"

"Pfftt," Greg said shaking his head. "No one checked these things. I expect half the cameras on site were probably out of action and the footage recorded from those that did work was never reviewed... they were a deterrent."

"Are you saying Ben didn't erase the footage as the prosecution alleged?"

He held his hands up. "I'm saying there's no way of knowing what he did or didn't do." He smiled apologetically. "I did tell your colleagues this at the time."

"And in court?"

"Well," he said quietly, staring at some nondescript point on the wall, "no one really asked me much about it. I must say I was surprised Ben's defence didn't mention it."

"Was it in your statement?"

"I don't recall." Greg frowned. "Probably."

"So, what made you change your mind to think that Ben was guilty?"

"I guess... the DNA evidence, the pornography found on his computer... Not that that is necessarily conclusive. Before I found my faith, I would occasionally look at... as most men do, and it doesn't make them killers." He coughed. "There was also the confession of course," his frown deepened, "and everyone thought he was. No one believed he hadn't done it by the end of the trial week. Not even me and, as I said, I spoke for him."

Greg's mobile beeped a notification and he absently picked it up and looked at the screen.

"Where were you going when you were seen leaving on the gate camera footage that night?" Tom asked.

Greg appeared distracted by his mobile and he shook his head, placing it back down on the desk, face down. "I–I'm sorry. What did you ask?"

"That night, when you left your office, where were you going?"

"Oh... um... I had that function I mentioned. A Rotary Club event... a dinner for some fundraiser or another. I don't recall what it was for exactly, but I was the main speaker or host for the evening. I do remember I was in a rush. I'd brought my change of clothes with me to the office because I knew I'd be going straight from there to the hotel, where the dinner was to be held. I arrived with only minutes to spare, but that was me back then. I'm pleased to say I've slowed it all down a bit in the last few years."

"How many people were in attendance that night?"

Greg concentrated. "Quite a few... one hundred, perhaps more. It was quite a successful do, if I remember right. It went on rather late, finished around one o'clock in the morning."

"And you left your office at what time?" Tom asked.

Greg blew out his cheeks. "I'm afraid you're testing my memory there, Inspector." His brow creased. "Do you not have that information from my statement?"

Tom nodded.

"In your statement you said you had to be at the function by 8.30 PM."

Greg thought about it. "That sounds about right. So, I would have left here around fifteen to twenty minutes earlier."

"You left at quarter past, according to your statement and the time stamp of the gate camera."

He nodded. "Yes, that sounds right, but as I say, it was a long time ago. I'm sure everyone at the event must have confirmed the starting time?"

"They did. Eight-thirty sharp."

"Well, there you go." Greg looked perplexed. "Why do you ask?"

Tom smiled. "Just recapping all the timings. Just routine. Tell me, did you see anyone else around the site as you left that night? Strange cars, someone hanging around outside who perhaps shouldn't have been there?"

Greg shook his head. "No, not at all. I don't remember seeing anyone at all. If I had, I would have said so at the time."

Tom smiled. "Of course. It's always worth asking. Do you have any idea why Angela Dale might have been at your business that night?"

"Other than to see Ben Crake, you mean?"

Tom nodded.

"No, I can't think of any reason why she would be there."

"Presumably, you knew her well?"

"Angela? Yes, of course. She was like a daughter to me. She was close with Susan and the families were very close for a number of years. I didn't see as much of her once Henry and I parted as business partners. I think Henry found it harder going once I wasn't there to help, but then that was one of the reasons why I jumped ship; I could see what was coming and I wanted no part of it."

"What did you think about her?"

"Angela?" Greg clarified and Tom nodded. "Nice girl. Bright, fun. I think she gave her parents some sleepless nights as she got older… nothing horrific, mind you. I've known of much worse, but she was extremely outgoing, vivacious you might say."

"Much like Susan?"

Greg was taken aback. "Susan?"

"Well, you said they were friends. Friends often have shared interests."

He shook his head. "By that time, Susan was more friendly with Jack. I think Angela was a bit more advanced than my daughter, if you know what I mean?"

Tom smiled. "I understand. What does your daughter do?"

"She works for the family firm… although, I must admit that she doesn't do a great deal to earn her money."

"You pay her well?"

Greg Brock's expression darkened. "Why do you ask?"

"Her friend told us she works in administration."

"Yes."

Tom waited but no further information was forthcoming and he let it slide.

"I gather Susan and Jack have become close again recently."

He looked at Tom searchingly. "Is that a question, Inspector?"

It may have been Tom's intuition but Greg Brock's tone seemed to have changed.

"An observation."

Greg momentarily wrinkled his nose. "They were close to the events of a few years ago. I suppose it's only natural, what with Ben coming out of prison. Bringing it all back, I suppose."

"Yes, that's true. What are your feelings towards Ben now?"

He turned the corners of his mouth down, appearing thoughtful. "I'm not sure. I suppose that depends on the outcome of all of this. What will happen to him? I mean, he's not cleared, as I understand it."

"There will be a further review of the case. Perhaps he will face a retrial or he could be acquitted entirely."

Greg bobbed his head sagely. "In which case, I dare say there will be many of us who will owe that young man an apology."

Tom figured he'd gleaned as much information as he could from this exchange. Olivia's doubts were at the forefront of his mind, although he didn't share her certainty that Greg Brock had anything to hide. Unless she wasn't telling him everything she knew, and there was that distinct possibility bearing in mind her distrust of the police, if not him personally.

He thanked Greg for seeing him and the two men rose. When they reached the front door, Tom turned back to him.

"Have you spoken to your daughter about all of this?"

"Recently?" Greg asked. "No, I haven't seen much of her since I returned from Africa, to be honest. If she's been supporting Jack, then that might explain it."

"And your wife?"

"I don't understand."

"It must be reopening old wounds."

"Marsha is very keen to support Henry and Marie. Marie especially, but I don't know if there is much for us to speak about really. Not until this mess with Ben is resolved one way or another. I have to say I'm feeling more than a little guilty now that you bring it all up."

"Guilty? About what?"

"Ben… and our treatment of him. If he is innocent of that awful crime, then we have condemned an innocent man and branded him terribly. Should he be acquitted… well, it will take more than that for people to forgive him around here. I preach forgiveness, Inspector and I can tell you this, the words are easy but the action is hard."

"Mud sticks," Tom said.

Greg nodded. "Yes, it does."

"I asked you what you thought about Angela. But what did you think about Ben, seeing as you knew him so well?"

"Strange lad, I have to say. Introverted. A definite lack of confidence. He was a bit of a mummy's boy. Needed a father figure in his life, I should imagine."

"Did you know his father?"

Greg shook his head. "I don't remember him ever being on the scene."

"And you were surprised that he could be considered a murderer?"

"I was, yes. Ben was quiet… a loner. Sometimes, these people make for soft targets whereas the real evil looks much more like what you see in the mirror." Tom met his eye and Greg shook himself out of his thoughts. "Sorry, that's maybe a little deep. I just mean that evil doesn't always appear with horns. Often, evil approaches quietly and wearing a warm smile."

"I understand," Tom said. "Let's hope we can clear this up one way or the other once and for all."

"Might I suggest you do so quickly, Inspector? For everyone's sake."

CHAPTER TWENTY-ONE

TOM ARRIVED BACK at the station late in the afternoon. On his way to the ops room, he glanced into the canteen only to see Tamara deep in conversation with Chief Superintendent Watts as they stood with their back to the dropped shutters between them and the kitchen. This late on a Sunday, most officers were finished for the day and those on late-turn would have to either fend for themselves or make use of the vending machines.

The sight of Watts made him feel uneasy, bearing in mind what Olivia had told him. Watts had never given him cause to doubt him in the past, being a competent, if publicity hungry and controversy-shy, senior officer. However, this was a case like no other; one that brought a family member under suspicion in what was a narrow list of suspects.

Without being seen, Tom made his way up to ops, entering to see Eric shutting down his computer and Cassie speaking to someone he didn't recognise. Eric looked up at Tom and smiled glumly, tilting his head towards the other two who noted Tom's arrival. Cassie looked stern and the other man, in his late forties, pale-faced and slender, smiled a greeting. It struck him as artificial, a smile dictated by protocol and manners rather than a genuine expression.

"Sir," Cassie said formally as he approached, "this is DCI Morris from West Midlands."

The man thrust out his hand and Tom took it. The handshake was weak and effeminate, although he met Tom's eye as they made contact.

"Hello, sir," Tom said, shooting Cassie a slightly perplexed look as DCI Morris immediately let the grip drop and turned to look at the information boards.

"You've provided a comprehensive review of the details, Tom," Morris said without conviction. He turned back to Tom. "My team will be grateful when they arrive tomorrow."

"Your team?"

"Yes. We're taking over the Dale case, effective immediately."

Tom was about to respond when Tamara and

Chief Superintendent Watts entered the room. Tamara looked shocked to see him standing there and she hurried over.

"Tom, I see you've been introduced to DCI Morris. I wanted to speak to you first, but I missed you on the way in."

Watts joined them, exchanging brief pleasantries with Morris and then his eyes flitted between Tom and Tamara. "You've both made great strides in this investigation, but now it's clear that the remains found out in Ringstead belong to Angela Dale, there really is no alternative than to pass the investigation over to the review team from West Midlands CID."

Tom frowned. "We will be on hand to provide assistance."

"That won't be necessary, Tom," Morris said. "I think it is best for all concerned if the locals step aside." The rebuke was far stronger than Tom cared to hear. "I'm sure you understand, Tom," Morris said. "Fresh sets of eyes and all that."

Tom didn't understand at all. He and his team had had no involvement in the previous case and the man's attitude struck him as someone dismissing regional CID as worthless in favour of his own officers.

"Of course, sir," Tom said, keeping his tone even. He caught Tamara's look in the corner of his eye. She knew what he was thinking and when he glanced towards her, as Morris and Watts switched their conversation towards protocol discussions around media announcements, Tamara shook her head almost imperceptibly. He held his tongue, indicating towards his office with a nod.

"Excuse us, would you?" Tamara said but the two men merely glanced in her direction as she and Tom moved off. Cassie had already returned to her desk and was gathering files. Tom led Tamara into his office and closed the door.

"This is nonsense," Tom said, his frustration bubbling to the surface.

Tamara raised her hands before her, a gesture to placate him. "Come on, we knew this day would come. Crake's release was always going to spark a review and us finding Angela has expedited it."

"We're just getting going and what happens now?" Tom cast a dark glance through the window to DCI Morris but was careful to ensure it wasn't clear that he was venting. "His lot aren't going to know anything about what it's like living around here. Bypassing us will only slow things down."

"I know. I've had this conversation with Watts."

"Speaking of whom," Tom said. "He has questions to answer."

Something in his tone must have piqued her interest because Tamara cocked her head. "Questions about what?" Whether she realised she'd lowered her voice or not, Tom didn't know.

"All this incongruity around Charlie Babcock's statements along with those of others pushing us towards him."

He dropped it as a brief knock on his office door was followed by the chief superintendent, DCI Morris in tow, entering without being bidden.

"Tamara, Tom," he said, frowning, "I understand that this must be galling for you, but I have every faith in DCI Morris and his team to get to the bottom of it. No doubt, they'll expect an early briefing from you—"

"Actually, that won't be required, Chief Superintendent," Morris said. "I'm sure the case files will be more than adequate."

"Oh… well," Watts said, "I suppose so."

Morris looked between Tom and Tamara. "But if your team could have any relevant documentation ready for us first thing, then that would be appreciated." He looked behind them into ops. "This is a little smaller than I'm used to for an incident room. Is there anywhere a little larger? My team will be tripping over one another out there."

Tamara pursed her lips. "I'm sure we can find you something suitable."

"Excellent, Tamara. Thank you," Morris said, smiling. "What's your broadband like around here?"

"Decent," Tom said flatly, irritated. Tamara noticed.

"Right, well, if there's anything else you need."

"No, I think I have everything covered, Tamara. Thank you. I'll head off and check into my hotel. Get myself prepared for tomorrow."

Watts cleared his throat. "If you would like a recommendation for somewhere to eat, I know of a cracking little restaurant that does great seafood. If you care to join me?"

"No, thank you. I prefer to maintain boundaries between my team and the locals, sir. It keeps things neat and tidy."

"Oh, right," Watts said, visibly disappointed.

"I'm sure you understand why, sir?"

"Of course," Watts said. Clearly he didn't. Tom found himself questioning why the chief superintendent was so keen; courtesy or something else?

"It'll be nice for your team to get back to everyday policing again," Morris said, looking at Tamara. "We'll do the heavy lifting on this one and let you all get back to normal. Have a good evening, everyone." He looked at Watts. "Goodnight sir."

Tamara smiled. Tom knew it was forced but Morris didn't notice as he turned to leave. Almost as an afterthought, Morris turned to the Chief Superintendent.

"Could one of your chaps organise a press conference for tomorrow, sir?"

"Yes… yes, of course."

"Midday would be good."

Watts nodded. "I'll see to it."

The chief superintendent's keenness to assist had dissipated and his expression darkened as Morris thanked him and left the office.

"What does he think we do around here; arrest shoplifters and kids throwing bags of flour at old ladies?" he grumbled.

"The superstars are in the building," Tamara said, arching her eyebrows.

Watts glanced at her, bobbing his head. Wrinkling his nose, he shook his head. "Oh well, I suppose it's not our problem anymore."

"Sir?" Tom asked. Watts looked at him enquiringly. "Can I ask you about Charles Babcock?"

Watts inclined his head, his eyes narrowing. Tamara initially seemed surprised but as she read Tom's expression it shifted to concern.

"Charles?" Watts asked.

"He is your nephew, isn't he, sir?"

Watts drew himself upright but his expression was fixed. He offered a curt nod. "Yes. He is my brother-in-law's son. Why do you ask?"

Tamara's mouth fell open and then she bit her lower lip. "Sir, Charles Babcock was a suspect in the Angela—"

"I'm well aware, Tamara," Watts said sharply. He looked at Tom. "Is there something on your mind, Tom?"

"Why didn't you disclose this information?"

Watts kept his tone even, his response measured. "In the original investigation or now?"

"Both."

"The original investigation team were well aware, although it had no bearing on the case."

"No bearing?" Tamara said before Tom had a chance to. "Your nephew was a suspect in a murder inquiry."

Watts shook his head. "We had already identified our chief suspect, quickly found corroborating strong evidence to strongly suggest we had our man." He shook his head. "Charlie was a victim, just as much as any of Angela's other family or friends. As I said, no bearing."

"You should have recused yourself, sir," Tom said.

Watts turned on him. "It sounds like you have something else to say, Detective Inspector."

Tom averted his eyes from Watts' scrutiny, fearing he'd overstepped the line. Tamara sought to intervene.

"Sir, it wasn't appropriate."

"I will decide whether that is the case or not, Tamara," he said sternly. "We had our chief suspect in custody. Charles was due to be attending the Royal Military Academy at Sandhurst in the following months. I saw no reason to drag the young man through the mud prior to that."

"That wasn't your call, sir," Tamara said.

Watts stared hard at her and then his eyes fell upon Tom. "Are you suggesting something untoward has happened here?"

Tamara stepped forward. "I'm sure that's not what Tom is suggesting."

"Who took his statement?" Tom asked.

"I don't understand why you're asking."

"Because what he told you back then doesn't tie up with what we are learning today, so something has gone awry, sir."

Watts' gaze narrowed. "I don't appreciate your tone, Inspector. What exactly are you implying?"

Tom shrugged. "I'm trying to understand the apparent inconsistency between what people were saying and what was officially taken down during the investigation."

"No, Tom, that is not what you are doing at all. You're suggesting there has been malpractice during the investigation. At least have the courage to say so, man!"

Tamara stepped forward, coming between the two men. "I think we all need to take a moment and consider what we say next before this escalates."

Watts glared at her and then Tom, bristling with indignation. He nodded to her and looked hard at Tom. "I can see you're frustrated at leaving this investigation before its conclusion, Tom. However, I would advise you to think twice before you raise unfounded allegations in the future."

Tom remained steadfast and silent. Watts lingered, hopeful of a response but when none was forthcoming, he left the office without a backward glance. Tamara let out a slow breath and rolled her eyes at Tom.

"Perhaps, in future, you should raise such concerns with me first. What do you think?"

Tom's shoulders sagged as he looked to the ceiling and drew a deep breath. "Probably be wise."

"Certainly, for your career," she said, cutting a wry smile.

Tom laughed, more from relief than humour. Cassie appeared at the door, raising her eyebrows and inclining her head towards where Watts had stomped out of the ops room in apparent disgust.

"All is not well in paradise?" she asked.

Tom looked away and Tamara quickly changed the subject. "Have you gathered everything for DCI Morris?"

"I gave him his travel pack as he left," Cassie said. "Bit spivvy, isn't he?"

Tamara sighed and Cassie shrugged. "Well he is! Thinks he's it. If his team are anything like him, then I'm happy to be out of it. Is he any good?"

Tamara nodded. "Supposed to be, yes. You get yourself off home, Cass."

Cassie shook her head. "Nope. I'm the CID cover, but I've sent Eric home. At least I'll be able to get back to my other cases. I've not looked at them since all this went off."

Tamara smiled. Tom, meanwhile, had taken his seat and was lost in thought, one hand resting on his chin. Cassie smiled at Tamara and left.

"What are you going to do this evening, Tom?" Tamara said, perching herself on the edge of his desk.

Breaking away from his thoughts, Tom sighed and glanced at his watch. "I promised to take Saffy to the circus this weekend."

"You're cutting it fine. Tonight's the last night."

Tom waved away her concerns. "I bought tickets for the three of us on Friday. If I couldn't make it, Alice would take her by herself."

"DCI Morris to the rescue then, huh?"

Tom smiled.

CHAPTER TWENTY-TWO

SAFFY GASPED, along with the majority of the audience as the woman was released forty feet above the ground, watching as she twisted herself through a double somersault before being caught with apparent effortless ease by a man suspended upside down from a trapeze, hanging by his knees. It was a move so well-choreographed that it was seamless.

The routine continued, perfectly supported by a rendition of Holst's 'Jupiter' providing tumultuous orchestral moments in tandem with the thrilling display. Tom was in awe of how well drilled the acrobats must be to pull it off. And then it was over, the lights going out with the final fling in sync with the last beat of the drum. The audience were on their feet applauding. Alice leaned into Tom so that he could hear above the cheering.

"Do you remember when we first started dating and you told me you could do a back flip?"

He looked at her and smiled, still clapping. "I remember it was about fourth on the list of requirements you had for any boyfriend."

"You never did prove it."

Tom cocked his head. "You stuck around though."

She laughed as they retook their seats.

"And don't think you'll have me trying now," he said. "I'll put my back out."

The ringmaster, illuminated by a spotlight, came to the centre of the ring, a piece of paper in hand.

"Let's hear it one more time for the greatest of all flying trapeze artists!" he called and the audience offered another enthusiastic response as the family of aerial gymnasts came to the fore and took a bow. Saffy applauded, grinning ear to ear. "And before we welcome our next act to the ring, we have another draw from our raffle."

Saffy turned to her mum and held out her hand for the raffle tickets. Alice obliged and Saffy clutched them in both hands as if they were cold, hard cash, waiting expectantly. The ringmaster was well into his pitch by now, building the excitement. Alice turned to Tom.

"I found out why Mum has been so coy about her treatments recently."

Tom gave her an inquisitive look, seeing the concern etched into her face. "What's going on?"

"The latest round of chemo hasn't gone well." Alice was looking down towards the ringmaster, but she wasn't really looking at him, staring straight ahead. "It's not looking good."

Tom touched her forearm, encouraging her to look at him. "What did she say?"

"Her consultant has put her forward for a new clinical trial."

"That's good, isn't it?"

Alice grimaced. "But he's not confident that she'll be well enough to proceed with it. He told her she needs to have her affairs in order."

Tom let out a deep breath, taking her hand in his and squeezing it gently. Alice forced a smile.

"That's us!" Saffy screamed. Both of them looked at her, Saffy brandishing a strip of five three-digit numbers printed on thin, green paper. "We won!"

Tom and Alice exchanged glances, unsure as they'd been so preoccupied that they hadn't heard the announcement.

"Ticket number four hundred and thirty!" the ringmaster called again, his eyes searching the audience for a claimant. Tom checked the ticket and nodded, smiling.

"Here!" he shouted. The ringmaster looked in his direction and Saffy leapt up and down on the spot to ensure they were seen, waving the tickets like a mad woman. Tom touched her arm and gestured for her to head down to collect the prize. Saffy, needing no further encouragement slipped out into the aisle and took off at speed to the ring, a spotlight tracking her all the way. Tom turned to Alice, who was smiling, but he could see her eyes were moist. "I'm here for you," he said. "We'll all face it together."

She nodded and leaned into him, their foreheads touching momentarily, before they watched Saffy collect her prize, a cuddly toy elephant, which was almost as big as she was. Miraculously, she managed to carry it back to her seat without stumbling on the steps, receiving her own round of applause. Alice looped an arm around her daughter and pulled her in for a hug.

Tom smiled and turned his attention back to the ring, his attention drawn to two figures below them, off to their left. Two women, one older than the other, and she was remonstrating with her, trying to lead the younger away. Tom recognised Marsha and Susan Brock. Susan was seemingly reluctant to go with her mother, dragging her arm away which only seemed to incense her mother.

Tom touched Alice's forearm, getting her attention just as the next act was introduced. "I'll be right back."

Alice nodded and Tom got out of his seat, apologising as he squeezed past others to his left. The Brocks were on the move and he lost sight of them as he descended to the arena floor, following their route away from the audience and into the darker depths of the big top. A shout went up from the audience as the next act began, Tom seeing the knife thrower line up his first throw, hurling several blades, one after another, at a target fifteen feet away. Only now did he realise it wasn't Daniel Turner, but another whom he hadn't met before.

Pausing at the straw-bale barrier, separating the ring from the walkway and the audience, Tom looked for Turner's assistant. She stepped into the spotlight, taking up a position in front of the circular, wooden target as the thrower retrieved his blades. He turned and demonstrated that the target was mounted and could spin. He then set about shackling his assistant to the disc by her wrists and ankles. Whoever she was, it wasn't Aislene.

Tom set off in search of Marsha and Susan, unsure of why his curiosity was piqued. Behind the entrance to the arena a huge navy blue curtain hung from scaffolding above, masking the acts readying themselves to enter and take centre stage. Two further curtains hung to the left and right ensuring the audience members at the extremities could not see the build-up from their vantage points.

The area was a hive of activity with one person controlling sound and another operating the lighting sequences, all prearranged and practised to perfection. Performers were readying themselves, adjusting clothing or carrying out last-minute inspections of props or clothing. No one noticed him and he passed by unchallenged. He almost collided with the Brocks as he rounded a corner behind a raised platform that would be wheeled forward into the arena at some point later in the performance.

"…want to know where…" Susan was heard saying as her mother cut her off, scoffing.

"You shouldn't be around these people!"

Both women were startled by Tom's appearance beside them and he regretted not having been able to hear more of their conversation.

"Ladies," Tom said, looking between them. Susan was open mouthed whereas Marsha lowered her eyes and bit her bottom lip. "What are you doing back here this evening?"

Neither seemed willing to answer.

"Good evening, Inspector Janssen," Susan said with reticence.

"No Jack with you this time, Susan?"

Marsha shot her daughter a dark look and Susan was visibly uncomfortable.

"No, I don't know where Jack is tonight."

Tom nodded. "What is it you want to know, Susan?"

She was shocked, suddenly fearful. Perhaps scared of how much he'd overheard.

"I… I…"

Tom was irritated. So many people wanted the truth about what happened to Angela and yet no one seemed willing to be honest with those tasked with getting to the bottom of it.

"You're testing my patience, Susan."

Marsha was indignant. "You shouldn't speak to my daughter like that. She's done nothing wrong."

Tom ignored the comment. "Susan, what is it you think these people are hiding?"

"I'm looking for Jack. I thought he might be here."

"In search of answers?"

"Aislene knows *something,*" Susan protested.

"How can you be so sure?"

She shook her head. "Jack is adamant that they know what happened or, at least, they can help to prove it."

"Okay. Why is Jack so sure?"

"Aislene saw Angela with someone that week-end. She said as much when Angela went missing."

"She wasn't so sure when she spoke to us."

Susan looked at her mother who frowned. "She

didn't want to get involved. I begged her, so did Jack. He got angry with her but DT got involved and for a moment I was really worried it was all going to kick off. DT said that you – the police – had their guy… and there was no need for Aislene to get involved in something that was none of their business."

"Inferring that Ben was guilty?"

She nodded. "And that's why we were here the other day… and now."

"Ben's been released and Jack thinks Aislene holds the evidence that could put Ben back in prison?"

"Exactly."

Tom felt his anger rising. "Then why didn't you damn well tell us this as soon as we asked?"

"Because these people won't go to the police… they don't *trust you*. And can you blame them?"

"Susan!" Marsha said. She turned to Tom. "I'm so sorry, Inspector. Susan is not normally… like this."

Tom held up his hand. "It is okay, Mrs Brock. I understand where she's coming from. Relations between the travelling communities and the police are often strained." He looked at Susan. "But you still should have told me. You came here alone tonight?"

Susan nodded.

"So, where's Jack?"

She shook her head. "I thought he might be here."

Tom inclined his head.

"It's true! I thought… hoped, he would be."

"Oi! What are you lot doing back here?"

Tom turned to see Ian Gallagher approaching, a headset in place over one ear with a wraparound microphone by his mouth, clutching a clipboard.

"Ah, sorry, Inspector," he said, recognising Tom. "I didn't realise it was you. It's all a bit chaotic around here tonight."

"I noticed some change of faces out there," Tom said, looking at the curtain as if he could see through it to the circus arena beyond.

"You wouldn't believe it! Acts going AWOL an hour before the show begins. It's taken some rejigging I can tell you."

Tom smiled. "You wouldn't notice. It's been great."

Gallagher's face lit up. "Oh, you're not here officially then?"

"No, I brought the family."

He was puzzled. "You'll not be seeing much back here." His eyes flitted between all of them, lingering on Susan. "In fact, none of you should be back here at all, to be honest." He gestured with an open palm, directing them to the nearest exit behind them.

"Yes, of course," Marsha said. "Sorry." She took

Susan by the elbow and assertively guided her to the exit; only once did she look back at Tom who watched them go.

"What's all that about then?" Gallagher asked.

Tom shook his head. "I wish I knew. I really do."

"I don't suppose you brought Cassandra with you, by any chance?"

"Cassie? No."

Gallagher smiled wryly. "Shame that. I wouldn't mind seeing her again."

"I'll pass it on."

"Maybe next time. We leave tomorrow."

"Early start packing up?"

"Work starts as soon as you lot leave tonight Inspector. It'll pretty much just be the big top that has to come down tomorrow."

"No rest for the wicked?"

"Blessed is he who has found his work; let him ask no other… something or other, Inspector."

"Are you a religious man, Mr Gallagher?"

"That's not scripture, Inspector. That was Carlyle… Robert or Thomas. I can't remember which."

"Robert is an actor, if that helps?"

"Must be the other then," he said, holding up his hand to indicate he needed to concentrate as someone spoke into his earpiece. "Are you bloody kidding me?"

Tom saw his exasperation was genuine and

pointed to the exit, silently excusing himself. Gallagher started mouthing obscenities into his microphone and stalked off in the opposite direction. The cool breeze struck him as he stepped out from the cover of the tent. The warmth provided by the crowd of several hundred sitting closely together inside masked the real temperature. The cheering and applause of the audience was muted here, mixed as it was with the sound of the wind rattling in across The Wash.

He saw the Brocks in the distance as they reached the car park. Marsha unlocked her burgundy BMW and pointedly instructed Susan to get into the passenger side. There was a brief standoff before Susan relented and got in. He couldn't help but wonder what all that was about, a mother's fear for her daughter's safety no doubt.

Regretting not asking Gallagher where Aislene and her partner, Daniel Turner were, he gave thought to where Jack Dale was and what he was up to. He couldn't help but think the disappearing acts were somehow related. The crowd roared and Tom realised he'd been gone for some time. He hurried back inside and found his way back to his seat. Alice gave him a quizzical look and he waved it away with a flick of his hand, sitting down beside her and slipping an arm around her waist.

CHAPTER TWENTY-THREE

CASSIE DREW her raincoat around her. She could taste the salt in the air and smell the onset of the coming rain. The wind whipped her hair across her face and she wished she'd tied it back when she left for work this morning. Another car passed them, ushered through by a uniformed officer controlling traffic on the quiet coast road, now that one lane was closed off. The car inched by them as both driver and passenger tried to see what was going on beyond the taped cordon, illuminated by flashing blue lights.

PC Marshall returned from his patrol car; shoulder-mounted radio pressed as close to his ear as possible to hear the reply from central.

"Whose car is it, Sheriff?" Cassie asked, addressing him by his nickname.

Marshall looked over at the body lying on the grass verge – currently being appraised by Dr Williams – thrown there having been struck by a passing car, and then to a white minivan parked in the lay-by thirty yards further along the road. It was beaten up, rusting around the rear doors and wheel arches. The uniformed officers had found it unlocked and with the keys in the ignition. Cassie doubted it had a valid MOT. At least not a legitimate one.

"The van's registered to *Myriad Entertainments,*" Marshall said. "They're based in Lowestoft, Suffolk."

"That's the lot who run the circus in town at the moment, right?"

Marshall shrugged. "If you say so."

Behind him, Fiona Williams rose from her haunches and beckoned Cassie over to her.

"Thanks, Sheriff," Cassie said. The constable smiled. Crossing the short distance to the grass verge, she came alongside the doctor just as the first spots of rain could be felt on her face. "What do you think?"

Fiona Williams wrinkled her nose. "Well, you were right to call me out, Cass." She shook her head. "This isn't your standard hit-and-run," she said, glumly. "No doubt your technicians will be able to confirm it, but I think he was struck somewhere back there." She pointed down the road in the direction of the lay-by. "You see the impact point on both his legs." Cassie looked down. Both legs lay offset at unnatural angles at the kneecap. "I think he was thrown up and over the roof of the car, likely hitting the windscreen on the way."

"If we can find the car, then we'll certainly see that damage," Cassie said.

Fiona nodded. "Before landing in a heap on the road behind."

Cassie grimaced as she looked at the dead man. "That made a bit of a mess of him."

Blood was pooled beneath the body, although it had ceased to flow soon after death.

"That's why I don't think it's standard," the doctor said. "The damage to his legs is consistent with riding up and over the car. Plenty of stats to prove that from these injuries, but I think the car stopped and came back for a second pass."

Cassie frowned. "You think he was purposefully run over again?"

Dr Williams inclined her head, pursing her lips. "I can't say it was deliberate. After all, I'm not in the driver's head, but look at the injuries. The clothing is shredded in places along the front; light fitting jacket and tee-shirt beneath. The jeans are harder wearing but even they have been torn. I think the car came back and ran him over. This time, seeing as he was on the ground, unconscious or not, he had no chance of getting out of the way with his legs smashed as they are. I reckon he was caught under the vehicle and dragged along the road, finally working free and ending up where we find him now. It's the only way to explain the injuries."

Cassie looked at the man's face, but only briefly before looking away. "Well, he may have been a real heart breaker or had looks that only his mother could love, but we'll never know by the state of him," she said, shaking her head.

"Delightfully put, DS Knight. Any idea who he is?"

Cassie shook her head. "Not carrying any ID and there's nothing in the van either. It's registered to the company putting on the circus, so it's fair to say it's one of their people."

"Presuming this man goes with the van?" Dr Williams said.

"No idea why they'd both be out here otherwise. I guess I'll go over there once we're through here and see who's missing."

Dr Williams frowned. "Not a nice way to go."

"Is there ever a nice way to go?"

"True enough. How long has he been lying here?"

"Not long. Someone came across him soon after, I guess?"

"Yes," Cassie nodded. "Another driver almost collided with a red car on a bend a quarter of a mile up the road. It was being driven erratically. Shook the driver up and she slowed, catching sight of our guy on the verge." She checked her watch. "That was barely three quarters of an hour ago."

"Well, the human body cools by roughly one to two degrees an hour after death occurs. He's outside, exposed to the elements, so I'd say he is at the higher end of the cooling scale. Although, the temperature at the body's core holds longer despite the elements. I'd say an hour, hour and a half at the most."

They were illuminated by the headlights of another vehicle drawing up at the cordon. It was the crime scene investigation team. Cassie smiled at the doctor. "Thanks for coming out, Fiona. Sorry to put a dampener on your Sunday."

"Well, I do get paid, Cassie," she said with a smile.

"Yeah, sometimes it's just not enough though, is it?"

"Considering a change of career, Detective Sergeant?"

Cassie laughed. "Primary school teacher, perhaps."

Dr Williams arched her eyebrows. "I'm not sure that's any less stressful, although far fewer bodies."

"One would hope," Cassie said, beckoning the

first technician over. The rain was falling steadily now and she was keen to have the body under cover as soon as possible. In the dark it was hard to tell, but you never know, there may be trace evidence present that could be washed away.

THE FINALE of the performance took the roof off. Everyone in the audience was up on their feet applauding, bathed in a colourful light show accompanying the final acts. Each act was introduced back into the arena to acknowledge the applause. The acrobats tumbled in in style, whereas others came back riding horses, providing yet more entertainment. Tom glanced past Alice at Saffy who was utterly bewitched by the entire show.

And then it was over, the colourful lights replaced by white lights, suspended high above them in the gantry, to see by and to enable everyone to leave the tent safely. A few remained in their seats, keen to avoid the rush to the car park. Saffy looked up at both Tom and Alice, grinning maniacally.

"I want to join the circus!" she stated.

Alice and Tom exchanged looks.

"Now see what you've gone and done!" Alice said, much to Saffy's amusement.

"Can I?" Saffy asked, pleading whilst hanging onto her mother's dress.

"What is it you want to do in the circus?" Tom asked.

"Acrobat… no, wait…" she thought hard. "Fire breather," she announced victoriously, wide-eyed. "A fire-breathing acrobat!"

Tom frowned. "You want to be a dragon?"

"That could be my stage name," she said, smiling.

Alice rolled her eyes. "Wasn't there a prime minister who ran away to join the circus once?"

Tom concentrated. "You're thinking of John Major, and his father was a performer. So, maybe it'd be closer to say John ran away from the circus to become a politician."

Alice smiled. "Close enough." Something caught her eye and she strained her neck to see over and through the crowd. "Isn't that Cassie?"

Tom followed her gaze, struggling to see through the press of people.

"You didn't say she was coming too."

"She wasn't. She's on shift this evening. I wonder what's going on?"

"Do you want to go and ask?" Alice asked.

Tom met her eye and shrugged. "Nah, I'll find out tomorrow."

However, he lingered as they got up to join the exodus, his eyes following Cassie as she made her way to the rear and out of sight.

"Oh, for heaven's sake, Tom. Just go and ask."

He met her eye. She wasn't annoyed. Amused was closer to it.

"You don't mind?"

"Heck no. You'll only be texting her within the hour if you don't anyway."

He laughed.

"Can I come and see Aunty Cass?" Saffy asked.

"No, you can come and wait with me in the car," Alice said. Saffy was disappointed. "Aunty Cass is working and you can tell her about your new career path next time we see her."

"Aunty Cass would let me join the circus."

Alice raised her eyebrows and smiled. "Aunty Cass would let you juggle chainsaws if you asked her."

"Yes, she's fun," Saffy said, grinning.

"I'll see you in the car," Tom said, passing her his keys.

Alice nodded and the two of them set off down the steps to ground-floor level. The crowd was thinning now as the tent emptied. Tom made his way down as he had done before during the show and slipped through the break in the curtains.

Cassie was talking to Ian Gallagher. He approached them and Cassie smiled.

"Did you enjoy the show?" she asked.

"Loved it," Tom said, more to Gallagher than to her. "What brings you here?"

"Trying to identify a hit-and-run."

Tom knew it wasn't a CID role to find and notify next of kin in a traffic accident, so he was curious as to why Cassie was here. Not that he said as much.

Gallagher was concerned, standing hands on hips, his brow deep set in a frown. "As far as I know, we're only missing two; DT and Aislene."

Cassie looked at Tom. Something in her eyes told him she was suppressing her surprise.

"When did you last see them?" Cassie asked, making a note.

Gallagher thought about it. "They were here for the lunchtime performance, but I didn't see them after… three-ish, I guess. Have they been in an accident?"

"I'm afraid it would appear so."

"Are they going to be all right?" Gallagher asked.

Cassie looked at Tom and then back at Gallagher. "Can I ask who DT… Daniel's next of kin is?"

"That'll be his dad, Cory. He's the lead in the acrobats. What's going on, is DT okay?"

"I think I need to speak to his father."

"And Aislene? What about her?"

Cassie shook her head. "As far as we know, she wasn't involved in the accident."

Gallagher thrust his hand into his pocket and took out his mobile. "I'll call her." He dialled her number and waited. "Damn it! Straight to voicemail, same as earlier."

Tom caught Gallagher's attention. "Maybe you could go and find Cory Turner for us?"

"Y–Yes, of course." He looked at Cassie, nodded and went to find the acrobat.

Once Tom was sure they were alone, he asked, "What's going on?"

"I'm not sure, but I'll tell you what I know. There's been a hit-and-run. One male, dead at the scene. It likely happened two hours ago," she said, checking her watch. "It seemed odd, so I called Fiona out and she reckons it was arguably deliberate; he was struck and then the driver returned and ran him over a second time, just to make certain they'd got him, you know."

"Not a second car accidentally driving over the body having not seen them? It happens a lot with motorcycle accidents."

Cassie paused for thought. "Maybe, but it's out in the middle of nowhere. Why would he park up in a lay-by and stand in the road? I checked his van; started first time. No idea how because it's a heap, but they must keep things ticking over around here."

"Without their vehicles, they can't earn, so that

stands to reason. Have you still got people on the scene?"

"Yeah, SOCO are processing it. Sheriff's out there as well."

"Right, have him widen the search to see if Aislene is there somewhere. Maybe she was pitched into a field or is lying in a ditch or something."

Cassie nodded, reaching for her mobile. "Good call."

"Do you know if Ben Crake or Jack Dale have a car?"

Cassie concentrated, already with her mobile pressed to her ear. She shook her head. "Ben? Not as far as I know, but I haven't a clue about Jack. Why?"

"Something Susan Brock said to me earlier, that's all."

"Susan was here?" Cassie asked, just as PC Marshall answered his phone. "Sheriff, I need you and whoever else you have there to spread out a bit and see if you can find another body. We're looking for a female, white, in her twenties and was likely with the deceased. Keep me posted, yeah?"

She put the mobile away. Cory Turner strode into view with Ian Gallagher a half step behind. She bit her bottom lip. "I hate this bit."

Tom nodded. "I'll take Alice and Saffy home, and then I'll be back."

"No need," Cassie said. "You go home. I'll have a poke around here and give you a call in a bit."

"Are you sure?" Tom asked.

"Yes," she implored him. "Go and be with your family for an hour or so. They'll forget what you look like otherwise." Before Tom could answer, she stepped away and moved to meet Daniel Turner's father.

CHAPTER TWENTY-FOUR

IAN GALLAGHER LED CASSIE through the community of tightly packed caravans and mobile homes that made up the accommodation for those associated with the circus. Many of them had Transit vans or SUVs parked behind or alongside them. Children ran between them hollering and shouting, excited to be moving to their next destination. Whilst most people were already setting about taking down the scaffolds and packing up equipment, others were readying their vehicles and packing their belongings for departure. Some would leave straight away and begin preparations of the next site before the bulk of the crew arrived throughout the coming week.

"Where did you say you were heading?" Cassie asked.

"Great Yarmouth. Then we are going to Ely before breaking for the winter holiday in December for Christmas and New Year," he said over his shoulder, sidestepping a boy barely in his teens and casually taking a swipe at the back of his head as he passed. "Get out of it, Bobby!" Gallagher sighed, shaking his head as he watched the boy run off, grinning back at him as he caught up with his friends. "It's been a tough season this one. I think we're all looking forward to a break."

"How has it been tough?" Cassie asked, looking around them at the hive of activity on site. Having performed one show on Friday and two each day of the weekend, the team were already dismantling everything at a rate of knots. They certainly didn't take things easy in this line of work.

Gallagher looked glum. "Attendances have been down… and no one is really sure why." He shrugged. "Maybe we need to move further afield and tap a new audience. I don't know. Opinion is divided."

"Do you work as some sort of collective; shared profits and that?"

He scoffed. "I'd love it if we did! No, we all have to negotiate our own rates and, like anything else, it comes down to a mixture of things; talent, experience… who you're related to."

"Nepotism in the circus?"

Gallagher looked at her sternly. "Things in our community aren't all that different from life in yours. You'd be surprised, DS Knight."

She cocked her head. "I am every time I visit."

His gaze lingered on her for a moment as they walked. She wasn't being sarcastic for once. He seemed to accept the comment at face value. Slowing his pace as they approached a motorhome, Gallagher pointed to it.

"This is theirs."

It was fairly large, but she'd seen bigger, in a reasonable condition, but it certainly wasn't new. A box trailer was set behind it and Cassie assumed that was what they used to transport their stage props, clothing and materials.

Cassie tried the door but it was locked.

"Do you have a key?"

Gallagher shook his head. Cassie was disappointed. The windows were shrouded by net curtains and even with her face pressed against the Perspex windows, she couldn't make out any detail in the dark interior.

"Shame. I really want to have a poke around inside."

"Don't you need a warrant for that?"

Cassie smiled at him. "I'm not gathering evidence. I want to find her and make sure she's safe."

"Ah… yeah, of course."

Gallagher glanced around to see if they were alone. The site was busy but DT and Aislene's motor home was at the rear of the field, on the periphery of all the vehicles parked up. No one was paying them any attention. Reaching into his back pocket, he produced a slim black pouch and eased himself past Cassie. She watched as he opened it, taking out two narrow metal implements. They looked akin to stainless-steel tweezers, only with one arm missing. The end of the first was pointed and the other had a misshapen head.

He glanced at her, and then cast another look around them before gently slipping both into the lock on the door, one at the top and the other below. Cassie turned her back and took a step to her right, providing him cover.

"This won't take a sec," he said, and moments later, he tried the door and it opened.

"I do not want to know how or why you learned to do that," Cassie said, shaking her head.

Gallagher grinned. "My dad worked as a locksmith for years. I used to go with him on jobs."

She nodded. "I believe you, but thousands wouldn't."

He moved aside and Cassie stepped up into the mobile home, searching for a light switch either side of the door. Illuminating the interior, she looked from left to right. The front seats were both captain's chairs and were facing inwards. Behind these, against the side wall was a small two-seater that doubled as a sofa and another single chair, also swivelled to face inwards, was opposite it. Directly in front of her was the kitchen with an oven and hot plate, sink and food prep area. Looking to her left Cassie saw a closed door that she presumed was the toilet and shower room and at the back of the motorhome was a dining table with wrap-around seating. No doubt this doubled as a bed.

The interior was cluttered and untidy. It must be difficult to manage your entire life in such a space. To Cassie, it felt cramped and claustrophobic. Gallagher had entered behind her and must have read the expression on her face.

"To us, it's home."

She smiled. "Anything seem odd or out of place to you?" she asked, moving through the space, taking in every detail.

"Um..." Gallagher looked around. "No, can't say it does."

Cassie opened the kitchen cabinets, inspecting the contents and finding what one might expect. There was nothing unusual. Moving to the rear, there were storage compartments built in everywhere to utilise the space. Casually opening them, she rifled through the contents: clothing, paperwork and assorted items collected over time.

In an overhead compartment, she found a mobile phone box which looked brand new and she took it out. The box felt light and, having opened it, aside from the phone not being there, you'd have thought the cellophane wrapping had only just been removed. A printed label on the exterior denoted the barcode and beneath that was the model of phone, as well as the IMEI and serial numbers. The majority of the packaging was still inside, including the laminated card with the mobile and SIM card number.

Holding the card up for Gallagher to see, she asked, "Do you recognise this number?"

He frowned, typing the digits into his own phone before shaking his head.

"It's not one I have for DT or Aislene."

Cassie took out her own mobile and photographed the details on the card as well as the box before typing out a message. She attached the photos and then hit send before calling Eric. It took several rings before he answered.

"Eric, I've just sent you some details of a mobile phone. I reckon it's being used as a burner."

"Whose is it?" he asked, sounding groggy. Cassie checked the time. He might have got an early night and she felt bad for waking him.

"Either Daniel Turner's or his partner, Aislene. Maybe both."

"I… thought we were off that case?"

"Things have moved on, Eric. All hands to the pumps and all that!"

"Okay… I'll head into the office. I take it you need it all now?"

"Yep, everything we can find out and we need it now." She glanced at Gallagher, wondering if she should say more in front of him or not. "It's important, Eric. Really important."

"I'm on it."

She hung up, reading Gallagher's expression as he analysed her.

"What do you think is going on?" he asked, concern edging into his tone.

"To be honest, I don't know," she said. "The best thing we can do is to keep looking."

She resumed her search, retrieving a shoe box from the same compartment where she'd found the mobile phone. It felt too light to contain shoes and she put it on the table, lifting the lid.

"Well, well, well," she said, arching her eyebrows. She looked at Gallagher, indicating the contents with a nod. "Is this normal?"

He crossed to stand alongside and looked past her, exhaling through pursed lips.

"Bloody hell. No, it's not. Not in my van anyway."

The box was full of cash. Not used notes, but bundled sets of twenty-pound notes, neatly stacked and wrapped with paper bands as if they were freshly withdrawn from the bank. It was hard to say if this was recent because the UK Mint was printing twenties on polymer now rather than paper and these new notes remained clean and shiny in appearance. Even so, the paper ties suggested they were fresh.

Cassie photographed them in situ before picking up the money. At a rough count, bundled as they were in groups of five hundred, Cassie figured there was at least ten thousand pounds in that box, but likely to be more.

"Cheeky sods," Gallagher muttered.

"What's that?"

"Oh… nothing," he said, embarrassed. "DT owes me a ton since… forever. He's been fobbing me off for weeks, and I really needed the money too."

"Has he seemed flush with cash recently?"

"No… I'd say quite the opposite."

"Any idea where they might have got this from?"

Gallagher exhaled heavily, averting his eyes from her gaze.

"And don't give me any of your code of silence rubbish, Ian," she said, tilting her head and catching his eye. She indicated the money. "This is serious cash. It looks like Daniel is dead… and it's likely this money has something to do with it. What was he involved in?"

Gallagher shook his head. Cassie frowned.

"Honestly!" he said. "I really don't know. I mean, he sold a bit of weed on the side in the past, but not in any quantities that would generate a store of cash like that!" He pointed at the money, shaking his head in disbelief. "Look at it! That's a shed load of cash."

Cassie nodded. Flicking through the bundles, she figured they had all come to DT and Aislene in one go rather than the stash building up over time.

"So, he was dealing?"

Gallagher scoffed. "In the past! Like I said, and nothing on this scale. Not to my knowledge."

"And you would know?"

"Of course I would know." He threw his hands wide. "We would all know!"

"Okay. What about recently. What's he been like? Aislene as well."

"I don't know… what do you mean?"

"Behaviour. Happy, sad… cock-a-hoop?"

Gallagher's brow creased as he concentrated. "I suppose they've been all right. No, better than all right. Pleading poverty, the lying scrote, but apart from that."

"What about the money he owed you? Did you think he was going to pay you back?"

"Yeah, yeah, I did. DT was a bit of a scoundrel, but he was okay. He'd always come good. He told me he was sorting some things out, things he'd been working on for a while, and that he'd see me right, if I gave him a few more weeks."

"How did you take that?"

He shrugged. "At first, I thought he was mugging me off a bit, you know? But, as I said, he always comes good. If I'd known he had this, I'd have kicked his teeth in."

Cassie inclined her head.

"Well, metaphorically speaking," he said quietly. "DT can take care of himself."

Cassie pondered all of this. It was one thing to keep the money secret, but if you owed a friend a pittance in comparison; why not pay up? Unless the money was set aside for something else or he genuinely didn't have it.

"Maybe he was telling the truth," she said aloud.

"What's that you say?"

"Oh, nothing," she said, waving away his question. "Before, just now, you said at first you thought he was mugging you off. What about after? It sounds like you had another thought."

"Yeah… well, I wondered if he might be off. Him and Aislene like, you know?"

"Off where? Leaving the circus?"

He nodded. "Aye, yeah. DT is a real performer. I mean, everyone is decent… all of the performers are skilled in what they do, but DT is something else. He's the real star of the show. Back when he was with his family in the acrobatic show, he was the star then too. He was always pushing it that little bit further than anyone else. Pushing all of them to go that bit extra, one more twist, if you like? Not that he was arrogant or anything… but damn he was good, and everyone knew it."

"He formed his own act."

"Yeah. And it's the best one too." He shook his head. "We really missed him tonight. I mean, the others are still good, entertaining, but DT is special. That's why I thought he might be moving on. It's no secret that other shows have tried to poach him before."

"But he always stayed?"

"Yeah, he did… family loyalty and that, but recently… what with the way things have been going financially for the show, it kinda made sense that they – DT and Aislene – might take up one of the offers. There's huge money available for some of the bigger shows."

"But they'd expect more too, though, right? Like you said, your world isn't too dissimilar from mine."

"Yeah, that's true. You earn your money, right enough."

"Big fish in a small pond or minnow in a lake," she argued.

"You're not wrong," Gallagher said. "And despite all his bravado… I still wondered whether he could succeed in that environment." He looked at the cash again. "But I guess he had something else in mind. You really think this might have got him killed? I thought you told his old man it was a hit-and-run?"

"Perhaps that's what we're supposed to think."

CHAPTER TWENTY-FIVE

TOM LEANED over and kissed Saffy's forehead. Her eyes didn't open but she grasped her duvet and pulled it up under her chin, exhaling deeply as her grip tightened on the material. He was surprised how easily the little girl nodded off, having done so in the car on the way home. Exhilarated by the entire show, Saffy had been full-on immediately after the performance. However, even having finished off a stick of candy floss almost as big as she was – aside from the clumps she tore off and handed to both Tom and Alice – she'd still fallen asleep on the drive home.

Switching on her night light, Tom reached for the elephant she'd won at the circus and placed it at the foot of her bed. Backing out of the room, he eased the door to, but left a gap allowing a sliver of light from the landing to penetrate the room.

He made his way downstairs, Russell, their ever-present terrier, padding out to meet him. Alice was in the kitchen making herself a cup of decaf tea and turned as he entered, head down flicking through screens on his mobile.

"Do you have to go in?"

He nodded, glumly, looking up and placing his mobile on the breakfast bar.

"Yes. I'm afraid I don't know when I'll be back either."

"I thought you said someone else was taking over the case?"

"They are, but not officially until tomorrow morning and," he sighed, "this might not even be related."

"Have you heard from Tamara?"

"No. I sent her a message but she's not picked it up yet."

Alice was deflated. The stress of dealing with her mum's illness in the past months had been hard enough but it was approached in the belief that the situation was improving. That bubble had burst and Alice had been holding it in, likely to avoid Saffy being upset, and now he had to go back to work.

Reaching out, he drew her to him and hugged her tightly, Alice putting her head on his chest.

"We will talk about all of this," he said. "Just as soon as I get home. Maybe once Saffy's at school, we could—"

Alice withdrew from him a little, angling her face up towards his. "I have to be on the ward for eight-thirty. Saffy's booked into breakfast club."

Tom inwardly cursed.

"We'll make time. I promise."

She nodded, smiling weakly. Tom kissed her and she responded briefly before placing her hands on his chest and gently pushing him away.

"You need to go and do your stuff, Detective Inspector," she said, her voice cracking slightly. He dabbed at the corner of her left eye with his sleeve and smiled warmly.

"I love you," he said.

"I love you too," Alice replied.

Tom's mobile rang and he shook his head, scooping it up and glancing at the screen. He was surprised. It was Olivia Goldman.

"I need to take this," he said, apologetically. Alice patted his chest with her palms.

"Go and do what you need to do."

He smiled, backing away and silently mouthing the words *I love you* once again as he answered the ringing phone.

"Tom, I'm so sorry to trouble you this late on a Sunday."

"That's okay, Olivia," he said, opening the front

door and levering the dog out of the way with the side of his foot, blocking him from following him outside. "I'm working. What can I do for you?"

"It's Ben…"

Her tone was off. She was on speaker; he was sure of that but there was something else. Something was wrong.

"What is it?"

"I don't know. I check in with him every day. I have done since he came out of prison." She hesitated. "I've been worrying about his mental health for a while, and I thought it would get better when he came home but…"

"It hasn't?" Tom asked, getting into his car.

"No. I thought being in his own home, surrounded by memories of better times would help, but I think the loss of his mother and those last years of her life are affecting him more than I realised."

"How was he last time you spoke?"

"I've been calling him every day, and yesterday I felt he was doing all right, but today… I've been calling and calling…"

"No answer?"

"No. I'm on my way over there now," she said, fearful. "If there's no answer when I get there… I know I have no right to ask this of you, but you did say you were willing to help Ben if he needed it."

"That's okay," Tom said. "I'm in the car now, so

I can swing by as well. Tell me, does Ben own a car?"

"A car? I don't think so… Why do you ask?"

"Probably nothing. I can be at Ben's in about ten minutes."

"I'm just pulling up now," she said. "It's in total darkness…"

"Don't go in without me."

"But I'm here now. He might need—"

"Olivia. Do not enter the property until I get there," Tom said, instinctively putting his foot down. The revs picked up as he accelerated. The sound of Olivia's engine died as she switched it off and he could sense she was deliberating whether to ignore his instruction. "Please, Olivia. Something is happening here tonight, and I don't know what you might be walking into."

"I'll think about it."

"Olivia. Olivia!" Tom shook his head; the call had ended. "Damn it."

Tom pulled out onto the wrong side of the road and sped past two cars sitting on the bumper of a little Suzuki hatchback sticking to a constant speed several miles per hour below the designated speed limit. Fortunately, this late on a Sunday night, he didn't face any further traffic delays and he turned into the driveway of Ben Crake's home only a few minutes later.

Olivia's car was parked near to the garage but

there was no sign of her. Tom got out and hurried up to the front door, pressing the doorbell. The shrill ring sounded inside the house but it remained in darkness. Tom stepped back from the porch and cast a look through each of the front-facing windows. The curtains were drawn and he could see neither light nor movement within. Cursing under his breath, he headed to his right and down the side of the house on a cracked and broken concrete path separating the house from the garage.

The net curtain hanging across the kitchen window was only partially obscuring the interior. The kitchen was an absolute mess. The house looked abandoned. Coming to the rear, he found the French doors open out onto the patio, the glass pane by the handle was smashed and the glass had shattered into pieces which lay on the floor of the rear reception room.

Using the torch on his mobile phone, Tom illuminated the interior. Aside from the forced entry, there was no sign of damage to anything else inside. Quickly dialling the control room, he requested uniform support at the address and hesitantly entered the property. Restraining himself from calling out to either Ben or Olivia, he made his way across the room and tried the nearest light switch but nothing came on. He entered the interior hall. It was here that he heard moaning. It ceased only a moment later and he hadn't been able to determine from where it had come. Realising he was breathing more heavily, Tom tentatively progressed through the house, angling the beam of light from left to right, careful to ensure he didn't receive an unwanted surprise without at least some warning.

The kitchen was still empty, the smell of stale air and alcohol lingering, akin to an old public house. In the dining room an antique clock ticking in the silence sounded like a hammer on an anvil. Turning his attention back to the hall, there were three doors ahead of him. One was a metre up on his right and the remaining two were to either side of the hall giving access to the bedrooms at the front.

The first door was into the bathroom. It was a tight space with a dated three-piece suite, avocado green with a shower head over the bath. The curtain was mouldy and missing several rings. The basin was full of water to a level practically overflowing, whatever was submerged almost causing the water to cascade over the rim and down onto the heavily worn and stained carpet below. The air reeked of bleach.

Of the remaining two doors, the one to the right was ajar and he approached it slowly. He could hear movement coming from within and he braced himself as he came to it. The door flew open, and someone came at him out of the dark, lunging at him with a wild overhead swing. Tom swerved to his right and then shoved his would-be assailant in the opposite direction with a forceful shoulder barge. She shrieked as she overbalanced and stumbled against the front door.

Tom turned the beam of light onto her, seeing Olivia Goldman doubled over, grimacing.

"Olivia!"

"Bloody hell, Tom!" she shouted at him. "You could have told me it was you."

"And you should have waited outside like I damn well asked!"

She grinned, righting herself and getting her breath back. "I never was very good at doing as I was told." She pointed into the bedroom. "Ben's in there."

"What's going on with the lights?"

She shook her head. "I've no idea."

Tom crossed the threshold into the bedroom, hovering in the doorway. His mobile cast a bright light over Ben Crake. Dressed only in a pair of jeans and socks, he was curled up in a ball on the bed, knees tucked up into his chest, hugging them fiercely with both arms. He was sobbing uncontrollably, his long hair curling around his face, damp, greasy and matted.

"I haven't been able to get any sense out of him," Olivia said, standing beside Tom. "I was sitting with him and stroking his back when I heard someone creeping around." She shot him a withering look. "That was you, by the way."

He ignored the jibe, moving the light away from him, fearful that the brightness would blind him and only heighten his emotions and lead to further escalation.

"Has he said anything at all?"

"He thought I was his mum," Olivia said, looking around the room. "I think this was her bedroom."

Tom cast the light around and saw the floral-print wallpaper, similar bedspread. In front of the window was a table and chair with a three-faced mirror pointing into the room. A dresser was set to the right of the window with vases, picture frames and some ornamental nick-nacks on top of it. The room was like a mausoleum to Ben's deceased mother.

"Is he having a breakdown?" Tom asked.

"Don't know about that, but he's hammered, in case you hadn't noticed," Olivia said.

"I'll check the fuse box and see what's going on."

He located the main fuse panel. Worryingly, it hadn't been upgraded since the original installation. The fuses looked sound, if dated and terrifyingly basic. However, he found the root cause. Returning to the bedroom, he found Ben sitting up, perched on the edge of the bed with his feet on the floor, Olivia by his side with a supportive arm around his shoulder. Ben had regained some of his composure.

Ben was dishevelled. He hadn't shaved since Tom's previous visit, his facial hair growing in clumps. The jeans he wore were soiled, mud up both trouser legs and particularly heavy below the knee. It looked fresh, still damp and the smell of earth reached his nose.

"Did you find out why we're in darkness?" Olivia asked.

Tom nodded. "When did they come round, Ben?"

Ben looked up at him. Only now did Tom see the swelling and reddening of the skin around his left eye which was almost completely closed. "Who?"

"The power company."

"Oh… right." He shrugged. "Yesterday… day before. I don't remember."

Olivia looked up at Tom.

"They've fitted a prepayment meter. You have to take the key to a service point, like your local post office, charge it and then put the key into the box.Did they leave you a key?"

He looked at Tom, confused. His one good eye narrowing.

"A key… for the electric? I… don't know."

They weren't going to get far with this conversation. Ben Crake's upper body was scratched across his shoulders and chest, as if he'd dived headfirst through a holly bush or similar. The skin of his neck was also red and sore.

"Who have you been fighting with, Ben?" Tom asked.

Ben looked at the floor in front of him, unflinching.

Olivia gently shook him with the arm wrapped around his shoulder. "Ben? What's happened." She glanced at Tom, concerned. "You can tell us."

"I don't know," he all but whispered.

"Have you been here all day, Ben?" Tom asked. He nodded but didn't speak or look up. "Do you have a car?"

Olivia shot Tom an inquisitive look and was no doubt readying herself to ask why he'd asked that question for a second time this evening, but he held up a hand, indicating she should say nothing. For once, she followed the instruction.

"No..." Ben said, glancing at Tom and then sideways at Olivia. "My mum did, so I guess I have hers."

"Where is it?"

"In the garage."

"Is it locked?"

Ben shrugged. Tom gestured for Olivia to keep an eye on Ben, and he went back into the hall, unlocked the front door and stepped out onto the driveway just as a patrol car rounded the corner, blue lights flashing. Tom waved them down and the driver lowered his window.

"False alarm," Tom said. "But stick around for a few minutes, would you?"

The driver nodded and wound the window up. The earlier rain had passed swiftly but the night was cold, and the constables were happy to stay in the car. They switched off the lights, keeping the engine, and more importantly, the heating, ticking over.

The garage door was unlocked but it couldn't have been opened for quite some time. The runners were stuck on the up-and-over door and for a moment, Tom thought it wasn't going to budge, but for Tom's immense strength it might not have. There was a fraction of give and then the door shrieked and juddered as Tom lifted it up, turning the beam of light from his mobile onto the interior. The garage was empty.

Returning to the house, Tom spotted a broken bamboo cane lying in the overgrown, weed-infested flower bed beneath the window to the left of the front door. He picked it up and took it inside. Looking in on the bedroom, he found Olivia had managed to find Ben a clean shirt to put on and he was currently sipping from a glass of water. Tom bypassed the room unnoticed and wandered along the hall and into the bathroom.

Using the cane, he lifted the material soaking in the basin of bleach and water, draping it over the side of the bath. It was a white T-shirt, the front emblazoned with a printed logo of Leicester Tigers Rugby team. It was clearly old, the colours of the logo faded, and the collar and waist edges were tatty. Why the need to soak it in bleach?

Walking back into the bedroom, both Ben and Olivia looked up at him.

"Ben, you're going to need to answer some questions and it's for the best if you're truthful with me."

He nodded slowly, his haunted expression clouding with fear.

"It wasn't my fault. I swear."

"You've been fighting, haven't you?" Tom asked.

Ben nodded.

"Why is your T-shirt soaking in bleach?"

Olivia cocked her head but said nothing.

"It's stained," Ben said. He glanced at Olivia sitting beside him. "Mum says you have to soak it as soon as you can."

"In bleach?" Tom asked. Ben averted his eyes. "What is it stained with, Ben?"

"Blood."

Tom and Olivia exchanged a glance. Tom saw the knuckle on Ben's right hand was cut and bruised.

"Your blood?"

Ben shook his head, uncertain and disconsolate. "Um... I don't think so."

Tom excused himself from the room, holding up his mobile to Olivia to indicate he was going to make a call. She silently mouthed she would remain with Ben.

CHAPTER TWENTY-SIX

TAMARA'S MOBILE PHONE RANG. She tutted, considering leaving it and allowing voicemail to pick it up. David sensed her restlessness.

"Do you want to get that?" he asked.

"I'd better. At this time of night, it might be important."

She put her glass of wine down and disentangled herself from him before rising from the sofa, adjusting her jumper and running a hand through her hair, sweeping it away from her face. David hunted for the remote control and paused the film they were watching.

"As long as it's not your mum asking what time I'm bringing you home."

Tamara smiled back at him. "I'm a grown up now. I don't have to be home until eleven."

He grinned, picking up his own glass and re-filling it. “Well, that’s certainly an improvement. Your mum and dad must be going soft in their old age.”

“It’s Tom,” she said, smiling and answering as he gestured with the bottle towards her glass. She nodded and he topped it up. “Hey, Tom. What’s up?”

“We have a situation developing tonight that you need to be aware of.”

His tone was serious and any alcohol-induced softening of her awareness was forgotten. “What’s going on?”

David looked over at her, his forehead creased with concern.

“Earlier this evening Cassie attended a hit-and-run. One male deceased at the scene. It looks like it’s Daniel Turner and we’re confident it’s not an accident.”

“He was targeted?”

“The driver turned around and took another pass at him. Perhaps to make absolutely certain. He couldn’t be identified at the scene, but he took off after the lunchtime performance and didn’t show for the evening finale. His partner, Aislene, is also missing.”

Tamara sat down on the edge of the sofa beside David who nursed his glass of wine.

“Why am I certain you’re about to add to this?”

"I'm at Ben Crake's at the moment. He's been involved in some kind of an incident and he's not in good shape," he said. "He admits he's been fighting, and by all accounts it looks like he's given as good as he got but… he's in a mess; intoxicated, possibly high and prone to moments of rambling incoherence. He'd left clothes soaking in bleach in his bathroom and his mother's car is missing from the garage. I think I need to have him assessed by mental health. I'm not convinced I can trust anything I get out of him right now."

"That bad?"

"Afraid so, yes. Cassie is at the circus now going through their digs trying to make some sense of all this. Turner was out in the sticks, somewhere he didn't really have any business being when he should have been preparing for the final show."

"You think he was meeting someone?"

"Stands to reason."

"And Aislene?"

Tom sucked air through his teeth. "We're still looking. I was at the circus tonight to see the show. I bumped into Susan and Marsha Brock. They were there looking for Jack Dale. They tried to deflect it, but they were worried about something. Susan has no idea where he is tonight. They left after I spoke to them, and it all looked very fraught."

Tamara bit her lower lip, thinking hard. David stroked her back affectionately and she stood up, walking away from him, not caring for the distraction.

"What do you need from me?" she asked. Tom appeared on top of it, but maybe there was something she could do.

"I have uniform here at Ben's. They can babysit him until we can get someone out to assess him. If he's passed fit, I'll have him brought to the station for questioning. In the meantime, Cassie's working the circus and Eric is on his way to the station. Cass found evidence of a burner phone at their place, but no sign of the mobile itself. With a bit of luck, we'll get a hit on the network. Once we have a lead on where Aislene might be we need to get to her. If we get a lead anyway."

"Sounds good," Tamara said, thinking hard. "Perhaps we should get uniform to swing by and check on Charlie Babcock and Mick George to see if they're about."

"The person who found Turner at the side of the road described a red car driving erratically close to the scene. I'm wondering if Ben Crake inherited a red car from his mother."

"Okay. Keep me posted. If you need me in, just shout, whatever the time is."

"Will do. Sorry to interrupt your evening."

Tamara hung up, looking to the heavens and exhaling.

"What's going on?" David asked.

She turned to face him, shaking her head. "That case I no longer had to think about… has just gone off like a grenade."

"Who's in the blast radius?" he asked, sipping from his glass.

She laughed, but without humour. "At the moment, I couldn't even tell you who threw the thing! Here," she said, passing him her glass of wine, "you'd better finish this."

"Anything to help," David said, exaggerating a winning smile.

TOM PUT his mobile away and gestured to the two uniformed constables to join him. They got out of their car, pulling their Hi-Viz coats on as they crossed to join him.

"I need you to get a mental health worker out here to carry out an assessment."

"On a Sunday night? That'll take hours!" one bemoaned, reining in the protest as he caught Tom's expression. "Sorry, sir."

"Stay with him and don't leave him alone. He's disturbed, under the influence and could well be a danger to himself," he looked them both up and down, "and possibly to the two of you."

"Sir," they said in unison.

"You think he did it, don't you?"

Tom turned to see Olivia Goldman standing in the doorway, arms folded defiantly across her chest.

"After everything you've said, you're the same as the rest of them."

Tom held up a hand to placate her. She was seething. He gestured for the officers to go inside, one of them putting a call into the control room to request a mental health assessment.

Olivia walked over to Tom, her lip curling as she readied herself to give him a piece of her mind. He sought to head her off.

"Olivia, we don't know what has happened tonight—"

"But you think he ran that… that Turner guy from the circus over, don't you? And what… kidnapped his girlfriend?"

"I never said that!" Tom countered, wondering just how long she'd been hovering in the background whilst he was on the phone to Tamara.

"Sounds like it to me!"

"Oh, come on, Olivia," Tom snapped, pointing back into the house. "He's in there, half-cut and likely as high as a kite, babbling. He's admitted he's been in a fight and he's bleaching his clothes to destroy the evidence—"

She stepped towards him aggressively, shaking with controlled fury. "You don't know that's the reason—"

"No, I'm sure he's just been reading *Good Housekeeping* from cover to cover." She hesitated and he saw the despair in her expression. She'd clearly given a lot of herself to get Ben Crake to this point and it was all starting to unravel at pace. He softened his tone. "Look, I don't know what's gone on tonight. Not yet. No one does but, we can agree, we need to find Aislene and once everyone's safe then we can get to the bottom of it. Yes?"

She nodded.

"The best thing you can do for me, and for Ben, is to stay with him until the nurse gets here. Ben will likely respond better to you than he will to my officers." He looked her in the eye. "Can you do that for me? I'll keep an open mind, I promise."

"I can do that," she said, turning towards the house. Tom took out his phone to call Cassie for an update. Olivia stopped, speaking to him over her shoulder. "It's an old Mazda 3."

Tom looked up. "What is?"

"The car Ben's mum used to drive." She nodded at the open garage. "No one sold it off when she died. It should be in the garage."

Tom followed her gaze. "You're sure?"

"It was there last week when Ben got home. I saw it myself."

"Colour?"

"Red."

Tom exhaled.

"But it couldn't have been Ben."

"You sound pretty certain of that," Tom said.

She shrugged. "That's one thing I can be sure of. Unless they've started giving driving lessons in Category A prisons."

Tom sighed. "He can't drive?"

"He could never afford the lessons. He's only financially sound now because his mum had a decent life insurance policy. Otherwise, he'd be sleeping in a bus shelter someplace right now." She stared hard at him. "You're focussing on the wrong man, Tom. Some things never change."

Without another word, Olivia went back into the house. Tom changed his mind and called Eric.

"Hi, Boss."

"Are you at the station?" Tom asked.

"I am. What do you need?"

"Ben Crake has a car. A red Mazda 3. I've no idea of the index and it is likely still registered in his mum's name. Ben doesn't seem to be on top of his admin… or much at all. Find out the details and get it out there for everyone to look for."

"You think that was the car used to knock down Daniel Turner?"

"I think it quite likely, yes. It's not here at Crake's home and apparently, he doesn't have a licence. Can you double check that for me?"

"Yep, can do. Although, you don't need a licence to drive a car if you're planning to use it as a weapon."

"And the eyewitness said the red car seen nearby was being driven erratically," Tom said. "So, even if he can't officially drive a car, he's still in the frame. Any joy on the burner mobile?"

"I'm awaiting data from the mobile phone networks. For any transcripts and so on, we'll likely have to wait for a warrant, but I sweet-talked my way to the tower data on the grounds it could save the life of a missing person."

"Good work, Eric." He was about to say goodbye and had a thought. "Did you do the background research on the Dales? Jack, in particular?"

"Yes, I did. What do you want to know?"

"Does he own a car? I bumped into Susan Brock earlier and she was out looking for him, seemed concerned for his welfare, but now I'm thinking—"

"She might be concerned for what he was planning to do?" Eric finished.

"Exactly."

"Wait one," Eric said. Tom heard a desk drawer sliding open and Eric shifting some paper in the background, the line crackling as he picked up his mobile again. "Jack hasn't got a vehicle registered to him, but his parents have two cars against their names, and he would likely have access to them. His dad has a 02-plate Audi and his mum… a Ford Focus."

"Colour?"

"Red."

"You're sure?"

"That's what it says here."

"Okay. I'm going over to see if Jack has resurfaced from his earlier disappearing act. Let's see what he has to say for himself."

"Do you want me to meet you there?"

"No, keep on with the tower data. The minimum we need to know is where that phone's been and with a bit of luck it's visible now and will lead us to Aislene. While you're waiting, go over the files looking for any property, land or remote locations that Jack Dale, Ben Crake, or even Charlie Babcock for that matter, might have access to. Anything that could help narrow down the search parameters for Aislene."

Eric exhaled deeply. "There's nothing to say they will have left her in one of their own places. It'd be a bit obvious."

"Yes, I know it's a long shot," Tom said, "but it's still a possibility. If they're acting off the cuff, then they might not have thought it through."

"On it," Eric said, hanging up.

Tom held the mobile in his hands for a moment, contemplating the situation. His eye drifted to the empty garage, turning scenarios over and over in his mind. Despite what he'd just said to Eric, there was another possible reason as to why this was falling into place as it was. The majority of people locally still considered Ben Crake to be guilty. A man tantalisingly close to *getting away with murder*. If someone wanted a guy to take the fall for this, then what better candidate could there be?

He was snapped from his reverie by a sound behind him as he was joined by a constable.

"Social worker is coming out," he said. "Mental health nurses are in short supply apparently."

"Whatever you do, make sure he can't harm himself."

"Babysitting a scumbag like that—"

Tom glared at him, and the officer took on a conciliatory stance.

"We'll see him right, sir. I promise."

CHAPTER TWENTY-SEVEN

THE LIGHTS WERE STILL on when Tom arrived at the Dales' house. It was approaching half-eleven now and almost every other house in the street was already in darkness. Rain was falling again and the temperature falling rapidly away. Time was a real factor now. The ambiguity around Aislene's whereabouts would likely prove fatal to her if she was exposed to the elements.

Tom approached the house, detouring around the two cars parked at the front. They were as Eric described. Susan Brock's Mercedes was also present. Tom was drawn to the red Ford. The exterior was immaculately clean. The rain settling on the car was pooling in little bubbles, indicating the surface was treated with a wax or similar. Peering inside, the interior was quite the opposite. Loose paper, old receipts and random bits and pieces were scattered around the cabin and the upholstery needed a good clean and vacuum.

He couldn't find any tell-tale damage at the front of the car, gently passing his hand over the end of the bonnet, the surface was free of dents or scratches beyond the expected stone chips. In this light there wasn't much point in getting underneath the car to see if there was any indication of a person being dragged recently.

"Oi! What do you think you're doing?"

Tom stroked the front wing as he turned to face Henry Dale, standing on the front step of his house, arms folded tightly across his chest, his immense frame casting a large shadow across the ground. Tom stepped from behind the car and into the light emanating from inside the house. Henry visibly shifted uncomfortably, his expression softening.

"I'm sorry, Inspector. I didn't recognise you."

"That's okay, Mr Dale," Tom said. "I'm pleased I haven't had to wake you. I'd like to speak to Jack, please."

"Um..." Henry glanced over his shoulder, back into the house. "I think he might have gone to bed—"

Tom came to stand before him. "It's not a request, Henry."

Henry took a breath before offering a curt nod, stepping back and beckoning Tom inside. Entering the kitchen diner at the rear of the house, Jack Dale was sitting at the dining table, staring at Tom, his expression akin to a rabbit caught in the headlights. Susan was sitting next to him, the fingers of her left hand interlaced with those of his right. She avoided direct eye contact with Tom.

Marie Dale was in the kitchen area; her demeanour was troubled.

"Inspector Janssen is here to see you, son," Henry said, leading Tom into the room. He was nervous too. It was evident in his tone.

"I see you found Jack," Tom said to Susan.

She nodded but said nothing.

"Where have you been, Jack?" Tom asked, casting an eye over the young man. He looked pale, his hair was damp but was unlikely caused by being caught in the rain. His hair was neatly combed, and it shone, much as it does fresh after a shower. His clothing looked fresh as well, neatly pressed as if it'd just come out of a drawer or wardrobe. You could still see the creases where his T-shirt was folded. A large welt had formed on the side of his cheek, close to his eye, and Tom's gaze lowered to his hands, resting on the table. Reflexively, Jack put his hands into his lap and out of sight. His knuckles were scratched and swollen though.

Jack shrugged, looking around in an attempt to appear casual. "Out and about. You know? I just needed some space."

"Driving?"

Jack looked up at Tom. "A bit."

"Where did you go?"

He shrugged. "I don't know really. Just out."

"See anyone?"

Jack tried to swallow, with difficulty.

"What's all this about, Inspector?" Henry asked. "It's a little late for cryptic questions—"

"A man was run over and killed tonight," Tom said. "It is possible he is loosely connected to the investigation into Angela's murder. This man and his partner have been of interest to Jack recently."

Tom turned his gaze onto Jack who in turn exchanged a confused look with Susan.

"I don't understand…" Jack said. "What has this got to do with me?"

"We think Daniel Turner is dead."

"That's not me," Jack mumbled, shaking his head.

"He may have been struck by a red hatchback, and we believe it was deliberate."

"It wasn't me!" Jack said, horrified. "I swear. It wasn't me."

"Then you had better tell me where you were tonight and why Susan was so distressed at not being able to find you."

Jack's eyes flitted between his parents. He was on the verge of tears, panic rising. "I'm sorry, Mum," he said. "I know I promised to stay away from him… but I couldn't."

"Oh Jack… what have you done?" Marie asked, nervously fiddling with the pendant hanging around her neck.

"You went to see Ben Crake, didn't you?" Tom asked.

He nodded, averting his eyes from Tom's gaze and down at the table. Tears flowed, dropping to the surface. Susan squeezed his hand.

"I just wanted him to admit what he'd done," Jack said. "I took your car, Mum. That's where I went. I sat outside and when I saw him stumbling back from the shops… I… followed him." He looked up at Tom. "I didn't know what I was going to do… it's not like I planned it."

"You confronted him?"

He nodded. "He was at the front door. He was so pissed; he'd dropped his keys and was trying to pick them up."

"What happened?"

Jack took a deep breath, steadying himself. "Like you said, I confronted him. I demanded he tell me why he did what he did to Angela…"

"And?" Tom pressed.

Jack shook his head. "He denied it. He told me

he loved Angela… that he would never have hurt her. He started to cry. I couldn't believe it. Even now, he was still lying, putting on this act of his – at least that's what went through my head – and I felt it all coming out, the anger, the frustration… the injustice of it all. And I…"

"You attacked him?"

He nodded silently.

"Did Ben not fight back?" Henry asked.

Jack looked at his father. "Not at first. I was punching and kicking him." He looked heavenward. "I've no idea how many times… or even if the blows were landing. Ben curled up in a ball on the floor… it was pathetic. I screamed at him; told him I was going to kill him just like he did my sister." He stared at Tom, tears flowing freely now. "I know it was stupid, but I took a knife with me just in case."

"A knife!" Marie exclaimed. "Oh Jack, whatever were you thinking?"

"I'm sorry, Mum. I wasn't thinking. I was so angry… and I pulled the knife out and… when I grabbed him, everything changed."

"He fought back," Tom said.

"Yeah," Jack said, his head dropping. "I couldn't handle him. I've never known Ben to be so… so aggressive, so violent."

"You see, Inspector?" Henry said angrily. "Ben

Crake can be a monster and you lot let him back out on the street."

"Self-defence, Henry," Tom said, jabbing a finger pointedly at Jack. "By his own admission, your son initiated the assault. Prisons are violent places, particularly for those serving offences against women. Ben would have to have learned to fight or he wouldn't make it. If anything, it sounds like he restrained himself until he had no other option and the survival instinct kicked in."

Henry was indignant but clearly found the logic hard to counter. Jack steadied himself. His breathing was heavy, and Tom wondered if he was about to have a panic attack.

"I thought Ben was going to kill me… I really did."

"How did it end?" Tom asked.

Jack shook his head. "He… just stopped. He was on top of me… I could taste blood in my mouth… running down my face. I realised later on my nose was bleeding. My anger was gone, and I was scared. And I mean proper scared… terrified. Ben stood over me, a wild-eyed maniacal look on his face… and then he cried. He just stood there… crying." He shrugged "And then he wandered away, picked up his bags and went inside. I'm sorry… so, so sorry," Jack said. "I just lost it. I should never have gone there tonight."

"And that's the only place you went to?"

Jack frowned, shaking his head. "Like I said, I drove around a bit… probably for hours, I'm not sure. After I'd parked up somewhere and managed to stem the bleeding anyway." He looked at Susan, smiling apologetically. "I ignored the calls on my phone. I was embarrassed and didn't know what to tell you…" he looked at his parents in turn, "any of you."

"What about Daniel Turner?" Tom asked. "Did you call and arrange to meet him or Aislene?"

"No! I told you, that wasn't me."

"You'd better be telling me the—"

"It is the truth!" Jack said. "I went to Ben's place and attacked him. I'll admit that, but… what you're talking about, it wasn't me. It couldn't have been."

"Where's the knife now?" Tom asked.

Jack and Susan exchanged a glance and he nodded. Susan turned to Tom.

"It's in my car, Inspector."

The gravity of the situation hung heavily in the air. The mood was solemn.

"Jack, you said Ben was stumbling on his way home."

"Yes. He was smashed. I could smell the booze on him, and his bag was full of carry-outs. He was on a proper bender. I was surprised he was able to walk… let alone fight."

"I see." Tom turned to Susan. "Let's go and get that knife, shall we?"

He indicated the door and Susan released Jack's hand, rising slowly from her chair. Marie took the vacated seat next to her son, putting a supporting arm across his shoulder.

"What happens now, Inspector?" Henry asked.

"One thing at a time, Henry," Tom said, falling into step with Susan and following her out to her car.

The rain had eased now. Susan unlocked her car, opening the passenger side door.

"We put it in the glove box," she said, reaching inside.

"I think it's best if you let me handle it," Tom said, stopping her in her tracks. She backed out of his way, and he slid into the seat before opening the compartment. Inside was a hunting knife, the blade of which was approximately six inches long. It was like something out of a horror film. He glanced up at Susan, shaking his head. "Does Jack have many things like this?"

Susan looked uncomfortable. "I didn't even know he had that one."

The blade looked clean, unused. Almost brand new. Why anyone in the UK needed such a weapon was beyond him. It was something of a craze in the cities these days; Zombie knives, they were called. Jack Dale was far from the type one might expect to own something like this. Tom found it perturbing that he took it with him to confront Ben with.

"He's changed," Susan said bitterly. "All of this… ever since Angela disappeared. He's just so different now. He carries the weight of it everywhere he goes. Not only his own emotions but his parents' as well." She shook her head. "When I think back to that night – the night Angela went missing – Jack was so carefree. Mum dropped me off at the circus that evening for the performance… and Jack was so bright and full of life. We felt like we had the world at our feet, and nothing was going to stop us."

Tom carefully picked the knife up, his sleeve over the handle, intending to take it to his car where he had some evidence bags in the boot.

"Life has a way of hammering the enthusiasm out of you," he said, as she closed the door and locked her car. "Often there's nothing you can do about it either."

"I just can't believe he went to see Ben like that."

"Hatred can blind us to reality," Tom said. "Emotions are powerful and when we feel powerless, we can react without thinking."

"Is that what you think happened tonight, between Jack and Ben?"

Tom nodded towards the knife. "When you take something like this along, it's hard to believe there wasn't an element of planning involved. Jack's in a great deal of trouble."

"I know," she said quietly. "But I believe him when he says he didn't drive his car into DT. I really do."

Tom nodded. He wasn't so sure.

CHAPTER TWENTY-EIGHT

TOM'S MOBILE RANG. It was Cassie and Tom struggled to take in the information, she was speaking too fast.

"Cassie, slow down," Tom said. "Where are you?"

"I checked in with Eric. The service provider just got back to him. The burner we're tracking is connected to one tower on the network. I'm heading there now. The signal is strong, so it's close."

A car horn blared in the background and Cassie cursed.

"Try and get there in one piece," Tom said. "A mobile tower covers a lot of ground—"

"Eric found a strip of land once owned by Crake's grandfather. There's some document archived in the land registry that shows it was passed to him by a local landowner for some unspecified reason. It's located between the Fring Estate and Docking. Internet satellite images show a building on it. It might be an old barn or something. Who can tell when you zoom in. Too much of a coincidence?"

"Were we aware of this previously?" Tom asked, hurrying to his own car.

"Not as far as I know. Eric found it. I'm almost there."

"Wait for support, Cass."

"Uniform are en-route."

"I'll be there as soon as I can."

He hung up, clambering into the driver's seat. The phone switched to the car's Bluetooth connection, and he called Eric, firing the engine into life. Eric picked up immediately.

"I've spoken to Cassie, Eric. I'm already on my way there. Have an ambulance meet us, will you?"

The back roads criss-crossing rural Norfolk were narrow, often with high verges and hedgerows to either side. Fortunately, it was so dark the headlights of any oncoming vehicle would reveal their presence and give him enough time to react. At least, Tom hoped so. Zipping along lanes and cutting through from village to village, he hoped the discovery would not be in vain.

The roads widened the closer he came to his

destination; the metal roads cutting through sweeping, open farmland to either side. The clouds parted as the rainstorm cleared leaving in its wake a damp and murky landscape lit by a sliver of moonlight. He didn't need to slow the car in search of the building, blue lights illuminated the immediate area for half a mile in every direction.

A track, almost invisible from the roadside, the entrance overgrown by foliage, stretched off into the darkness. Tom turned onto it and bounced his way along the dirt track, wheels slipping in the mud, until he pulled up behind a liveried police car. The track was so narrow that they were forced to park bumper to bumper.

Cassie's car was in front of two police cars and Tom found a gate at the head of the track, barring entrance to a small yard with a dilapidated aircraft-hangar style barn on the northern end of the plot. The gate was chained, the padlock securing it in place rusted so badly that removing it without bolt cutters would be nigh on impossible.

Multiple torch beams were moving around the site, searching, probing the darkness. Tom vaulted the gate and moved to join them.

"Here!"

Tom followed the shout into the barn, everyone quickly converging on the same location. Cassie came alongside Tom, and they arrived at the same time. The barn was full of rusting machinery, rotting wooden crates and was evidently home to various species of wildlife. There were weeds and assorted foliage growing through holes and tears in the fabric of the building, such was its state of disrepair.

At the far end of the barn was another room, partitioned off with basic stud work, a solitary door and windows that were all smashed and broken; the result of vandals now likely long since grown into adulthood. PC Marshall, kneeling, angled the beam of his torch towards them and then down to the floor, allowing them to see the glass at the entrance.

Lying at his feet was Aislene Turner, her hands bound behind her back, her legs bound at the ankles. Blood trickled from a head wound but Tom could see it was still flowing. Her heart was still pumping.

Marshall looked up at them, concerned. "I have a pulse, but it's faint."

"Ambulance is on the way," Tom said. "Free her and put her in the recovery position. Do what you can. Everyone else, spread out and search this place."

"Sir?"

He looked around. A constable gestured for him to follow. Cassie joined him and the officer led them back out of the barn and around to the north face of the barn. Less than twenty feet away was another structure, little more than the size of a domestic garage. The front had two doors, one of which was ajar. The officer approached it, easing the door open. The hinges were rusty, shrieking against the pressure of the movement with the weight of the door.

They all raised their torches. Inside was a red Mazda 3. Tom inspected the front of the car. There was a visible impact point to the left of the grille where the bonnet curved down at the front to meet it. The windscreen was also cracked in the top left corner on the nearside.

"Well, I think we found our murder weapon," Cassie said.

Tom nodded. "But why leave Daniel by the side of the road and bring Aislene way out here?"

Cassie clicked her tongue against the roof of her mouth. "You've got me there."

There was enough room to allow a person to move along either side of the car. Tom indicated for Cassie to go down one side and he went down the other. Reluctant to search the car, and thereby destroy any evidence, both of them shone their lights onto the interior.

"You had the number for the burner phone, didn't you? That's how you could track it here."

Cassie nodded. "We called it from the circus, but it went to voicemail."

Tom cocked his head at that. "It didn't ring at all?"

Cassie shook her head. "No, why?"

"There's a signal out here," he said, his eyes scanning the interior. "And there it is."

The beam of his torch lit up a mobile phone in the passenger side footwell. "Can you call it now, please?"

Cassie obliged and the screen illuminated as the call connected. Tom held up his hand, indicating for her to wait. The phone rang for twenty seconds or so before the screen went dark.

"That's voicemail," she said.

"And before, at the circus, how long did it ring for?"

Cassie shook her head. "It didn't. It cut straight to voicemail. What's going on?"

"My thoughts exactly."

Cassie frowned. "I found a lot of cash in the Turner's motorhome. It looked recently drawn too."

Tom considered it. "Blackmail?"

"My first thought, yes."

"Maybe Jack Dale was right after all, and the Turners knew something critical."

"And then used it to their advantage," Cassie said. "Ian Gallagher said Daniel told him he was sorting out something big. Maybe this was it; blackmailing Ben Crake with whatever they knew about him and Angela, and whatever happened that night six years ago. Ben inherited a fair bit of money, right?"

"Yes," Tom said, nodding.

Cassie shrugged. "Maybe they got greedy and asked for more."

"And this was his reply?"

"Why not? Ben would do anything not to go back to prison, don't you think?"

"Yeah, maybe," Tom said but he was less than convinced. "Have the car sealed off and get forensics out here."

The sirens of the ambulance signalled its arrival.

"Let's hope Aislene makes it and can tell us what the hell has happened tonight," Tom said.

"What about Ben Crake?"

"We already have officers with him. If he hasn't been sectioned, he'll be on his way to the station."

Tom took out his mobile and called Eric.

"Eric, you said the burner was connected to this particular tower. Does the data indicate when it came into range?"

"Er… should do, yes. Hang on," he said, tapping away on his keyboard. "Did you find Aislene?"

"Yes, the ambulance crew are here now."

"Is she okay?" Eric asked, pausing in his search.

"Touch and go, I reckon."

"Right, I have it." Eric took a breath. "What do you want to know?"

"When did the mobile connect to this particular tower?"

Eric paused as he filtered through the information.

"It popped up on the network at 10:31 pm," Eric said.

Tom looked at Cassie, repeating the time, "10:31."

"Yep. Is that significant?"

"It just might be, Eric. Thank you."

"Oh, before you go," Eric said. "You know you had me looking for property, obscure connections to land and such?"

"Yes. What about it?"

"I found something. The woodland where we found Angela Dale's body. You'll never believe it."

Tom listened as Eric explained what he'd found out, the pieces starting to come together in his mind. He hung up, fixing Cassie with his gaze.

"What is it?" she asked.

"The burner mobile connected to the tower at 10:31, which was why your call earlier went to straight to voicemail."

"The phone was out of coverage."

"Or switched off," Tom said. "Either way, it found its way here at 10:31."

"And? So what?"

"Cassie, I was with Ben Crake at 10.31… and I think we can likely rule out him working with an accomplice because everyone in this town hates the guy."

Cassie inclined her head. "You think this is a stitch-up?"

He nodded. "I do. And what's more, I think I can prove it."

CHAPTER TWENTY-NINE

Tom pulled up at the gated entrance, lowering his window. Tamara looked at him before he reached out to press the button for the intercom.

"You're sure about this?" she asked. It was more of a clarification of his confidence than doubt in his conclusion. Otherwise, she wouldn't allow him to take this step.

"I'm sure."

He pressed the button for the intercom. It was the early hours of the morning, but this couldn't wait. He pressed it again, repeatedly. Eventually, a groggy voice came through the crackly speaker.

"Yes?"

"Mr Brock, it's DI Janssen. Can you buzz me in please?"

"Have you any idea what time it is?"

"I do, Mr Brock."

He waited and when he didn't comment further, a buzzer sounded, and the gates opened. Tom accelerated and the uniform patrol car tailing them followed. The drive curved around to the front of the house where Tom parked outside the front door. Both he and Tamara got out, Tamara signalling to the accompanying officers to wait by the car.

The front door opened, and Greg Brock received them, drawing his dressing gown tightly about him, feeling the chill of the early hours. He was clearly unhappy at their presence.

"I apologise for the lateness of the hour, Mr Brock, but it is important. May we come inside?"

"Yes, yes of course," he said, standing aside and letting them enter. He cast a glance out at the waiting officers standing beside their car, turning to Tom, fearful. "Is everything all right. Something hasn't happened to Susan, has it?"

Tom shook his head. "I spoke to Susan earlier, at the Dales' home. She appeared well. Perhaps she has stayed there to support Jack after the events of tonight."

Greg Brock frowned, his eyes flitting between them. "Why? What's happened?"

"What is it, love?" Marsha called from her position above them on the landing, peering down into the atrium. "What's going on?"

"Nothing, darling. You can go back to—"

"Perhaps your wife should join us?" Tamara said. Greg looked at her and then up at his wife. Marsha made her way around the landing and descended towards them.

"Is Susan okay?" she asked.

"She's fine, love," Greg said, shaking his head. "I've no idea what's going on, I really don't."

"Where were you tonight, Greg?" Tom asked. "Between the hours of eight and eleven?"

"At home," Marsha said.

"In the office," Greg said, both speaking at the same time. The couple looked at one another. "I went into the office and then I came home, didn't I love?"

"That's okay," Tom said. "For the avoidance of doubt, we'll be able to track the GPS signal from your mobile phone and know exactly where you were. Unless you remembered to leave your mobile behind when you set out to murder Daniel Turner."

Greg's mouth fell open, his eyes fixed on Tom.

"Is this a joke? What are you talking about?" he asked, shaking his head. "I don't know anyone by that name."

"He works for the circus," Tom said, "and he's been blackmailing you in relation to Angela Dale's murder. Most likely, he's been doing so for years, only now – what with the release of Ben Crake from prison – the stakes are even higher as we're looking into the case from scratch. Someone has a lot to lose."

Greg looked at his wife, then Tamara. "This is insane! Blackmail? What on earth could he be blackmailing me with?" He waved a pointed finger at Tom. "You know damn well I couldn't have killed Angela. I was at a Rotary Club dinner in front of a hundred people! You saw me leaving work on camera." He laughed, incredulous. "Unless you're suggesting I have the ability to be in two places at once, you should think again."

Tom shook his head. "I didn't say you killed Angela. You're right. You couldn't have done it."

"There you go," Greg said, throwing his hands in the air.

"How about you, Marsha?" Tom asked, turning to face her.

Marsha Brock was startled by Tom's sudden attention. "I… I… I was in Ely that day. I'm sure you know this."

"I know that was what is in your statement, Marsha," Tom said. "Although, if you're going to go to the trouble of fabricating an alibi, then you really should have run it past your daughter."

Marsha looked pleadingly at her husband. He was agitated.

"Inspector Janssen. I must protest at this."

"You may protest as much as you like," Tom said, holding a hand up to them both, "but Susan told me a matter of hours ago that Marsha dropped her off at the circus to meet her friends in time for the evening performance. You couldn't have been in Ely golfing all day and not returned until late that night, and also been up here on the north coast in time to drop Susan at the circus in the afternoon. That wouldn't make any sense at all."

Greg Brock opened his mouth to protest again but said nothing. Marsha implored him with her eyes. Tom turned his attention back to Greg.

"How long had you been having an affair with Angela, Greg?"

"What?" he said, glaring at Tom. "You've lost the plot, man."

"It puzzled me, for a time. Henry and Marie Dale telling us how Angela always had money; material items that far outstripped her ability to pay for them. Her work didn't pay much, and the family were struggling financially. Who in her circle could have funded her? I even considered that maybe she was selling herself, but as far as I can tell she wasn't the type. Have you always had a temptation for younger women or did you only have eyes for Angela?"

"How dare you!"

"No, sir. How dare you. You allowed a troubled young man to go to prison for the most heinous of crimes when you knew he was innocent. You even spoke for him at his trial."

Greg sank to the bottom tread of the stairs, burying his face in his palms. Marsha placed her hands on his shoulders, aghast.

"It's not like that at all. You have no idea what you're talking about."

"Perhaps not. However, the young woman you left for dead tonight, in the old barn belonging to Ben Crake," he stared hard at Greg, forcing him to maintain the eye contact, "is still alive. We got to her in time."

"I don't know what you're talking about!"

"She has an interesting story to tell," Tom said, clocking a brief glance his way from Tamara.

Tom met Marsha's eye. "It's over, Marsha. What you both did back then, along with your attempts now to keep it concealed have ruined lives. And it's all been for nothing."

Marsha's head lowered.

"You suspected your husband was cheating on you. All those extra hours he put in at work. Secret text conversations, suspicious purchases of jewellery or tech that never seemed to appear, perhaps?" She was fighting back tears. "So, you followed Greg that night, or waited outside the office to try and catch him out. What a surprise it must have been for you to find out it was one of your daughter's friends. A family friend at that."

Marsha gently squeezed her husband's shoulders one more time, before she took her hands off him and steadied herself on the banister.

"I didn't want to believe it," she said, shaking her head. "Not again."

"Marsha!"

"Enough, Greg!" she snapped. "I've had enough of it. All of it!" She took a breath, pursing her lips momentarily. "My husband has a wandering eye, Inspector. He is a wonderful man, truly. He would do anything for me, but… I am not enough for him. I never have been."

"You walked in on them?"

"Marsha, think, damn you!"

She turned on her husband, growling. "You've had it your way for years, Gregory! I'm making the decision now."

Greg looked away, humbled.

"No, Inspector. I didn't walk in on them, but it wasn't for the lack of trying, I assure you," she said, dejected. "They must have heard me coming… sensed I was there, maybe. I don't know. In any event," she steadied herself, pausing for breath, "Greg was alone in his office when I walked in. I was embarrassed. Humiliated. Greg berated me for doubting him." She inclined her head and smiled ruefully. "And I *doubted him*. I truly did. I left the office, angry and uncertain. Doubting myself as much as my husband. Although, he has a Machiavellian way of making me think these things are all in my head."

"But you waited outside in your car, watching to see who came out, didn't you?"

She slowly nodded. "I watched Greg leave... alone. I wondered whether I'd made a mistake and that it was all my imagination, just as Greg said it was. And then I saw her... running through the rain, a big smile on her face." She glanced at Tom apologetically, "Ben was following after her. He never caught her up, giving up and watching her as she ran off down the road. I watched her too. She was smiling... laughing... at me!"

"What did you do?" Tom asked.

Marsha shook her head, her gaze fixed on some far-off point in the distance. "I didn't think. I was angry... so, bloody angry. I drove the car after her, unsure of what I'd do when I caught up to her."

"And then?"

Marsha's gaze drifted across to Tom, her expression emotionless, her tone flat.

"I didn't stop... not until I'd hit her. Maybe it was the noise of the rain or the wind... but she didn't look round. I don't think she ever knew it was me... or what I had done, let alone why." Marsha took a deep breath, releasing it slowly. It was as if a weight had lifted from her. "I stopped the car and walked back to see her. She was staring up at the sky, unblinking. I knew she was dead there and then. I suppose, thinking about it, I could have left her there. Another victim of a tragic road accident."

"So why didn't you?" Tom asked. "Why didn't you leave her there?"

Marsha shot him a steeled look. "Because I wanted Greg to suffer. I wanted him to suffer like he made me suffer… and I wanted him to know it was me."

Greg, who'd been sitting in silence, staring at the floor whilst listening to his wife, slowly raised his head to look at her, tears in his eyes.

"I wronged you, Marsha. I didn't realise how badly… not until I came home that night."

"Where was Angela?" Tom asked.

"In the car," Marsha said. "I managed to put her in the passenger seat and clipped her in. We drove around for a while. All that time, I thought at any moment I would begin to panic but," she chuckled, "it actually got easier. I felt in control of my life. For the first time in years, I had the power over our family, the business… even our marriage. I could take it all away in an instant."

Greg looked devastated. As much as his wife appeared free of the weight of their shared secret, Greg was crestfallen. He glumly met Tom's eye.

"I came home from the dinner. Marsha was waiting for me… blood on her hands, dried into her clothing… waiting for me. Waiting to show me." He looked at his wife with obvious compassion. "She was ready to go to the police, to hand herself in."

"But she didn't," Tom said.

Greg shook his head. "No. I stopped her."

"You couldn't handle the thought of your life falling apart?" Tom asked.

Greg laughed then, but it was a sound without genuine humour. "No, that wasn't it at all, Inspector. I doubt you'll believe me, but I felt responsible. It was *my fault*. I did this to Marsha. It was me who led Angela to her death." He shook his head. "No, I wasn't prepared to let Marsha throw her life away like that. I wasn't going to allow Susan to share in that shame. Angela was already dead. How many more lives needed to be ruined?"

"So, you covered it up."

"Yes," he said, nodding solemnly. "I hid the body. I cleaned the car, and I destroyed my wife's clothing."

"You hid her in a freezer?"

He nodded again. "It was supposed to be temporary. That night, by the time I'd realised what had gone on, it was too late to take her… to take the body somewhere else. I resolved to do it the following night, but," he shook his head, "by that time everyone was out looking for her. I thought it best to leave it until the dust settled. I mean, we were discreet, careful. I was confident no one was going to come looking for her here."

"You hadn't counted on Ben Crake and his schoolboy obsession with Angela though."

"No, that's true. I had no idea. I knew they were at school together and that she said he was a little odd, but I knew that myself. He'd been around us for much of his life. His mother was something of an oddball as well. How was I to know that he'd become a suspect, the *only* suspect as it turned out."

"You erased the camera footage showing you and Angela together, didn't you?"

He nodded. "I did, yes. But what I told you about the footage of Ben and Angela was true. I genuinely didn't know it was on a separate feed otherwise I would have destroyed that too. I wasn't looking to scapegoat the lad. Angela was dead. There was nothing I could do about that. I was trying to protect those around me."

"And yet, you let Ben go down for what you and your wife did." Tom was angry now. These people making out that they were the victims, rather than Angela and Ben.

"I didn't for a second believe that he would be convicted! You have to believe that Inspector," Greg said. "He was an innocent… quite a simple lad, to be honest. How could any reasonable jury convict him? It was madness."

"Someone had to pay, Greg. The public need to

believe they are safe in their beds at night and to know that someone had to pay."

"Well, that's not our fault!"

Tom shook his head in disgust. "You ruined a young man's life to protect your own—"

"What should I have done? You tell me. Thrown my wife into prison, the mother of my only daughter? Could you have done that?"

"You should have done the right thing, Greg." Tom's eyes flitted between the two of them. They both avoided his gaze. "You should have done the right thing."

"Yes, well… it's a bit late for that now."

"You kept Angela in the freezer, here at the house?"

Greg shook his head. "In the barn, out the back. We have a number of chillers and freezers left over from when we were processing a lot of food on site." He sighed. "Business hasn't been great these past five years or so, despite outward appearances. The redevelopment of the barn is necessary to try and… rejuvenate the business. When we realised that was what we had to do…"

"You needed to move Angela."

"Yes. I know it will probably sound strange, but it was almost easier to pretend she wasn't there. I knew I should move her… but… it never felt like the right time."

"When it came to it, you took her out of the

freezer to dispose of her… but where to do it?" Tom said. "One of my officers came across a useful bit of intelligence that had passed everyone by upon discovering Angela's remains. That patch of woodland belongs to you."

Greg nodded. "Yes. We purchased it years ago, planned to make it into our own piece of tranquil paradise."

"Nowhere better to keep your trophy, is there?" Tom asked. Greg looked horrified. "All these years and you still couldn't bring yourself to part with her, could you? You will have had ample opportunity and yet, you couldn't do it. You wanted to own her in life, and you couldn't allow yourself to be parted in death."

"It wasn't like that," Greg muttered.

"So, you say."

"I cared for her, damn you!"

"Did you care for her while you were cutting her into pieces and packing her into bin bags… throwing her out like rubbish?"

Greg was silent.

"I take it Daniel Turner threatened to expose you?"

"Scum. That's all he is… he didn't do anything for any purpose other than his own financial reward."

"Why did you kill him?" Tom asked.

Greg looked at him. "Is he dead then?"

"Yes."

Greg looked away. "I won't lose any sleep over him. My only mistake was agreeing to pay him so soon."

"What did he know?"

"Not as much as he thought. He saw me with Angela one afternoon… when we had all gone to the circus." Greg looked at his wife who made to leave but Tamara stopped her, placing a restraining hand on her arm. She didn't want to hear this, but she would have to. "We stole a moment, Angela and me. I don't think it was an issue until the police started asking questions. At the time, Turner didn't want to get involved or so he said. He was no friend of the police."

"Only now, with Ben's release, everything hitting the headlines again and the potential for a new inquiry."

"Exactly. He remembered me from the time… sought to turn it to his advantage. I was too willing to pay. It only encouraged him. He must have realised I had more to hide than he'd originally thought, and he wanted more."

"So, you arranged to meet?"

"He started messaging and calling from an unidentified number," Greg said, shaking his head, "at all times of the day and night. Once he had my attention… that was when he revealed himself."

"How much for his silence?"

"Five thousand," Greg said, sitting upright. "At first. I paid. Then he asked for more… putting it to me. How much was I prepared to pay for his silence?" He met Tom's gaze, holding it. "Whatever I offered it would never be enough. He would come back again and again and again! We would have his shadow hanging over us forever more. I had a decision to make. Just as I had one to make when," he glanced at his wife, shooting her a supportive, apologetic smile "… with Angela. This one was easier, I have to say."

"But you didn't count on Aislene, did you?"

"He was supposed to come alone. I didn't know that she was there."

"And you stole Ben's car from his garage to make it look like it was him. Where was your compassion for his suffering?"

"It was easy to get the car. His house was wide open, and Ben was passed out drunk on the living-room floor. I knew I was putting him under pressure again, but I didn't think you would be *stupid* enough to make the same mistake again and blame an innocent man. Lightning doesn't strike twice, does it? I was only trying to muddy the waters… to deflect your investigation—"

"A plan that fell apart as soon as you caught sight of Aislene."

Greg nodded. "I was driving off. The adrenalin was pumping. I wanted to get away from there as quickly as possible but then I saw her, running over to him and crouching over his body. How could I leave her?" He sighed. "She shouldn't have been there."

"You thought you had everything within your control. Only it wasn't Daniel Turner who saw you and Angela together that day at the circus."

Greg's head snapped up.

"It was Aislene. She told her partner and he hatched the blackmail plan. You were never going to get away with this. For all of your efforts, six years ago and now, you have arrived at the same destination. Only now, the fall out is even worse. More lives destroyed… more pain. All of your good works and your faith… it's all just a façade. You're a pathetic, weak little man."

Greg stuck out his chest, his lip curling as he spoke. "And yet it took you long enough to get here."

Tom controlled his response, holding his tongue. There was more he needed to achieve here and riling Greg Brock further would no doubt mean he would fail.

"Where is Angela?" he asked. "If you have any shred of decency left in you, the least you can do is tell us where the remainder of her body can be found so she can be laid to rest with dignity."

Greg lifted his head, nodding slowly. "I moved her in the dead of night. I took her to the woods – I knew no one would ever uncover her there – and buried her in the shadow of one of my favourite trees. It is a beautiful spot. I have sat there in the evening sunshine on many an occasion." He sighed. "Only when I returned home, did I realise I'd left a couple of bags behind. I don't know how that happened. I was doing it in the dark, hurrying. I got careless. It was far too early in the morning by then to go out again. The sun was rising, and people were already arriving for work."

"So, what did you do?"

He inclined his head, refusing to meet Tom's gaze. "We have had a lot of contractors here… and there's been a great deal of debris, old junk and rubble to clear. A lot of skips passing between here and the landfill site near Edgefield, the one just south of Holt…" He shrugged. "I didn't know what else to do."

Tom felt a wave of revulsion pass over him. There was no way they'd be able to locate her remains in that site. Countless searches had taken place in similar landfill locations in the past in search of missing bodies. No one had ever been successful, unless searched on the same day. By the look on Tamara's face, she felt the same. Tamara had listened to enough. She walked to the front door, opened it and beckoned the waiting officers to come inside. Any further could be said in a formal interview.

The Brocks were taken into custody, Tamara standing alongside Tom as they were placed in separate police cars for the short journey to the station.

"That was quite a gamble you took there," she said.

"What's that?"

"The whole *Aislene has an interesting story to tell* part."

He shrugged. "Well, I'm sure she will have when she wakes up."

"If she wakes up."

"I didn't say she had told us her story, only that she has an interesting one to tell. Circus life by itself must be more interesting than most."

Tamara shook her head, smiling. "Greg wouldn't have broken if Marsha hadn't."

Tom nodded, the police cars setting off.

"She's been harbouring that secret, holding in the guilt for so long that it's been eating her from the inside out." He looked at Tamara glumly. "For what it's worth, I reckon she was telling the truth. Had it been down to her, she would have handed herself in the next day. But men like that… men like Greg, insist on keeping control. Whatever he says, he did what he did for his own selfish gain. Whitewashing his character with charity works and presenting himself to the world as something he isn't works for him, but not his wife. I almost feel sorry for her."

"Almost?"

He shrugged. "She allowed her friends to suffer for years not knowing the fate of their daughter. I've no doubt Greg has exerted coercive control over her… but even so."

Tamara sighed. "It's a hell of a job we have to do, isn't it?"

"Yes, it is," Tom said, glumly. "We'd better go over and see Henry and Marie Dale."

"It's late. Should we leave it until the morning?"

"I think we should go now. They've waited long enough."

CHAPTER THIRTY

Olivia Goldman sat stone-faced while Tom outlined the arrests they'd made the previous night. Following their initial detention, Greg refused to speak, insisting on communicating with his solicitor before agreeing to an interview. Marsha, on the other hand, waved her rights to legal representation and engaged with them at the first opportunity; evidently keen to release everything she'd held inside for so many years. It was damning testimony and all the legal trickery in the world would do little to aid Greg's case.

"Thank you for filling me in," Olivia said, her eyes drifting to the information boards of the ops room.

"I trust you will be discreet with this information until it is official," Tom said.

"Of course. All I ever wanted was to see justice done." She smiled coyly. "That sounds so cheesy, doesn't it?"

Tom laughed. "Well, without your persistence on Ben's behalf it is likely he would still be sitting in a prison cell right now. Your conviction in his cause is arguably what made the difference."

"I wasn't sure though."

"About what?"

"Ben. His innocence." She looked almost apologetic. "I really wasn't. It was a hunch that something wasn't right."

Tom arched his eyebrows. "You travelled an awfully long way on a hunch."

She laughed. "Yes, I did. Pretty pleased that it worked out. Although, my money was on Charlie Babcock. His family connections to the investigating officer in the case… the inconsistency of his story…"

"And that he was booted out of the academy at Sandhurst for inappropriately touching another cadet."

"Really?" Olivia asked.

Tom nodded. "We've just heard back from the Ministry of Defence. It was never taken to court, military or civil, but Charlie certainly left under a cloud."

"The army protecting their reputation as normal."

"I'm afraid it does look that way, yes."

Their attention was drawn to movement in the corridor outside the ops room. Chief Superintendent Watts strode purposefully past with a face like thunder, quickly disappearing from view, just before Tamara entered the room with DCI Morris a step behind. The two of them made a beeline for Tom and Olivia.

"Someone isn't happy," Tom said.

Tamara nodded but didn't comment. It was Morris who spoke first.

"Well, it looks like your team has left me nothing to do," he said, looking from Tamara to Tom and momentarily at Olivia. He didn't ask who she was but he clearly hadn't come across her before. He must have assumed she was a member of CID. No one saw fit to correct him. "A good job, done by all."

He was irritated. Tom could tell. Unsurprising, he supposed bearing in mind Morris had been drafted in to review a high-profile murder case. Careers could be made off the back of such cases… or destroyed, Tom thought, contemplating his chief superintendent.

"I'm sorry you've had a wasted trip," Tamara said, not sorry at all.

Morris smiled. He knew she didn't mean it either.

"Yes, well. As I say, you've wrapped it up nicely." Another man came into ops, hovering at the entrance. He was part of the review team that were already arriving to take over the case. Morris spotted him and waved. The man left. "It looks like I have some admin to attend to," he said, excusing himself.

Tom smiled, holding his tongue until he was out of earshot.

"There are a lot of people who have driven all the way here only to be turned around and sent home again."

"Norfolk is a bugger to get into quickly," Tamara said. With no motorways in the county, and it being a large county, it often felt like it can take an age to get anywhere in Norfolk.

"And it takes just as much time to leave again," Tom added, folding his arms across his chest with a satisfied smile creeping across his lips.

"How is Ben?" Tamara asked.

Olivia looked glum. "I spoke to a nurse at the mental-health unit an hour ago. He had a difficult night. I should imagine he feels he's being incarcerated again. On top of everything else he's had going on… Six years of everyone you know believing you're a killer, prison… losing his mum while he was inside." She shook her head. "I'd like to think he will get the help he needs to find his way back, but I'm not optimistic. I'll be there for him when it comes to the compensation claim," she looked between them both, "not that it's about the money, but the chance of Ben leading any type of a normal life anytime soon is very unlikely."

Tom exhaled, his feeling of satisfaction dissipating. "I understand. He might need the money to pay for the help he needs. You've done a lot for him. You should be proud of yourself."

Olivia blushed.

"I mean it," Tom said. "You once told me you wanted to make a real difference to people's lives, and when it comes to Ben, you have. At least now, he has a chance."

"Speaking of the future," Olivia said, obviously keen to change the focus of conversation away from herself, "what happens to Watts?"

Tamara sucked air through her teeth. "There will still be an inquiry into the first investigation."

"Morris?" Tom asked.

Tamara shook her head. "No. They'll be bringing in a bigger fish to manage that. I expect our chief superintendent will be spending a lot of time in his garden very soon. And, judging by his reaction to the briefing this morning, he is well aware of that fact."

Olivia seemed pleased to hear that news although her expression clouded momentarily soon after.

"What is it?" Tom asked.

"Angela. You said Brock admitted to disposing of her remains in a landfill site?"

Tom nodded. "At least, he put the bags in a skip that was heading to landfill. Are we going to search for her?" he asked, looking at Tamara.

"We will, Angela and the family deserve the effort, but it all happened weeks ago. These sites are regularly bulldozed and added to daily. A specialist search team is on the way here. Usually, they search for people in collapsed buildings, disaster zones and the like, but they'll give it a shot. It's the least we can do for the Dales. Any word from the hospital regarding Aislene?"

Tom frowned. "Nothing new. She is in a medically induced coma. The next twenty-four to forty-eight hours will be critical. Her father is at her bedside. The head wound is such that even if she does make it through, she'll likely have brain damage." He shrugged. "Time will tell. All anyone can do is wait… and hope."

"Will you need her testimony?" Olivia asked. "For Greg Brock's trial?"

Tom shook his head. "We have their confessions, Marsha's in particular. Even if they withdraw them, we can still track the cash taken from Greg's bank account to prove the link. Daniel Turner was using a burner phone to make contact, but Greg was using his own, so there's a digital trail of their communication. The crown prosecution service still needs to assess the evidence before we can officially charge them, but we have enough. I'm sure."

CHAPTER THIRTY-ONE

Tom looked across the foyer. Alice's mum was fussing over her hair, making last-minute adjustments that really weren't necessary. The nerves were kicking in now and he took a deep breath to steady himself. Not that he doubted the decision for a moment. Tamara came in from outside, putting her mobile phone away. Alice offered her a wave and Tamara smiled, coming over to Tom, who was standing with Cassie, Eric and her partner, David.

"Looks like change at the top," she whispered, accepting the floral arrangement David had been looking after for her while she stepped out to take the call.

"The chief super?"

"Retiring."

Tom frowned. "Leaving quietly before he was pushed?"

"Oh, he was pushed all right. They had no choice, and neither did he. You can't get away with that sort of thing. Not these days."

"Although, being allowed to retire is a way of getting away with it," Tom countered. Tamara didn't disagree. "What about DCI Reynolds down in Suffolk?"

"Suspended pending conclusion of the inquiry."

"So, he'll resign as well then?"

"I wouldn't be surprised."

Tom found the conclusion of their investigation troubling to say the least, although he wouldn't shed a tear for the implosion of the careers of Chief Superintendent Watts or his one-time deputy, DCI Reynolds. Their professional fate was sealed through self-destructive acts, acts they thought they'd long since got away with. It was likely they believed they had the right man or, at least, Tom hoped they did, but they'd played fast and loose in a murder investigation. The idea they'd get to walk away with their pensions intact, if not their professional reputation was galling.

It was Marie and Henry Dale who Tom's thoughts turned to. Having finally been able to lay their daughter to rest, they now had to cope with the realisation that she died at the hands of their long-time friend, Marsha; Angela's killer so often standing beside them offering a supportive hand or a comforting word. He could still picture the devastated expression on Marie's face when he'd broken the news to them. The curl of Henry's top lip as years of anger and frustration spilled from his subconscious upon hearing his friend and former business partner had not only covered up his daughter's murder, but that he was also having a sexual relationship with her. It was yet another wound on top of those still yet to heal.

Tom hoped the family would support one another through it and they would merge united, but he'd seen more than enough of these cases to realise that was rarely the case. Revelations like these tore lives apart. Henry believed he should have seen the truth, Marie that her intuition should have alerted her, and then there was Jack; in a burgeoning relationship with Susan Brock. Another union that would not survive the uncovering of secrets long buried. It was a mess. Two families utterly destroyed, and Tom took little pleasure in the result they'd attained by solving Angela's murder. The Dales had a measure of closure, but he was in no doubt that their nightmare would go on.

"Having doubts?" Tamara asked him playfully.

Tom smiled, shaking his head.

"No, of course not. I was… somewhere else for a moment."

Saffy ran over, frowning as she stared up at Tom

whilst standing on her tiptoes. He leaned down, smiling.

"What's up, munchkin?"

"How long do I have to wear this?" she whispered conspiratorially from behind her hand, anxiously glancing at her mother.

"You look very pretty."

Saffy rolled her eyes, much as her mother does whenever Tom deflected a question he had no idea how to answer. The two women in his life were uncannily similar.

"But I can't run properly!" she whined, still keeping her voice low. "And these... things," she said, looking down at her shoes, "hurt my feet."

"When you run?"

She nodded.

"You're not supposed to run in the Registry Office, Saffy."

She exhaled theatrically much to both Tamara and David's amusement. Cassie snorted a laugh, quickly covering her mouth and trying to compose herself realising she'd drawn Alice's attention.

"How much longer?" Saffy asked.

Tom put his hands on her shoulders and turned her to face the entrance doors as he heard them opening. The first of two registrars stepped through, smiling at Tom and looking around for Alice. She appeared relieved when she saw Alice on the other side of the foyer.

"Do many people fail to show?" Tom asked quietly, reading her expression.

The registrar inclined her head. "You would be surprised. If you're ready, we can begin?"

Tom nodded and Alice hurried over to him, adjusting her dress, as the small party of guests, barely fifteen people in total, a mix of work colleagues, close friends and precious few family members, due to the short notice, began drifting into the ceremonial suite. Their photographer was busying herself in the background snapping pictures of both the couple and guests. They'd been very lucky she'd had a cancellation and been able to make it.

Alice came to stand before Tom. He smiled at her.

"You look beautiful," he said.

She put a hand on his chest and then held her palm up. "Don't make me cry. This make-up took forever, and I'd hate to have to look back on a photo album of me looking like a drag queen."

Alice's mum came alongside, patting the back of Tom's hand and then reaching up to adjust his tie. He accepted her assistance at the same time hoping it would pass quickly.

"Thank you for this, Tom," she said, leaving his tie and cupping his cheek affectionately.

He shook his head, taking her hand and kissing her cheek. The news of her diagnosis had rocked

Alice's world. All the optimism they'd felt in the previous months evaporated swiftly, replaced by the harsh reality that medicine couldn't work miracles. As she had told Alice at the time; a heart only has so many beats in it. It was her time, and she was prepared for it.

The conversation between Tom and Alice had been brief. The date of their wedding came forward from the following year. Their plans were curtailed. Not because they didn't have the time or the energy, not really. What was important was to make that commitment to one another in front of the people they loved more than any other. Sure, some noses were put out of joint when they realised they couldn't attend, but that was their issue.

For Tom and Alice, this felt proper. It felt right.

The guests were now seated, and the registrar beckoned them forward. Saffy was hopping around at their feet, full of energy and pride despite the white frock she was forced to wear. Before leaving them to go inside herself, Tamara gave Alice her floral bouquet, an arrangement of sunflowers to match those waiting for them in the courtyard garden outside where they would have the pictures taken.

Tom took Alice's hands in his own and drew her to him.

She smiled at him, taking a deep breath. "Last chance to change your mind."

He laughed. “Not likely.”

“Let’s go!” Saffy said, waving her own bouquet in the air at them. “Enough talking already.”

Eric overheard her and laughed. He was Tom’s best man, willingly stepping into the role when Tom’s oldest friend couldn’t get a flight in from Canada in time to make the ceremony. Tom nodded to Eric, and he gestured for the music to start.

“Come on then, soon-to-be Mrs Janssen. Let’s crack on.”

“Hang on,” Alice said, placing a restraining hand on his forearm. She looked at him sternly. “I thought we were going to break with tradition and you were going to take my name.”

Off guard, Tom didn’t know what to say. “I… thought you were joking.”

Alice smiled. “And in your job, you have to know when people are lying?”

Shaking his head, out of sight of everyone, he playfully patted her backside. “This level of back chat won’t play when we’re married, you know?”

“Yeah, we’ll see about that, Detective Inspector,” she said, and they entered the ceremonial suite side by side.

FREE BOOK GIVEAWAY

Visit the author's website at **www.jmdalgliesh.com** and sign up to the VIP Club and be the first to receive news and previews of forthcoming works.

Here you can download a FREE eBook novella exclusive to club members;

Life & Death - A Hidden Norfolk novella

Never miss a new release.

No spam, ever, guaranteed. You can unsubscribe at any time.

Enjoy this book? You could make a real difference.

Because reviews are critical to the success of an author's career, if you have enjoyed this novel, please do me a massive favour by entering one onto Amazon.

Type the following link into your internet search bar to go to the Amazon page and leave a review;

http://mybook.to/JMD-angel-of-death

If you prefer not to follow the link please visit the sales page where you purchased the title in order to leave a review.

Reviews increase visibility. Your help in leaving one would make a massive difference to this author and I would be very grateful.

PREVIEW - DEAD TO ME

HIDDEN NORFOLK BOOK 13

If the truth be told, this was a strange day. Upon reflection, it had been building for a while now and she should have known. There was the underlying tension hanging in the air over the last couple of days. The walking on eggshells, hoping not to be the one to trigger the anger, to be the one who causes everything to go off like it had done so many times before. Each step taken in the short walk home from school had felt heavier as the weight of what she might be walking into fed her anxiety. Although, anxiety is the fear of an uncertain outcome, the therapist told her. This isn't uncertain. This is happening again, and it is very, very real. You're not alone, mum. You're never alone.

The shouting has stopped. It's been at least five min-

utes. Too soon to allow a sense of relief to settle in though.

Hopping off her bed, she crossed the short distance between it and the rear-facing bedroom window, gently easing the net curtain aside to improve her view, but careful to stand back and keep out of sight. Daft really, seeing as this is her bedroom and the only person who would be moving the curtain was the occupant. The gentle breeze passing through the cracked window whistled momentarily. Glancing at her bedroom door, the chair still wedged underneath the handle to prevent anyone from entering unbidden, she felt safe.

He was there, standing in the garden in the sunshine, hands on his hips, a look of mild consternation on his face. Other than that, broadly emotionless... as always. What did he expect to happen? It was like watching a living statue, but one so beleaguered that it wished to decay, collapse and disappear from existence like many of those depicted in the books he loved to read. Fascinated by life as it was several thousand years ago... but far less interested in what was happening in front of his eyes.

There's the shouting again. A scream and a crash. He flinched. The statue actually flinched! A positive sign? Perhaps.

Locking her in the orangery probably wasn't a good idea. Another pane shatters and a wrought-iron chair clatters to the patio. Her father turned to his right as two figures approached. Police officers. A man and a woman. She was a fair bit shorter than him, blonde hair tied into a ponytail beneath her funny little hat, at the nape of her neck. They glance nervously towards the orangery, taking in the situation. Dad looks apologetic, like butter wouldn't melt. Mind you, he's probably at a loss at how to explain this one. Then again, he was a man skilled at fashioning excuses to explain away all manner of bumps, bruises and random injuries, all seemingly occurring through unfortunate and unavoidable mishap. Even the school seemed to buy into his nonsense. He was plausible, if nothing else.

One of the officers is walking away from her dad now, a large walkie-talkie pressed to her lips. The other one is still standing with dad. I wonder who called them? It wouldn't have been her father, that's for certain. *It will blow over. Don't worry.* That was pretty much his stock phrase. That and, *I'm sorry*. He said it so often these days that it was hard to feel any genuine passion contained within the words. If he was truly sorry, then he needed to work on his delivery because it had all the contrition of a puppy caught shredding a newspaper. The puppy couldn't stay either. *Too much work on top of everything else we have going on,* he said.

The policeman moved towards the orangery, ducking as something was thrown at him. I can't see her though. I hope she's alright. One of these days she won't be, and what will we do then?

Stepping away from the window, she went back to her bed and clambered in, pulling the covers over her and burying her head in the pillow. The screaming was starting again. It would last for hours. It always lasted for hours. The fear of what might happen to her mum came to mind followed by a selfish thought, one that made her feel guilty the moment it popped into her head. She always felt bad when her subconscious threw it at her, but it was a concern repeatedly raised. This is my future… and I don't want it, but how can I get out?

She drew the covers over head, trying to drown out the screams from the garden. It made little difference. It never did.

BOOKS BY J M DALGLIESH

One Lost Soul

Bury Your Past

Kill Our Sins

Tell No Tales

Hear No Evil

The Dead Call

Kill Them Cold

A Dark Sin

To Die For

Fool Me Twice

The Raven Song

Angel of Death

Dead to Me

Life and Death ***FREE** - visit jmdalgliesh.com

Divided House

Blacklight

The Dogs in the Street

Blood Money

Fear the Past

The Sixth Precept

Dark Yorkshire Books 1-3

Dark Yorkshire Books 4-6

Audiobooks

In the Hidden Norfolk Series

One Lost Soul
Bury Your Past
Kill Our Sins
Tell No Tales
Hear No Evil
The Dead Call
Kill Them Cold
A Dark Sin
To Die For
Fool Me Twice
The Raven Song

In the Dark Yorkshire Series

Divided House
Blacklight
The Dogs in the Street
Blood Money
Fear the Past
The Sixth Precept

Dark Yorkshire Books 1-3
Dark Yorkshire Books 4-6

Printed in Great Britain
by Amazon

14715848R00253